LOOKING FOR
GARBO

A NOVEL

LOOKING FOR
GARBO

A NOVEL

JON JAMES MILLER

bsp

Blank Slate Press | St. Louis, MO

bsp

Blank Slate Press | Saint Louis, MO 63116
Copyright © 2019 Jon James Miller
All rights reserved.

For information, contact:
Blank Slate Press
An imprint of Amphorae Publishing Group
a woman- and veteran-owned business
4168 Hartford Street, Saint Louis, MO 63116

Manufactured in the United States of America
Set in Breamcater and Adobe Caslon Pro
Interior designed by Kristina Blank Makansi
Cover designed by Kristina Blank Makansi
Jacket Images: MS *Kungsholm* , Ingen Uppgift [Public domain],
via Wikimedia Commons
Greta Garbo: Popperfoto Collection/Getty Images

Library of Congress Control Number: 2019933801
ISBN: 978-1-943075-55-3

For my mother Jean Dempsey,
and the love that has lasted a lifetime.

"Beauty will save the world."
Fyodor Dostoyevsky

LOOKING FOR GARBO
THE REAL STORY BEHIND THE NOVEL

At a dinner party in the 1960's, reclusive movie star Greta Garbo dropped a bombshell on her friend Sam Green. "Mr. Hitler was big on me," she told him. "He kept writing and inviting me to come to Germany, and if the war hadn't started when it did, I would have gone, and I would have taken a gun out of my purse and shot him, because I'm the only person who would not have been searched.'

Stunned, Green later said, "That's a direct quote. She said it to me over dinner, and it was so out of character. It wasn't her habit to make up such a story to stop a dinner party."

Garbo was not only serious, but actually volunteered to spy for the Allies and personally saved Jews in Denmark. Hitler, who owned his own copy of Camille, wrote her fan letters and considered her his ideal Aryan Goddess. But Hitler wasn't the only one obsessed with Garbo. Her every movement was recorded daily in the tabloids, and her refusal to give interviews in the 1930s only fueled the public's interest and efforts to catch her in candid moments. That's where Seth Moseley came in.

Author Jon James Miller met Seth while working in Los Angeles as a researcher on a documentary about famous kidnappings. Seth was the young, ambitious Associated Press reporter who got the scoop of the century when he interviewed Charles Lindbergh shortly after his baby had been abducted. But one of Seth's fondest memories was when he found Greta Garbo hiding in the men's room aboard the MS Kungsholm, a Swedish ocean liner, at the Port of New York in 1938.

Seth had boarded the ship with the Press Corps, all of whom received the tip that Garbo was secretly aboard. In exchange for not ratting her out, Garbo gave Seth an exclusive. And after his interview with Seth, Miller knew he had his protagonist for a novel.

Greta Garbo passed away in 1990, and Seth died in 2000. Their time together on the Kungsholm, back when Garbo was the most famous face of all and Seth Moseley was the beat reporter pursuing her is now the stuff of legend. But the fact that they became friends and respected each other was almost as unlikely as Garbo following through on her plot to kill Hitler and stop the war before it even had a chance to start.

—Jon James Miller

SETH

I could have done nothing. I could have remained on the darkening Promenade Deck of the S.S. *Athenia* and sipped sidecars, played whist or shuffleboard with the swells until the end came. But as doomed as the situation was, I had to see her one more time. A washed-up, lovesick, twenty-nine-year-old hack reporter with the story of a lifetime and very little lifetime left, I had to get back to Garbo.

I had joined the ship on a fishing expedition. The kind meant to hook the biggest catch ever for a newshound like me—a candid photograph of a movie star. And in 1939, the biggest star in the world was none other than Greta Garbo. I was lucky enough to catch up with her in the middle of the Atlantic, and no one or nothing was going to let her get away. Not even a second world war.

So, I took a chance and headed down the hollow-sounding ship corridors to Suite 313B. I put an ear to Garbo's locked door and listened. The room inside was silent. I knocked. Nothing. Was I too late? Had she been discovered? An electric shock ran through me. I backed across the empty hallway, then made a run for her door. I was going in no matter what.

The hinges gave way, and I burst into the darkened stateroom as a shot rang out and a bullet whizzed past my ear. *THWAK!* The molding of the doorframe exploded, wood fragments stabbing the side of my face and neck. I was sure whoever was on the other end of that loaded gun was readjusting his aim. It was over. I was a goner.

"Don't. Move," the low-contralto voice of a feminine silhouette commanded.

A shadow rose from the bed and moved toward me. An open-toed shoe dipped into the pool of light that spilled in from the doorway. Then came shapely, sun-kissed legs and swaying hips encased in a white pencil skirt below small, rounded breasts peeking out from the deep neckline of a tight, blue silk blouse. Then, finally, *The Face* was illuminated.

"I nearly killed you."

No two-dimensional black and white actress now, movie goddess Greta Garbo stood in vivid color glory before me, a .9mm semi-automatic pointed at my heart.

"I know," I managed to croak. The left side of my face throbbed and a trickle of warmth ran down my neck. I reached toward her. She lowered her gun and closed the space between us.

"Nazis," I whispered. I touched my bloody cheek, then my vision swam, my knees buckled, and I fell forward. She dropped the gun and caught me in her arms.

★ ★ ★

LOOKING FOR GARBO

LA-based prod co. seeks
true life stories about
movie star Greta G a r b o
TV-interview/comp. rates
Exclusives need only apply
Cont: James/818-509-3883

★ ★ ★

I. APPLEKNOCKERS

SETH

February 14, 2000—2:10 EST
Seth Moseley Interview—Norfolk, Connecticut
<u>**Greta Garbo Special**</u> **(Adversary Productions, Inc.)**

I'll start from the beginning. The year was 1939. The morning of September 1st, I was bellied up to the bar at Henson's, a rundown "black-and-tan" in the Bronx. That's what they called joints that served both blacks and whites. All of us were getting tight in the gray early half-light that seeped in through whitewashed windows turned amber by nicotine and dust.

The phone rang behind the bar. The barkeep, a former pugilist with the mangled face and outsized frame to prove it, answered the call. The bruiser listened with his cauliflower ear, then motioned me over. He handed me the phone.

"Seth Moseley," I said, putting on my best happy voice.

"You pathetic piece of shit," the voice on the other end growled. It was the editor-in-chief from *The Journal*.

"Boss," I said, "how'd you find me?"

"Who cares how I found you. You need to hustle your ass down to Jackson Heights."

"Jackson Heights? Why?"

"There's a ship coming up the Narrows. The *Athenia*."

"Yeah," I said. "Who's on it?"

"Garbo," he shouted. "Get me a candid, or don't bother coming back."

Then the line went dead. Message received.

Garbo was the hottest star on the silver screen in 1939. She had ruled Hollywood for an entire decade, adored and lusted after by more people the world over than anyone of her era. At $250,000 a year, she was also the highest paid and most influential actress on the planet. She was tops.

I'd met the actress for one fleeting moment in the early '30s when I was a copywriter at MGM Studios in Los Angeles, churning out fictitious stories for movie trade magazines. I'd heard Garbo was on the lot and wanted to see if she was as gorgeous in the flesh as she was on film. The first actress to French-kiss on silver nitrate in 1927's *Flesh and the Devil*.

Garbo was coming out of Louis B. Mayer's office when I saw her. Swathed in a fur coat, the young star looked sullen and kept her eyes to the ground. But then she looked up and caught my stare from across the corridor. Her blue eyes penetrated so deep, I remember taking a step back. She had a presence I hadn't felt before or since.

Garbo, the exotic creature from Sweden came to Hollywood to be the next vamp. Nobody knew then that she was more than the next "it" girl. She wouldn't merely play the role of a sex goddess on screen in pre-code melodramas. Garbo was destined to become Queen of Golden Age Hollywood, but she would become so much more. Just nobody could see it yet, including me.

I left Los Angeles not long after and came to New York. And after a string of high-profile pieces for legit papers, I fell face down on my luck. At twenty-nine, a run of bad bets at the track made me *persona non grata* in polite company and real newsrooms. On the lam from my bookie, I mostly hung out in derelict bars and took the occasional scandal sheet assignment for drinking money.

I stumbled out of Henson's that morning, my trusty Bell & Howell camera in hand, to see a streetcar hauling a hot load of sweaty, smelly assholes uptown. They were the working class. The chattel that made the city run. I was the hot, smelly asshole on the sidewalk, lollygagging my way down to the Narrows. It didn't help my attitude that it was the *silly season*. That's what we newshounds called late summer when editors resorted to—for lack of hard news—gimcrackery. Like the movements of movie stars and local color to sell papers. In short, I moseyed.

I was about to turn into the corner deli for a fried egg and bologna sandwich when two guys with tree trunks for arms shanghaied me from behind. I felt a hard, blunt hit to the noggin and crumbled to the sidewalk like a sack of shit. My audience on the streetcar rolled by, indifferent to my plight. I'd been jacked-up good.

"Moseley," one of the goons said. I flipped over like a fish and wall-eyed my assailants while sucking wind. "We been looking all over the city for ya."

It was Toes. A particularly gruesome-looking goon in the employ of Johnnie Roses, my bookie. Toes had a sidekick, Bernie, built like a brick shithouse. Bernie was a fairly amiable guy that Toes kept around to do the cleanup after he was done messing up Joes who owed Johnnie.

Toes was a tough act to follow. He tended to make a big mess.

"Hi, Toes," I uttered out my bleeding fish mouth. "How's it goin'?"

"Good," Toes said. "Bernie, get Moseley up off the street. We need some privacy."

Bernie lifted me like a straw man. He carried me toward a nearby alley. Toes carried the blackjack he'd used to clock me, a piece of rebar attached to a coiled spring and wrapped in leather. He knew better than anyone how to employ six ounces of metal slug to turn a willful asshole into a fearful supplicant. He took pride in his work, scouring the city for delinquent marks like me. I was in for a very painful treat.

"Johnnie says you're three weeks behind," Toes said as Bernie propped me up against the brick wall of the alley. "You like getting shit on by Lady Luck?"

"You know women," I said without irony. "Can't live with them, can't live—"

"You may not live at all after this one," Toes said, gangster-movie dialogue his specialty. "I don't gotta spell it out for ya, do I?"

"It means you're gonna hurt me,"

This made Toes smile. Smiling was good. I could work with smiling. This could still have a happy ending.

"Anything you'd care to say while you still have teeth?"

"Teeth," Bernie echoed, missing a few himself.

"Shut up, Bernie," Toes said. Bernie did as he was told and hunched back away from me.

"I got a lead on a big story," I said. "Gonna pay off big time, too. More than what I owe Johnnie and then some. Just need the morning to get it."

Toes stopped smiling. This was a bad development. I had it on good authority that once Toes stopped smiling, beating soon ensued. I had interviewed enough snitches and lowlifes in my time who'd run afoul of him to convince me of this fact.

"You think Bernie and I are a pair of appleknockers, Moseley?"

Appleknockers were synonymous with Upstaters. Upstaters were synonymous with know-nothing bumblefucks. The sort whose eyes any wiseguy worth his salt could pull the wool over. It was an insult that required an immediate retaliatory response. It was also an invitation to have the snot beaten out of me. I was determined for my snot to stay where it was.

"No way, Toes. No appleknockers here."

Toes was a sadist, given to theatrics. His influence was felt throughout the borough. It didn't matter if you were rich or poor. If you owed a debt, Toes came to collect. How he did it was left up to his own improvisation. I'd heard once a businessman had eaten dog dirt off the sidewalk because Toes had told him to. Another loser Toes depantsed and snipped his left nut off. How Toes chose which nut to cut was still open for debate among all the cub reporters covering the crime beat. Suffice it to say we newshounds stood united in our devotion to the family jewels. The thought of losing either one gave us a collective shudder, and I was no exception.

"Bernie, get his shoe off," Toes instructed.

Toes replaced the blackjack in his hand with a short blade from his double-breasted jacket pocket. I didn't struggle while Bernie took my left shoe and sock off. All struggling got you was another blow to the head. I wanted to keep those to a minimum so I could think.

Toes approached my naked foot. He held the pen knife with exceptional skill. I was about to experience the signature move for which he had earned his nom de plume. I secretly said goodbye to each and every one of them, not sure whose number was going to come up first. They were my digits not my nuts, thank Jesus. All the same, I hadn't truly appreciated the ten up until that moment. Where was a flat-foot when you needed one?

"Garbo," I suddenly screamed. "Garbo's in town."

"I love Garbo," Bernie intoned.

Toes hesitated. I'd gone off script, and he wasn't sure of his next line. So I filled in.

"My editor will pay top drawer if I can get a snap of her," I followed quickly. "I'll pay Johnnie back with interest."

Toes looked down at me. My toes and I looked up at him. Bernie, God love him, couldn't stand the dramatic tension. He looked at Toes, frozen over me about to strike, and decided to get in on the action of our little penny-dreadful in progress with an ad lib of his own.

"Maybe we should let him go," he said. "Just this once. Okay?"

The newfound love I felt for Bernie swelled my chest, but I dared not breathe a sigh of relief. I had to see where this was going first. It was never a good idea to raise expectations prematurely.

"You better not be trying to make a fool out of me, Moseley," Toes warned. "It could be bad for your health. And I ain't just talking about your toes."

"I promise," I said. "I won't disappoint."

"Could you get me Garbo's autograph?" Bernie said, still holding my shoe.

"Sure, Bernie." I held out my hand for sock and shoe. I would have promised delivering her up in the palm of my hand to get my scuffed, leather Florsheim back on.

★   ★   ★

In order to make sure I kept my word, Toes and Bernie escorted me down to the docks to meet the *Athenia*. The scene at Pier 80 was a bevy of activity. Droves of reporters from all the tabs were there, crawling all over the pier. Half the town had gotten the same tip. The dock was so thick with newsies not one of us stood a chance of an exclusive. My piggies cringed inside my shoes.

The sun was still rising when I first caught sight of the *Athenia* coming up the Narrows into port. In front of her a seaplane coasted on her pontoons, bringing mail from another ocean liner still days out at sea. Another fixed-wing seaplane hung from a crane above our heads. Loaded with fresh outgoing mail, no doubt, she waited to be hoisted onto the *Athenia*. The same ship I needed to be on.

I tried to explain to Toes that if I'd have any chance of getting to Garbo before the other shutterbugs, I'd have to proceed alone. Hitch a ride on the pilot boat about to head out to the British merchant vessel. But Toes wouldn't hear of it.

"I let you go," he said, "it makes me look like an apple-knocker."

"I have to get aboard that pilot boat to even have a chance of getting to the ship before these other mugs."

"Fine," he said, "we'll go with you."

"But," I protested, "I only have one press pass."

Toes took in the scene and stalled to figure the angles. He knew I knew he was taking a risk that I would run. Meanwhile, the *Athenia* came up the straits, getting bigger every minute. The fourteen-thousand-gross-ton ocean liner was cruising under auxiliary power, and the pilot boat was about to launch and rendezvous with her. Toes would have to make a decision soon.

"You swim?" he said.

"What?" Both Bernie and I turned to him.

"Did I stutter?" he snapped. "Can you swim?"

"No." I was surprised by the question. "Not a lick."

"Don't even try and run out on me, Moseley." he said and stared out at the ocean liner. "Any tomfoolery, I'll make it my mission in life to end yours. Got me?"

I was pretty sure it was a rhetorical question, but I wasn't going to take any risks by not answering.

"Yeah," I said and nodded violently.

I ran for the pilot boat. Ran like my life depended on it, my toes' lives, at least. No sooner had I flashed my press pass and jumped from pier to ship deck than the pilot boat was underway. For the hell of it, I turned and waved back at Toes and Bernie. Bernie waved back. Toes just glared at me. He knew I was a bad bet.

Fifteen minutes later, me and a couple dozen other hacks transferred from the pilot boat to the *Athenia*. We all spilled onto her Promenade Deck like so much fish guts. A contingent of British first officers in crisp whites were on hand to make sure we didn't run off anywhere aboard ship. It obviously wasn't the captain of the *Athenia*'s first merry-go-round with the American press.

Rumors out of Hollywood said that Garbo was retiring from films for good and that she'd secretly joined the ship the night before so as not to deal with the likes of us newshounds. Some jag-off paparazzi were even saying she was headed off to live in a castle on an island she'd purchased off Stockholm. I didn't pay no mind. I didn't care. I was just relieved to be away from Toes.

Captain James Cook, master of the *Athenia*, a large man with a blonde beard and bushy eyebrows, had his first officers herd us up to the port bow. He emerged from the bridge and made his way down the external steps. And before he even stepped on the deck, the reporters assailed him with questions. He shut us down but quick.

"I will not," he said in a loud voice with pitch-perfect English, "confirm or deny that anyone by the name of Greta Garbo is listed in our manifest." The captain then stared at us, daring us to question his authority. Which, of course, all of us did. And I knew how to talk to these Brits. Knew they liked to tell the truth. Ask them a direct question, and they most often answered truthfully out of reflex.

"Captain," I said, "Seth Moseley from *The Journal* here. Sir, has anyone joined the ship after leaving her berth in Montreal and before we came aboard this morning?"

Everyone turned. The captain stared at me, knitting his bushy eyebrows as he blinked.

"Affirmative," he said.

That got the crowd going. Confirming someone influential enough to organize a secret boarding after departure meant someone special aboard. A dignitary, for instance. Or a movie star, someone the caliber of Garbo. The newshounds could practically smell her.

"Garbo's been sighted in the salon," a reporter from *The Graphic* said, and a feeding frenzy immediately erupted.

We all broke ranks and ran down the Promenade, not a one of us sure where we were headed but determined nonetheless. We came en masse to open double doors with a gilded sign that read Grand Salon. The lot of us stormed inside without breaking stride.

Sure enough, we found ourselves in a nicely appointed, art-deco-designed watering hole. And, like many of the ravenous dog packs that ran free throughout the city in those days, we sniffed out our prey. A single girl sitting at the bar. She was the right age and at the right angle, had more than a passing resemblance to Garbo, the movie queen.

I could have told them she wasn't Garbo, even before I laid eyes on her. Garbo wouldn't be caught dead in such a public place. No, the girl was just another look-alike, one of thousands at the time. We almost scared the poor thing to death, all rushing her at once and popping flashbulbs in her pretty young face.

Her screams brought our shenanigans to an end. The captain took no time in issuing the order. His first officers, more now than I'd counted before, rushed into the salon and pushed us back out onto the Promenade Deck. We'd had our fun. Now all of us were to be booted from the ship as soon as *Athenia* docked in port.

Lady Luck looked like she'd run out on me for good. I stared over the railing to the portion of the deck I and my fellow hacks had been relegated to for the duration of the short trip into port. I eyeballed the waterline below. Must have been forty feet if it was an inch.

I hadn't lied to Toes. I didn't swim. So, I'd either have to learn fast or come up with another land-based solution to keeping my toes attached to the rest of me. They'd come with me this far, and I wasn't about to let them down. But short of Garbo miraculously materializing in front of my camera lens in the next couple of minutes, I'd have to come up with a plan of action. From here on in, my toes and I were on the run.

"As I live and breathe," a female voice said. I looked up into the eyes of Sylvia, a sob sister from *The Graphic*, a rival news rag that employed mostly female reporters. Sylvia eyeballed me while she smoked a cigarette at the railing.

"Funny meeting you here," I said with a nod.

"Yeah, real laughs." She blew out a trail of smoke. "What happened to you, Seth? You said you were going to call two weeks ago."

My mind raced for an answer. Sylvia was one in a long line of sob sisters, women who wrote the gossip columns, that I had loved and left hanging. My past was catching up with me in more ways than one today. I forced an easy smile while she stared, stone-faced, back at me.

"Yeah." I cleared my throat. "I was about to when something came up."

Sylvia took a deep drag off her cig then dropped it and crushed it under her heel. She walked from the railing to stand right in front of me, exhaled smoke straight into my face. I blinked and coughed while she leaned in to whisper in my ear.

"You'll never change, Seth Moseley," she said. Then she kissed me, long and hard, smack on the lips.

The newswoman pulled away, lifted her right hand to

my face. For a second, I thought she was going to slap me, not that I didn't deserve it. Instead, she wiped lipstick— "Cherries-in-snow," her signature color—from the corner of my mouth.

"Take care of yourself, Seth." She tapped the end of my nose. "The next woman you love may not be quite so forgiving."

Then Sylvia turned and walked down the Promenade Deck away from the dog pack of reporters. A shiver ran up and down my spine as if someone had just walked across my grave. Sylvia had rattled my cage more with that kiss than if she'd smacked me upside the head.

That was the power of women. Just when you thought you knew what they were going to do, they'd surprise you and do something completely unexpected. She reminded me of my one golden rule when it came to women: falling head over heels in love with a dame will only get you hurt, so love them and leave them as quick as you can.

Too bad I didn't heed Sylvia's warning until it was too late. Until I was in way over my head with the most beautiful and powerful woman on the planet.

2. ROPE-A-DOPE

JAMES

February 14, 2000—2:26 EST
Seth Moseley Interview

"Cut!"

My boss, documentary film producer Martin Hinkle, simmered in the chair opposite Seth, the ancient reporter. Tom, aka Video Guy of Norfolk, switched off his video camera mounted on a tripod in front of the two men. Two practicals—halogen lights affixed to six-foot metal stands placed on either corner of the tiny room—kept the room cooking.

"What," Martin demanded, "does any of this have to do with an exclusive on Greta Garbo?"

Seth put a hand up to cover his eyes from the glare. His nearly bald head gave off a faint blue hue, like a robin's egg, under the hot lights. His red-and-green plaid shirt hung loosely on his skeletal frame. His body was literally wasting away from its battle with emphysema. For the first time since we'd arrived, I could see in detail the frail old reporter I had talked to over the phone from across the country.

"If you'll indulge me," Seth said, enunciating each word. "It has everything to do with Garbo."

Seth lowered a thickly veined hand, index and forefinger stained brown from decades of handling nicotine, to once again reveal his wrinkled face under the stark incandescence. A plastic tube ran from his nose to a green oxygen tank behind his chair. He rotated his head to assess each one of us in turn. I wasn't prepared for the penetrating gaze of his deep-set brown eyes as he scrutinized me.

Seth Moseley had called me in response to an ad I'd blanketed in the classified section of numerous East Coast newspapers, searching for anyone still above ground with firsthand knowledge of Greta Garbo. I had an idea for a documentary on the movie star and talked Martin, my boss of five long years, into giving me a co-producer credit if I could get an exclusive.

"Get me something fresh and dirty on the dead star," Martin had said. He knew the old man had seen things that staggered the imagination. Seth Moseley had scooped the Lindbergh Baby Kidnapping, covered the Hindenburg Disaster and was on hand to witness burned bodies washing up on the Jersey Shore from the *Morro Castle* ocean liner fire. I couldn't get him to shut up over the phone. And his biggest story was what we had come all the way to Norfolk to hear—a Garbo story no one ever heard before.

My empty stomach shifted as I looked on in uncomfortable silence. I hadn't slept in over thirty-six hours. Hadn't eaten in over eight, and that meal had consisted of a bag of overly salty pretzels and a Diet Coke on the plane ride I couldn't afford. I glanced at the camera's eyepiece over Video Guy's shoulder and noticed how small Seth appeared. The old man smiled and licked his thin, cracked lips.

"All right," Martin barked. "Let's get to Garbo, shall we, Seth? And … action!"

But Seth just stared at Martin in silence. Martin looked back at Seth, incredulous. Video Guy turned and looked at me. We all shared a moment of suffocating silence. The room felt pressurized as I glanced wide-eyed over at the oxygen tank. I didn't dare move for fear of setting off a spark that would blow us all to kingdom come.

"Well?" Martin asked.

"Well what?" Seth said.

"What about Garbo?"

"Garbo?" Seth asked, apparently in full-on senior moment.

"Yeah," Martin goaded. "Garbo."

"But I already told you," Seth said, then laughed. "Garbo's the reason I went on the *Athenia* in the first place. That is my Garbo story."

Oh. Oh no. Tell me the old man didn't just say that. Video Guy stifled a laugh. I wanted to cry. Somebody needed to call the bomb squad. The only job I'd had since graduating film school was about to blow up in my face. All on account of an old man's shaggy-dog story.

"You," Martin said through gritted teeth, "we were under the distinct impression you were going to tell us an exclusive about Greta Garbo. The movie star? I'm doing a special on her. Remember?"

"Right," Seth said. "Right. Garbo."

"So," Martin said to himself, fighting to process the information, "Garbo was never on the ship? Just the look-a-like?"

"Yup," Seth said with a smile, then looked over and gave me a wink. "The hot tip we all got about Garbo being on the *Athenia* turned out to be just a bum steer."

"Oh, what fresh hell is this?" Martin groaned. Then his face turned bright red. "CUT!"

I watched intently while both men sat scrutinizing one another. One old and dying, the other growing more furious by the second. Seth had rope-a-doped Martin, and I had been his idiot accomplice. I had taken it on faith that he had a story, a Garbo exclusive. In my desperation to secure a co-producer credit, I'd fallen for the oldest trick in the book: the bait and switch. I burst out in a cold sweat while both men sat frozen in place. Video Guy turned off the lights.

I considered Seth's silhouette, backlit by the whiteout outside his little studio apartment's bay window. Squinted at him while he sat in his now shadowed throne. What in hell was going through his mind? What could possibly be his motive? Was he the type that reveled in wasting other people's valuable time? Happy to just not be alone?

I turned to Martin with morbid fascination. Waited for his tiny brain to assimilate this new information. So wildly out of his element now, there was no telling what he'd do next. Then Martin's body shook with rage. I checked the exit behind me. If needed, I could use Video Guy as a human shield.

The memory of the next half hour of my life remains a blur. I remember seeing Martin erupt out of his seat, the rest of us frozen in place. I remember glancing at Seth as he stared up from his chair with unabashed glee at Martin boiling over in front of him with a toxic mixture of anger and vitriol. I remember Video Guy, nimbly packing up his video equipment while navigating around Martin's flailing and convulsing body in the confined space.

The next thing I knew I was outside, snow falling horizontally as I watched Martin in the driver's seat of the rental car, warming it up. I could barely make out his face behind the icy, fogged windshield. But I could hear him just fine as he screamed, "You fuck!" over and over.

Video Guy finished loading his van, the engine idling, and came to stand beside me. To look at us, we could have been Laurel & Hardy in a previous life. I had spent countless childhood hours admiring their violent yet loving relationship on TV. Now I wanted to jump into the big guy's arms and have him hold me. Better yet, I looked up into the white heavens and prayed for a piano to materialize out of nowhere and drop on me. Put me out of my misery.

"Your boss," he said and watched Martin, "is pissed."

Martin beat his fists against the steering wheel, then the dash of the rental car. Video Guy stifled laughter.

"Yeah," I said and wished I could join in his amusement.

"I'll only charge you for a half day," he offered.

"Nah," I said. "Martin will pay for the full day."

We stood in quiet contemplation for another moment as the snow fell harder and Martin's blows softened in exhaustion. I shifted my weight in the snow, producing the sound a leather chair made when you shifted your buttocks. Like I'd farted. Video Guy turned to me and smiled. He lifted a massive arm and rested it on my shoulders. I sank lower in the snow.

"It's none of my business," he said, "but your boss is a real horse's ass. I like the old man better. Even if he is nuts."

"Yeah, thanks for the input."

Video Guy reached in his jacket with his other hand and extended me his card. I took it.

"If you're ever in the area again," he said, "give me a call."

Then Video Guy departed to the warmth of his van. A moment later, he and his vehicle were gone. I approached the passenger door of the rental car and opened it with caution. A rogue wave of snow entered the car and covered Martin.

"What do you think you're doing?" he asked, looking over at me like a crazed snowman.

"Going back with you?"

"Get. Out," Martin said calmly.

"Martin, come on," I said in a sycophantic squeak.

"No," he screamed. "You're fired. Get the fuck out."

Martin threw the car into reverse. The vehicle pulled away from the assisted-living home, snow flying forward from under the front tires. I barely had time to get out of the way of the open passenger door. Martin gunned the engine again. The lumbering automobile squealed in protest as he threw the Taurus into Drive. The back wheels spun wildly and sent rooster tails of snow in odd directions until the snow tires gained enough traction to propel the car onto the main road.

I stood alone in the tranquility of the snowstorm, then turned back to the assisted-living facility. A wrinkled mass of faces stared at me from behind the large windows of the lobby, some confused, yet most happy not to have missed the afternoon matinee I had produced for them. Finally, I had attracted an appreciative audience.

The onlookers scattered as I took a step back toward the door. Then the entire facility disappeared behind a wall of snow brought on by a violent gust. I stopped, frozen in place in the whiteout.

The realization that I'd just allowed myself to be stranded on this strange planet was accompanied by a blur of bright red out of the corner of my eye. I turned and saw a cardinal take flight in the driving snow. Watched his crimson wings fight silently to ascend, disappear into the blank canvas sky. There and then gone like the last five years of my life.

I had to go back in to the assisted-living facility. Re-enter the old man's world, now invisible behind the curtain of snow, long enough to arrange my own flight. Unable to see what lay ahead, I had to pick a direction and start over. So, I took a blind step forward and everything went from white to black.

3. SETH ON THE S.S. *ATHENIA*

JAMES

I woke up in a hospital bed with a headache and a hard-on. To my left was a window, frosted in the corners with snow crystals that glistened under an unseen sun. To my right was Seth, lying in his own bed not six feet away. He stared at me, the corners of his cracked lips turned upward.

"Good dream?" he asked and nodded his head to my waist. Thank god I was under a blanket.

As if this wasn't humiliation enough, a young, attractive nurse carrying a clipboard entered our room. The closer she got, the more attractive she was, and the more mortified I became. Seth laughed out loud while he watched as I tried to turn away from her, conceal the tent I was making out of my blanket. That's when I first noticed my right arm had an IV line attached to it. My nervous jerk resulted in a jolt of pain from pulling the line taut. I reacted by emitting a girlish scream.

"That's what you get for fidgeting," the nurse said and came around my bed.

She leaned in to inspect my arm. I watched the sunlight glow deep blue on contact with her long black hair. A dark wave cascaded down her face in slow motion as she leaned down. She parted the wave with both hands and put the black silk behind her ears. I felt the incredible urge to run my fingers through her hair. Drown myself in it. In this perfect stranger.

"No permanent damage," she said and gave me a jolt of electricity when her fingertips made contact with my forearm. I needed to make the moment last. Keep her near to gaze at her face. Smell her scent. Touch creamy white skin. Behold red ruby lips. A crimson pout beneath the brightest hazel-colored eyes.

"What happened?" I looked up at her like a drunken man.

"You slipped and hit a patch of black ice," she said, then looked up and caught me gawking at her. She didn't pull back or run away. "With your head."

"Cracked your noggin pretty good, too, from what the paramedics tell," Seth chimed in. "Good thing head wounds produce so much blood, or they wouldn't have found you."

"Found me?" I said, disturbed by the image he conjured.

"You were stumbling your way into the woods," she said.

"Like a wounded animal," Seth ad-libbed. "Headed off to a secret burial ground to die."

I didn't have to wonder why. The old man had driven me crazy. I remembered that much. Getting fired from my job, then stranded. The insult that led to my injury. I had been headed back into his apartment to make plans for going God-knows-where. After that, nothing. Just darkness. Darkness until now with this raven-haired angel staring down at me.

"I should inform the doctor you're conscious," she said and began to pull away.

"Wait." I reached a hand up to hold her wrist. To get her to stay. Please stay. "How did the medics get there so fast?"

"Every time we get a Nor'easter," she said, "they're dispatched to the assisted-living facility. Good thing too, or we might not have found you 'til spring thaw."

Good thing was right. But that didn't explain why the old man was there. In my room. Making my head throb harder.

"Allow me to introduce you two," Seth interjected. "Sarah, this is Jimmy."

"James," I corrected him and kept my eyes on her. "What's he here for?"

Seth laughed. I was pretty sure he was the architect of us landing in the same room together. Hell, why not? He had his L.A. audience back. And then some. If only Sarah and I could be alone. What, James? Then what would you do?

"Mr. Moseley's medical condition," she said, "is confidential."

"They say I've got pneumonia," he blurted. "Lucky for you, huh, kid?"

Lucky? Not quite. Lucky would've been never having heard of Seth Moseley at all. Never come all this way only to end up with a big fat goose egg. Less than zero except for the beautiful woman now standing in front of me. I hoped Nurse Sarah was the silver lining to my very dark cloud.

"Jim-boy came all the way from Hollywood to get my story," Seth bragged. The smug bastard. The old man didn't have a problem talking to women. He didn't have a problem talking, period.

"Is that so?" Sarah said, then reached up to my IV stand, slowed down my saline drip by depressing the thingamajig on the clear, plastic tubing. She tapped the base of the bag with her finger. My heart beat a little faster.

"I'm going to make him famous," Seth gushed. "That is, if you think he'll live."

Make him go away, Lord. Don't kill him, just make him go away. I lifted my unencumbered left hand, felt my bandaged and throbbing head. I had to believe Seth was the real pain in my neck that was making my head throb.

I looked up at Sarah and smiled. She leaned in again to inspect my head bandage. In my imagination, she was moving in slow motion again. Like Grace Kelly leaning into a kiss with injured Jimmy Stewart in Hitchcock's *Rear Window*. As her face approached mine, a band of tiny freckles bridging her nose came into sharp focus.

I started to count them, when I realized she was looking straight into me. Her retinas were bottomless pools of black, surrounded by the purest hazel striations I'd ever seen. Her eyes looked like two massive storm systems you'd see on Jupiter.

They were beautiful and ferocious at the same time. Then I caught the reflection of myself staring at Sarah in the eye of each storm. I was tiny. Insignificant. I looked like a field mouse that'd come in from the cold and found himself sniffing her intoxicating scent. Getting warm and high on a mixture of soap, moisturizer and sweet, sweet sweat. Maybe a little lavender water, too? I had to get to know this woman.

"He'll live," Sarah said. The words smacked me back into reality, as I blinked my reflection away. She reached out and caught the tip of my chin between her thumb and forefinger. Lavender fingernails with little white flowers painted on them. Then gently, playfully she pulled my lower lip out and waggled it in her grip. "But only if he watches where he's going from now on."

She let go and leaned back to look at me. Was that a wink? My resolve to be in her world stiffened anew.

"I need to get an emergency contact number for you," she said, brandished her clip chart and clicked her pen. "Mother, father, next of kin?"

"No," I said.

"Wife?" she asked.

"No."

"No one?" she asked. "No one we should contact?"

"Nope," I said.

Sarah shrugged and checked a box with the flick of a pen. Then she put her hand back down on my forearm. A gesture she probably made with a thousand patients before, but to me felt special. Little white flowers stared up at me from her lavender fingernails.

"Well, you have me now," she said. "And I know this old guy here is awful fond of you."

I turned to Seth. He beamed a toothy smile at me.

"How long do I have to be in here?" I said, staring at him.

"You've suffered a concussion," she said, all business now. "We'll need to observe you for at least twenty-four hours. So, I suggest you sit back, relax and enjoy our Norfolk hospitality."

Sarah came around my bed to stand between the two of us.

"Can I get either of you gentlemen anything?" she said, looking at both of us in turn, "before I go fetch the doctor?"

"Codeine and bourbon," Seth said.

Sarah smiled at Seth. I could tell she'd dealt with his kind before. Maybe a lot before. Maybe him before. Made sense this wasn't Sarah's first rodeo with the old reporter. Made sense and made me nervous. What had he told her while I was out?

"Sorry, Seth," she said. She didn't bat an eye or miss a beat. "But we want to keep you sharp and lucid so you can tell young James here your story."

With a quick smile and lovely turn of her powder-blue scrubs, Sarah was out the door and gone. Seth gave a gratified chuckle, obviously happy with himself. I looked over at him.

"Codeine and bourbon?" I said. "Those were Talullah Bankhead's final words."

"Yeah," he said. "She was a great gal."

"You met her?"

"Yup," he said and raised an eyebrow. "She was a wild one, all right."

The image of Talullah flashing her crotch on a small boat came to mind. I'd read that on the set of Alfred Hitchcock's *Lifeboat*, she'd refused to wear underwear. Hitchcock had been noted as saying he didn't know whether it was a problem for the makeup or hairdressing department. Tallulah and Seth. Of course, they had known each other.

"I wish I was dead," I said to the open doorway.

"Why on earth would you say that?" Seth asked.

"I had a hard-on with a girl in the room." My head was throbbing harder by the minute.

Seth shook his head. "Better than having a hard-on without a girl in the room."

"Don't you ever get embarrassed?"

"What's to get embarrassed about?" he said. "I'd give anything for some lead in my pencil."

"It's graphite."

"What?" Seth looked at me, perplexed.

"Pencils are filled with graphite, not lead."

"Jesus, kid," he said with an exasperated sigh. "You really do need to get laid, don't you?"

"Please," I begged, "can we stop talking about boners?"

Seth's laughter whacked me in the skull like a baseball bat. I feared the next curveball might do me in for good. Thankfully, his laughter quickly subsided.

"You really don't have anyone in your life?"

"You make me sound pathetic."

"No," he said. "Sad, maybe."

"Do you mind?" I shot back. "I've got more pressing matters right now."

"Like what?"

"Well, for starters." I raised my free arm up to grasp the hospital bed railing. The cold metal felt soothing. "I'm confined to a hospital room with you."

"Here we go again," he said with a snort.

"Frankly"—I scooted up on the bed a little—"I thought I was done with you."

"Hey, no one asked you to take a header out my front door. Okay?"

Silence passed between us. A steely, cold silence. I looked up at my IV drip and watched the droplets of saline form slowly, then fall the tiny distance from the mouth of the bag into the line. God, what I wouldn't do for a drink of something hard.

"Well," Seth said finally, "aren't you going to ask me?"

"Ask you what?" I stuck my hands under my damp armpits. I was sweating and freezing all at the same time.

"About Garbo," he said.

"We tried that once." I sat ramrod straight in my bed. "It didn't turn out so good, remember?"

"I didn't tell your hack boss," he said, "because he didn't deserve to hear it. The story I have to tell I've never told anyone before. Not even family."

"Why pick on me, then? A total stranger?"

Seth hesitated, cast his head down and plunged his skeletal facial features into shadow. Then he opened his eyes and looked over at me.

"Because—"

"Because what?"

"My story," he said, "it … it's special."

I heard a drum roll in my eardrums. The blood in my veins ran cold until I felt frozen solid from the inside. He had used the dreaded "S" word. I could have told him how many quacks and psychos had professed how special their story was, only to prove in the end to be complete bullshit. I could have told him. But I didn't care to.

He shifted in his bed and looked over at me. "Did you read the official record?"

"What?"

"The sinking of the S.S. *Athenia*? The one I sent you. Tell me you at least read it."

I had. Great Britain declared war on Germany at 11:15 a.m. EST on Sunday, September 3, 1939. Eight hours later, Nazi U-boat U-30 Commander Lieutenant Fritz-Julius Lemp sighted the *Athenia* off the Hebrides archipelago. She was running without lights. And against the Prize Rules, the Hague Convention and Der Führer's own rules of engagement, Lemp opened fire. The *Athenia* was torpedoed three times before Lemp fled the scene, taking the lives of one-hundred and twelve men, women and children, twenty-eight American. It was the shot heard round the world.

"Sure," I said. "So what?"

"So don't you think it's funny that a seasoned U-Boat Commander would open fire on a merchant vessel carrying civilians mere hours after war had been declared?" he said.

"There's nothing funny about it." I was serious as a heart attack. I set my jaw and registered my impatience.

"You know what I mean. Did you read the eye-witness accounts of the survivors?"

"Look, Seth—"

"They all said the *Athenia* had been fired upon, before the torpedoes even hit."

"I don't—"

"For a submarine, stealth is its most effective weapon." he yammered on. "Lemp wouldn't surface and give away his location just to fire his deck guns. Use your head, James."

"I thought I had," I said. "And instead I ended up in here with you."

"Mr. John Cudahy, the American Minister to Ireland, said that witnesses stated the *Athenia* had been struck amidships and was shortly afterwards struck again 'by a projectile shot through the air.' What does that tell you?"

"You're saying there was another ship present?" I said.

"Yes." Seth said. "Another enemy ship."

"Yet no evidence of another ship exists?"

"Right."

"Wrong," I said. "Nazis kept exact records of everything. How many ships they sank. How many bullets they used. How many Jews they incinerated. Why would the sinking of the *Athenia* be any different? Why a conspiracy?"

"Because," he said, "of her secret cargo."

A shot of anger flushed my cheeks, lit my face from within. Seth sat up in silence. Obviously, it was my call. Ante up or fold. I called.

"Okay, I give. What cargo?"

"Garbo."

"That's the most ludicrous thing I've ever heard."

"Is it?"

"Yeah, it is." I said. "What the hell would Nazis want with a movie star? They only had a world war on their hands. If I'd known that was the story you were going to tell Martin, I never would have come here in the first place."

"I told you it was a good story."

"You did," I said. "But you didn't mention it would cost me my job and the only contact I have in Hollywood."

"So why not let me make amends?" he said. "You heard the nurse. You're stuck here."

"Maybe so," I said. "But it doesn't mean I have to listen to your tall tales."

The old man's cheeks now flushed with anger. That made two of us. But instead of fanning the flames of contempt, I turned away. Stared off at a far wall rather than incite him or myself further.

"I see," he said. "Still thinking if you can just catch up to that boss of yours, he'll make it all better."

"How did we get back to Martin?" I motioned to throw

up my arms in disgust but knew from previous experience the IV line would not approve.

"His type will always be searching," Seth said. "He'll never find what he's looking for because it's not there. Because he doesn't have it in him."

"How the hell would you know?" I said. "You barely laid eyes on him."

"Trust me," he said. "I know a bad apple when I see one."

"Drop it, okay?" I said. "I'm done with all of it anyway. I quit."

"Maybe you shouldn't give up so easily," Seth said.

He sounded demoralized. I couldn't imagine why. If anyone should have been upset, it was me. But I was calm. For the first time in a long time, I felt centered.

"Maybe," I said, "you should mind your own damn business."

God, I was finally able to say what I needed to, in the moment. And it felt great. And whatever the reason the old man picked me to mess with before he dropped dead no longer mattered. I decided in that moment Seth Moseley was going to rattle my cage no more. No matter how hard he tried. No matter what.

"Maybe so," Seth said and didn't say another word.

That afternoon, Sarah came back with the doctor in tow and drew the curtain between Seth's bed and mine. Seth and I weren't on speaking terms, so I enjoyed the privacy. After the most cursory of examinations, the doctor prescribed a painkiller for my head and told Sarah that I should only have ice chips to quench my thirst for now. I didn't care. I had her watching over me.

Then Sarah brought both Seth and me dinner. He had an ice cream scoop of powdered mashed potatoes, several strips of turkey and peas. Mine consisted of a bowl of chicken broth (complete with crazy-straw) and blood red Jell-O cubes. I looked over at Seth and longed for his untouched, off-yellow potato snowball. He avoided all of it and quietly sipped a cup of tea Sarah had made especially for him.

The silent treatment between Seth and me continued on into the early evening. Seth had not spoken to me since I had told him to mind his own beeswax. Sarah must have sensed the rift between us. She came to our room at the end of her shift and turned on the TV, mounted between our two beds above the door. She sat down quietly at the bottom of my bed with the remote and channel-surfed, hunting and pecking until she came to the Turner Classic Movie Channel.

I looked up at the screen to see the word *Garbo* flash in bold black and white letters. Then the title *Queen Christina* came on, accompanied by the tinny sound of melody. I looked down and watched Sarah look up at the monitor. Her body literally perked up and came to attention. Why on earth would a young woman like her be interested in a movie that had been made some fifty years before she'd been born?

We all watched in silence as *Garbo* made her entrance. She was twenty-nine when the movie had been released in 1934. The same age I was now. Garbo's physical beauty was in full blossom, radiating out from the shitty little monitor demanding my attention. I glanced over and saw it had the same effect on old Seth.

We were all Garbo's subjects as she held court in the movie. Garbo as Queen Christina of Sweden addressed us with an unwavering gaze. She slammed her fist down on her throne:

"We have been fighting since I was in the cradle and many years before. There must be an end."

I had seen the movie before but felt I was hearing these words for the very first time. A gear in my head I never knew was there snapped into place. I looked at Sarah, then Seth. Surely they had heard the rattling machine-sound my skull had made? But they were still watching the screen. Enraptured with Garbo's presence.

I looked at Seth's profile as he stared proudly up at Garbo on the monitor. It reminded me of one of those early war posters, where Uncle Sam stood, shirtsleeves rolled up, gaze fixed on the stars. The posters that asked young men to come forward and fight for freedom and the American way of life. Except in my version, Uncle Sam was bed-ridden, weighed all of ninety-five pounds, and dying of emphysema.

"How did you know Garbo was on the *Athenia*," I heard myself ask, "when by all accounts she never left America from 1939 to 1945?"

"Simple," he said, without looking away from Garbo on the television. "I was on it with her."

"That was two days before France and England declared war on Germany," I said. "After Hitler invaded Poland."

"Yeah," he said, still attuned to the screen.

"The *Athenia* never made it to Europe," I said. "It was

lost at sea. You're telling me that you and Greta Garbo were aboard when the ship was sunk, though no records exist of either of you being rescued. How is that possible?"

Seth finally looked down. The television played in the background. Garbo herself now looked down on our little group, considered us in quiet contemplation from her private black-and-white bed chamber in ancient Sweden.

"That's because we weren't on the ship when she was hit." Seth had a distinct look of sadness in his eyes as the movie goddess watched from above.

"Where were you?" I said quietly.

"In the air overhead," he said, distracted.

Sarah turned to look at Seth. Her beautiful brow now crinkled in curiosity. He had hooked us both. I leaned over my hospital bed side rail. Stared straight at Seth, riveted, while beautiful young Sarah and Queen Garbo above her on the television looked on.

"Your story," I said, "does it have a wow finish?"

Seth looked over at me. The setting sun in the window behind me fired his pupils, like a golden-hued key light in an old Hollywood melodrama.

"Yeah," he said. "Wow."

4. SCARS IN THE ATMOSPHERE

SETH

The *Athenia* crept ever closer to port while the gaggle of reporters crowding the Promenade Deck all jockeyed for position. Everyone wanted to be first man off. The tip on Garbo being onboard was a bust, so it was every shutterbug for himself. Every hack with a Kodak was now looking for a story prior to deadline to earn his keep. Everybody but me. I just wanted to keep my toes.

A tab reporter's life was to always be one step ahead. But this was one time being out front wouldn't pay. I shrank back from the railing and moved to the rear of the wolf pack, shunning the refracted light coming off the water's surface like some bottom dweller might. If Toes wanted my toes, he'd have to come on board to get them.

My strategic retreat lured some unwelcome attention. I felt a presence from behind me. I knew it couldn't be Toes, because we hadn't made port yet. But that didn't make me any less jumpy.

"Moseley," a voice said over my left shoulder.

I turned to see Bill Evans, a mick from *The Mirror*, a rival tabloid rag. A harmless, dim-witted general pain-in-the-ass who I'd neither the time nor the patience to deal with.

"You look like forty-miles of rough road," he cackled.

"Shove off, Evans," I said. "Don't bother me."

"What's the matter, you *hang over* the railing, too long?" he said and laughed. "Hangover, get it?"

I got it all right, and I would have finished it, too, if I had the—*That's it!* He'd be just the diversion I needed. I glared at Evans and smiled. The schmuck was made-to-order.

"Funny," I said. "You write your own material? Or did *The Mirror* hire a monkey to do it for you?"

Evans had the kind of sarcastic smirk I would have been only too happy to remove with the business end of a shovel. Instead, I sharpened my tongue and hoped to inflict just enough injury to provoke the moron. I was a gambling man, after all, and I now had my money on Evans taking a fall and creating enough of a disturbance for me to disappear, toes intact.

"Haven't seen you around much," he said while several fellow hacks turned toward us, smelling trouble. "You been on a case, Moseley?" Then Evans licked his lips, his tell just before delivering a punch line. "A case of Scotch?"

Evans laughed a high-pitched hyena laugh. I let him enjoy himself. I found when engaged in verbal sparring, it was always good to let your opponent draw first blood. Or think they did. Evans had been nipping at my ankles for years. Now it was time to teach him a lesson and, at the same time, use him to save my own tail.

"That's a knee-slapper, all right," I encouraged him. "But ya know, you should be more thankful."

"How's that?" Evans mocked.

We had an audience. The reporters crowded around us, while I took a glance at the port looming ever closer. In a minute we'd be docked. Bernie and Toes would be looking for me. I had to buy myself some time to sneak away. Make myself scarce long enough to skip town or come up with the scratch to pay back Johnnie Roses, my marker. I turned back to Evans.

"God gave you opposable thumbs," I said. "So you can wipe your own ass and work a typewriter once in awhile." Then I went in for the kill. "Not that you could tell them apart with the crap copy you write."

The crowd erupted in gales of haughty laughter. The grin on Evan's face faded. I'd gotten to him. But I had to make sure he went for the bait. No time to lose.

"Crap," I added. "Get it?"

I could see in Evans's eyes that I'd succeeded in drawing a line in the sand. Now all I had to do was make sure he stepped over it. The smart man would have given up in the face of a superior intellect. But Evans wasn't smart. As I predicted, he pressed on with a losing concern.

"I guess what they say about you is true," he said. "You're all washed up. A has-been."

The crowd took a collective groan. They knew, as I did, where Evans was headed with this. They just didn't know I had led him there. I visually bristled and braced myself. Already had a line on what was coming next.

"Like your man Lindbergh," Evans said.

Now the crowd gasped in unison, drew back and gave Evans and me a wide berth. That was my cue. Evans knew, as did every man and woman on that deck, my history with the famous aviator. Lindbergh had given me the story of the century. My big break when I was still a greenhorn reporter. But that was a story for another day. Right now

I had other pressing matters. Like getting into a fistfight without getting my own teeth knocked out.

I knew my limitations. My upper body strength had not been taxed for some time beyond lifting a pint glass. Evans, on the other hand, was built like an Irish ox. I eyeballed his stocky six-foot frame and decided the best course of action was an uppercut. But I'd have to be quick and use the element of surprise to my full advantage. I'd only get one shot.

"You can lead a horse to water," I said, then motioned to turn away. "But you can't get him to shut the fuck up."

I was lucky. The air horn of the *Athenia* sounded above us and I took the opportunity to whip my right fist up under Evan's chin. A deafening siren accompanied the crowd of reporters as they made way for Evans, reeling back on his heels. They parted like the Red Sea as the Irishman hit the deck like 250-plus pounds of dead weight.

I felt the ship lurch to a halt as the ship's air horn continued to blow. And while everyone stood around, gawking at Evans slithering in pain on the deck, I made tracks for the first exit off that deck I could find.

My plan had been more pragmatic than elaborate. I'd succeeded in distracting the mob of reporters. Now I had to find a place to hide and wait out the goons waiting for me in port. My hand ached while I ran down a mahogany-lined hallway with chandeliers, plush red carpeting, and bevel-mirrored walls. My desperate visage stared back at me in the looking glass, like a bum who had stumbled his way into a foreign palace.

My stomach dropped when a young porter suddenly came out of a stateroom at the other end of the hallway.

I put on the brakes and broke into an uneasy smile. To my surprise, instead of ringing the ship's alarm, the young porter waved a white-gloved hand in a practiced, welcoming gesture.

"May I be of assistance," he said in English with a heavy and, I assumed, Swedish accent.

"Bathroom?" I said in a winded, plaintive voice.

"Of course, sir," he said. "There is a gentleman's room at the other end of the hall." Then he turned and gestured with the same hand for me to follow him. "Right this way."

"Excellent," I said.

We were both off like a shot down the hallway. He brought me, key in hand, to an overly ornate door adorned in black-lacquered high relief with cherubs and naked water nymphs. I didn't think I was about to enter a john as much as a church sanctuary.

The porter inserted the key and opened the door. I didn't have a plugged nickel to tip him, so I saluted him instead. He gave a confused smile in return. I piled into the black-and-white-tiled room while he looked on. I made my way over to the wash basin, feigning illness.

"Oh, *gaaaaaaaaaaawwwwwwdddd*!" I fake-vomited, the porcelain basin amplifying the sound.

"You'll be requiring of your privacy, sir," the porter said from the doorway. "I'll lock the door from the inside, so no one need disturbs you."

This kid was the answer to my immediate prayers. He turned the lock on the inside of the door for me, then proceeded to close it. I couldn't have come up with a better solution to my situation myself. Things were looking up.

"Much appreciated," I said.

The porter gone, I leaned up and took a look at myself in the mirror. I decided I wasn't such a chump after all. A little soap, a little cash and a lot of luck, and Seth Moseley would be back on top. I proceeded to turn on the water faucet and grabbed a fresh bar of soap on the basin. I was gonna start turning things around that very minute. Cleanliness was next to Godliness, something like that.

The bathroom was both nicely appointed and bigger than my apartment back in Hell's Kitchen. The daylight and sea air streaming in through the porthole over my right shoulder was delightful. I laughed at the idea of making this joint my new permanent address. Throw in room service, and I'd never leave.

Then I glanced up in the mirror and saw movement. Like an eclipse, something had passed in front of the porthole and obstructed the light. I turned in time to register someone dressed in a black cape, black floppy hat and velvet gloves with green piping standing before me. They must have been hiding in one of the stalls because I remember the porter had locked me in from the inside.

"Who the hell are you?" I said, my face and hands covered in soap lather.

My assailant—let's call him the masked musketeer just for shits-and-giggles—came at me wielding an object strikingly similar to a wrench. Swung down and caught me right in the noggin. Next thing I knew I was on my knees, staring down at the black-and-white floor tiles, now spinning like pinwheels blown by the hot winds of hell.

Hit over the head for the second time that day. The odds of a permanent mark, not to mention brain damage, were high. I fell to the floor like a rag doll. Gob-smacked the tile floor with my face. My ears heard the sickening thud my flesh made against the floor, while my eyes glared down into a rotating dark abyss. My gateway into oblivion.

The first thing I noticed when I regained consciousness was that the light in the room had changed. The second was that I had apparently pissed myself. A nasty habit I was determined to break myself of. Once people stopped accosting me, of course.

The cacophony of pain in my head couldn't be worse if somebody had ripped the two hemispheres of my brain apart and smashed them together like cymbals. My eyes ached in direct proportion to the light in the room. I had taken to the recessed shadows of a darkened bar for so long, my eyes had become allergic to light. And to getting my own porch lights punched out one too many times.

I got up on all fours and stared up at the porthole above me. A shimmering shaft of daylight now shot straight across the room. Even in my diminished capacity I deduced it must be around noon. The sun was on the rise. But I'd have to wait to take in the view. First, I had to figure out how to get myself up off the floor.

My stomach, back, and head all screamed at me in unison. I looked down at my hands and noticed the smallest vibration coming through the tile floor. It was like it was alive. I pondered this as I crawled my way back to the bank of basins, hoisted myself up on my knees, then theoretically to my feet. The whole procedure took far too long, but I wasn't in any position to argue the point.

I didn't bother looking in the mirror when I finally made it to my feet. I knew what I must have looked like and didn't need the stark truth to confirm it. So much for cleaning myself up. Someone obviously had taken exception to my appearance. Tried to wipe the smile off my face with a wrench.

I rested my haunches on the basin and faced the porthole. Gazed upon it as if in a trance. The color of the light had a beautiful pink tinge to it. My mouth hung open as I stared at the round disk of sky in front of me. Like the fancy dinner plates my mother had hung on the wall of our dining room. I used to stare up at them when I was a little sprig, eating my cream of mushroom soup.

My spell of nostalgia was broken when something flew by on the other side of the porthole, temporarily obstructing the light. Something big. Was that a … was that an albatross? No. No such bird existed on the Atlantic Ocean.

I got to my feet and slowly, oh, so slowly walked towards the porthole, careful to mind the light beam. I felt like a direct shot of sunlight might cause my head to spontaneously combust. I was already spinning. I didn't want to be on fire as well.

I came up to the edge of the open window and gingerly stared out. What I saw was not what I expected. No dock. No port of New York. In fact, nothing but open sea with pink and purple cotton-candy clouds above a continuous horizon. Then I looked at the sun. It wasn't morning, but late afternoon into early evening. The sun had aligned with the porthole on its descent into the west.

Holy shit. The ship was at sea. Headed towards Sweden. I was now officially a stowaway. I broke into a smile for the first time in a long time. Toes had figured I'd jump ship. He hadn't considered I'd stow away. Neither had I, for that matter. Someone had made that decision for me. I had no idea who or what the reason could possibly be, but I was thankful I was still intact. For the most part.

I stared out at the placid sea, a sheet of glass mirroring the heavens above. A reflection of the first star of the night bobbed on the surface. Like it had fallen there but was too hot to be extinguished. No. Not a star. The planet Venus.

Yeah, my world had been turned upside down, all right. In the last couple hours, I had been transported to another world entirely. This new one was more exotic, bigger and covered entirely with water. The *Athenia* encompassed my reality now. In order to survive, I'd have to get to know the floating city and her crew intimately. Once she stopped spinning.

5. VELVET GLOVES & SCREAMING MEEMIES
SETH

When I emerged from the men's room that evening, I was a little worse for wear. I walked down the mirrored hallway of First Class suites and immediately noticed my hair. Getting hit in the head with a wrench had given me a permanent part. I was also pretty sure my new coif broke some obscenity law. Mashed together, my black locks looked like a big fist giving me the finger in the mirror. Or a demented rooster.

The *Athenia*'s Promenade Deck was abuzz with activity, what with the dining saloons just letting out. Mothers lined the railing, gossiping, with babes in arms, their older children playing games, while husbands had repaired to the bar for cigars and digestives. The sea remained smooth as plate glass.

The ocean air on the open deck didn't revive as much as nauseate me. My skin had the ghostly pallor of a husk shed by a rattlesnake. What I needed to make myself right was a cigarette and a drink, both in the ship's salon. This was a tricky proposition, though. I wasn't a paying passenger and looked it. I hoped the ship's salon accepted

American greenbacks and no questions asked. I made my way through a gaggle of mothers and children, trying to avoid their stares.

I stepped into the ornate art-deco establishment made of glass and hardwood and felt eyes fall on me like bricks. You'd think I'd be good at walking into a bar with all the practice I'd had recently. But this joint was different. This was the kind of place guys like me entered through the kitchen to make a delivery or work the hot line. It had that rarified air I found suffocating. I felt as welcome as a spare prick in a honeymoon suite. But since I had nowhere else to go and solace lay just behind the bar, I pressed on.

I'd practiced grinning in the hall mirror before I came in. I thought a smile might improve my appearance, but I ended up looking like an idiot. Whoever said, "Smile and the world smiles with you," was a lying sack of shit. All cadavers smiled once their lips got eaten away. I was doing a bang-up impression of one when the barmaid approached me. It's to her credit she didn't start screaming right off the bat. Instead, she led me to an empty table in the corner.

"What may I get for you, sir?" the Swede said in pitch-perfect English.

"Bourbon and a beer chaser." I literally fell into the chair she kindly pulled out for me.

"Lager or pilsner?" she said.

"Yes," I said and placed my hands flat on the table top.

The raven-haired barmaid turned, and I caught a look at her shapely buttocks as she walked away. This was an encouraging sign. I hadn't expired yet, though you couldn't tell to smell me. She was back in the time it took the barkeep to draw the spirits and then placed them before me. I looked up at the young woman's open face and flashed my corpse smile.

"What's your name, beautiful?" I asked.

"Ingrid." She had a beautiful Swedish accent.

"I didn't know Swedes came in colors other than blonde."

"Some of us even keep our spots when we grow up." Her delivery so quick and deadpan that I almost did a double take.

"I guess I'm not the first Joe to crack wise to you today, huh?"

"That would depend."

"Depend on what?" I said.

"On whether your name is Joe."

Ingrid turned and left me to my libations before I could come up with a snappy rejoinder. For the next half hour, I watched her help other patrons as I downed the shot, then the pints. I couldn't help but admire how she charmed patrons without condescending to them. I especially liked the way she met people's gaze head on with a pleasant yet serious nature. She carried herself with a confidence and countenance that belied her apparent youth. By the time she came back to me, I was spreading my newfound sea legs and eager to enter into another round of spirited conversation.

"Another round?" Ingrid asked.

"Only if you'll join me."

She shook her head. "We aren't permitted to fraternize with the passengers."

"What about when you get off?"

"Then I go to bed."

"You're the boss," I replied.

Ingrid let the comment hang in the air. I felt like a trapeze artist high up on a tightrope about to lose his balance. I held my breath, unsure whether I'd gone over the line. She could tell her pause was having the desired effect and let me dangle there another few seconds. It served me right for working without a net.

"Maybe this one time," she said, "I can make an exception."

"Wonderful." I exhaled.

"What is your name?"

She put both her hands on the table and gave me a nice view of her cleavage. I stared into the dark-v her bosom created, drew a momentary blank on my own moniker. The power women possessed was stunning. I moved my eyes back to her face, rallied at the last minute.

"Seth," I said, relieved I'd managed to remember.

"I get off at nine." She straightened up until her shoulders arched backwards and her cleavage caught the light. There were freckles on her chest. Her spots were showing, and they were beautiful.

"I'll be waiting," I said.

I'd bought a pack of smokes before departing the bar and inhaled nicotine under the stars in the open air of the Promenade Deck. Mothers and their children had long since retired to their cabins. I stared out on the Atlantic with a sense of excitement. No better salve for a bruised male ego than a beautiful woman who agreed to meet up after work. Dilapidated, I was. Disheveled, for sure. But it hadn't seemed to harm my chances with the fairer sex. Ingrid had spied my charming nature through the detritus and couldn't help herself. If this was a fairy tale, I was prepared to cuddle up for the whole story.

While I waited for Ingrid, I heard a commotion in the Main Parlor off the deck. Light and smoke came from the darkened front entrance, and I could hear familiar, though hard-to-place, strains of melody coming from within. I doused my butt and headed over to the open archway.

I stayed in the shadows of the doorway and peered inside. There, on a large movie screen set up atop an elevated bandstand, a roomfull of passengers watched the glowing, gloriously huge face of Greta Garbo in the 1934 movie *Queen Christina*.

My heart skipped a beat. Garbo dressed as a young nobleman shimmered on the screen, augmented by the cigar and cigarette smoke that swirled and played in the horizontal column of light from the projector. Her majesty rode a white horse through the snow-covered Swedish countryside. In actuality, the landscape was a sound stage in Los Angeles covered in tons of dried potato flakes used to simulate snow under the hot lights. But Garbo always made make-believe convincing. The audience sat enraptured at her image. Men and women alike were mesmerized by her beauty.

I laughed. I had finally found Garbo. She'd been onboard the whole time, hiding in a film can waiting to be brought to life on a movie screen. I imagined what my editor, let alone Toes, would say if I told them. Then again, Garbo only meant money to them. To me as well, if I had any sense left.

I watched Garbo enter a Swedish inn and take off her potato-flake-covered overcoat and gloves. In the hands of any other actress, the concept of a beautiful woman masquerading as a young man would have been laughable. But this wasn't just any actress, this was Garbo. Her androgynous beauty fueled the mystery of her persona. She was more than a woman or man. She was something else altogether.

Then I felt the presence of someone on deck behind me. I turned ever so slowly in the dark shadow of the doorway and saw the caped and hooded figure that had brained me in the bathroom. Made up of shadows, the shrouded figure stopped just behind the periphery of light spilling out from the room and remained still as a phantom hovering just above the deck.

I stared at the ghostly apparition and wondered what the hell to do. I'd been lucky enough to go unobserved. Why the heck would anyone expect me to be crouched in the dark? But with the figure facing my direction, I knew I wouldn't be able to get a jump on it the way it had me. So, I resigned to remain still and observe. Glean whatever details I could of the character in the twilight.

There we remained, the phantom and I, until a small boy appeared in the doorway of the salon. Not a day over six, he peered into the darkness and must have seen enough to investigate further. My heartbeat accelerated as the boy passed me and made a beeline for the phantom.

I don't know what I expected, but I was surprised to see the dark figure just stand there while the boy walked up to it. He came to a stop and stared up at the shroud without an ounce of fear. The boy's curiosity had gotten the best of him. I watched slack-jawed.

Then the most amazing thing happened. The apparition spoke. "Why aren't you watching the movie," a low-contralto voice said. Male or female I couldn't tell.

"It's boring," the little boy replied.

"You don't like Queen Christina?"

"That's not her," the boy said and brought both hands up to his hips. Arms akimbo, he cocked his head up at the phantom. "That's just some actress pretending to be her."

I stifled a laugh. Straight out of the mouths of babes. Couldn't get anything passed this kid. But would the apparition feel the same way?

"Some actress?" It replied. "You don't know her name?"

"No," the boy said.

"Don't you think she's pretty?"

"No," he said again. "She's too skinny."

"Everyone's a critic," the phantom said. "Tell me, do you know how to swim?"

A shiver ran through my bones. That was the same question Toes had asked me, before he let me join the *Athenia*. I judged the distance between me, the boy, and the apparition. If the ghoul decided to bend down and throw the little tyke over its shoulder, I'd never make it before the kid hit seawater. Before he'd be lost forever.

"Yes, I'm a good swimmer," the boy said. "Why?"

"You think if I threw you overboard you could swim all the way to Sweden?"

"Why would you do that?"

"Because I don't like children," the phantom said. "Especially little boys."

Another shiver ran through my timbers. From behind the boy, I braced myself against the outer wall of the salon.

I wasn't good at the whole rescuing thing, but I considered making a run for it and snatching the boy if I had to. You never knew what a phantom would do faced with a fresh young soul staring up at it. At least I didn't.

"Why not?" the boy said. He'd missed his cue to turn and run back into the salon, back to safety. Instead, the little bugger stood his ground.

"They grow up to be little men,"

"I'm going to be a policeman when I grow up," the boy said, "and everyone will have to do as I say."

"Like I said."

Then a shadow overtook the boy from behind. I turned in time to see a man standing in the threshold of the salon, peering out where the boy and phantom were having their conversation.

"Tyler?" the man said. "Who are you talking to?"

I turned back to see the boy facing toward his father.

"This man who doesn't like little boys," he said matter-of-factly.

"What man?" the father said.

I turned with the boy to see that the phantom behind him had vanished. The three of us took turns looking up and down the deserted Promenade Deck as I held my breath. The goddamn ghoul was gone again.

"Come back in, Tyler," the father said. "Now."

Tyler complied, and I breathed a sigh of relief. I straightened up in the shadow of the doorway and peered inside. Garbo was sitting on her throne, glaring while she addresses her packed court.

"There are other things to live for than wars," she declared. *"I've had enough of them. We have been fighting since I was*

in the cradle and many years before. It is enough. I shall ask the powers to meet for a speedy and honorable peace." Then Garbo slammed her fist on her throne. *"There must be an end!"*

The audience—onscreen and off—sat in silent awe of the queen's presence. I was one of them.

"You need a bath," a young female voice behind me said.

Startled, I spun around and found Ingrid smiling back at me.

"How long have you been there?" I said, then sniffed myself. Ingrid had spoken the truth, though not exactly the first thing I wanted to hear from her lips.

"Not long," she said.

"Did you see someone in a cape and hood walking around out here?"

"No. Why?"

"No reason," I lied.

"Where's your suite?" Excellent question. Where was my nonexistent cabin? While I contemplated lying through my teeth to the beautiful Ingrid, my mind was occupied by the strangely familiar voice that had emanated from the phantom's shrouded face. A voice I could not place, yet swore I'd heard before.

"My suite?" I said. "I seem to have temporarily misplaced it."

Ingrid cocked her head and scrutinized me. Homeless and smelly, I became even more self-conscious. I smiled meekly at her. Then she took hold of my grimy hand and led the way down the darkened deck.

"Come with me," she said, and I left Garbo to her adoring fans.

★   ★   ★

Ingrid's quarters were located at the stern of the boat, where the ship's engine was the loudest and had the most vibration. The entire crew was berthed there except for the Captain and his First Officers. She led me into her cabin, and I immediately got an idea of the quality of woman I was dealing with. I had already figured that she was single, given her occupation and bare ring finger. She was a bit of a free spirit, as evidenced by how she had appointed her private quarters. Ingrid had an amazing collection of picture postcards from every port of call she had ever made: Poland, Belgium, France, London, New York, to name a few. The images went on and on, and I marveled at how well traveled she was at such a tender age.

I also admired the fact she had a private bath adjoining her cabin, which she instructed me to enter. I'm not the retiring type, but I did hesitate when given this command from such an attractive woman. I was filthy, don't get me wrong. Her room, on the other hand, was spotless with clean, pressed white linens and a bouquet of red roses. I was amazed the big blooms didn't explode on contact with my stench.

Ingrid walked into the white-and-black-tiled bathroom, turned on the shiny faucet handles, and drew me a bath. Then she turned and looked up at me with a somewhat curious, somewhat annoyed expression.

"What are you waiting for?" she said. "Undress."

I started to disrobe. I had expected Ingrid to leave the bathroom, but she merely rolled up her sleeves. With one hand, she checked the water temperature. With the other, she turned the hot water fixture adjacent to the faucet that fed the bath. I was down to my skivvies and feeling downright introverted when she turned again to assess my progress.

"Those too," she said, and pointed to my underwear.

This was new. While I was sure I had taken a bath sometime in the last month, I was equally confident it wasn't in the company of a beautiful young female. I wasn't exactly sure how Swedish people bathed, but I knew I didn't need to be babied. I stripped and stepped butt-naked into the tub. That was as far as I was going to let it go.

"Sit down," she said.

"I'm pretty sure I can handle things from here," I said, standing my ground.

"Looking at you," Ingrid replied, "would indicate otherwise. Now sit down. I haven't got all night."

The last time I had been given a bath, my Irish grandmother had washed me in the same basin with her pug, Mimi. Alva would use a washcloth similar in consistency to sandpaper and scrub Mimi and me so hard it was a wonder there was anything left of us.

Ingrid's bath elicited a much different response from me than Grandma Ratray's ever had. In any normal scenario, I would have taken this as an invitation to get better acquainted. But as I watched Ingrid wash my legs, it struck me that this girl was on the up and up. She was giving me a bath because I needed one. I decided to put the kibosh on the tub proceedings before I debased myself in front of either the young woman or the memory of dear, departed Screaming, or rather barking, Mimi.

"I'll take it from here, sister," I said, and snapped my legs together.

"Suit yourself," Ingrid said and handed me the washcloth and soap. "Save the bathwater when you're done. I'll use it to wash your undergarments in the morning."

Her stare telegraphed that fresh water was a precious commodity on ocean liners and not to be wasted. I nodded like an obedient schoolboy and made busy with the soap and cloth. Then Ingrid turned and walked out of the bathroom.

She left the door separating the two-room suite ajar. I could see from my vantage point the pale-skinned, dark-haired beauty disrobe. She couldn't have been more than twenty-two or twenty-three years old, with a short torso connecting athletic arms and legs that went on for days. Her eyes were a lapis blue, her height just enough below mine to make her tilt her chin up to look at me. But when she took off her top, my investigative reporter brain turned to mush. Robbed of my powers of detached observation, I lingered instead on her beautiful shapes and curves. The woman was no longer measurable by earthly dimensions. I sat in the water and drank her in.

Then something changed. At first, I didn't understand the image that interrupted my reverie and projected itself fleetingly onto the black-and-white tile of Ingrid's bathroom. Tile which was identical to that of the men's room in which I had been accosted earlier that day. Then the image flickered to life again, and I knew.

"Seth," she said from the other room. "Are you all right?"

I looked up. Ingrid stood in the threshold of the bathroom. I watched her pull the hairpin out of the black bun at the nape of her neck. Her dark, bosom-length tresses cascaded down around her beautifully shaped face, framing a concerned expression.

"Yeah," I said.

Ingrid broke out in a million-watt smile and momentarily lit up the bathroom like a marquee sign. Her moon-crescent eyes gave me a shiver while I sat in a puddle of my own filth.

"Don't forget to wash behind your ears," she said, turned, and walked naked toward her bed.

"I won't," I murmured and watched her get under the covers.

I turned back to the black-and-white tile, scrutinized the mental image now frozen upon it. I imagined Mimi the pug sitting in the tub beside me wailing a high-pitched warning to guard my privates while I still had them. But I was mesmerized by the image of the velvet gloves of my assailant, which were the same as the phantom's on the Promenade deck. And the very same ones worn by Garbo in *Queen Christina*. I double-checked my memory for telling details, but it was clear as day in front of me. The green piping was unmistakable, even in black and white on the screen. I was sure of it. Garbo was aboard in more than just smoke and light. And I failed to grab her when I had the chance, out of fear. I'd even been bested by a little boy.

But why would Garbo hide in the men's room, and why clock me? Screaming Mimi evaporated into thin air. I didn't need an imaginary, castrated dog to tell me when I was in hot water. I turned to the mysteriously accommodating young beauty who lay in wait in the next room. Ingrid dozed while I kept an eye peeled on her.

"Come soon," she said sleepily.

"Be there in a New York minute," I blurted and made splashing noises with bar soap and washcloth.

Something queer was going on aboard this tub we were sailing on. Lovely Ingrid had served herself up to me on a silver platter. She knew I needed help. Knew I was a fish out of water in the middle of the ocean. Ingrid knew a lot about me already, and I knew absolutely bupkis about her. I was a dumb sitting duck.

"Almost done," I said. Good and cooked was more like it. I lifted the washcloth and dutifully scrubbed behind my ears. Ingrid the Swedish barmaid was made-to-order, all right. Made me feel all tingly inside and want to believe she was just a swell kid with a heart of gold. Believe she had a soft spot for strangers in need of a bath and a place to hide out. And that's what scared me most.

6. THREE ON A MATCH
SETH

I looked at Ingrid sleeping next to me. Somewhere between midnight and 6 a.m., I'd fallen hard for this dame. I watched the shadows recede in her room and realized there was no going back. I was basking in the afterglow of our night together and didn't want the sun to rise over the ocean. First light brought the danger of ending what we had begun in the dark.

I had never equated love with sex before. I had never equated love with anything before, except maybe beer. But nestled next to Ingrid's naked body, and when she was on top of me, her hips synchronized to my own, when we fell into a natural rhythm, I felt a strange yearning. From the start, our bodies fit together like two interlocking jigsaw puzzle pieces. This newfound sense of belonging ran contrary to how little I knew about the person lying in my arms. As was the completely alien desire to want to care for and protect her.

Ingrid awoke and smiled up at me. She summoned the sun to rise in my eyes, and I smiled apishly back at her. I was thinking and acting like an ignoramus. I hoped I wouldn't have to say anything. The thought occurred to me she might not feel the same way about me as I did toward her. Blood turned cold in my veins with fear.

"Good morning, handsome," she said. If Ingrid noticed the sudden change in my body temperature, she didn't let on.

"Hi."

"You stay here." Ingrid kissed me, then slid out of bed. "I'll get us breakfast."

"Okay." I watched her skip naked into the bathroom.

The weather on the North Atlantic in September can be freezing, and her room was chilly. I curled under the covers and contemplated how it could be I was still in a woman's bed that I had had sex with the previous night. Usually, I couldn't get away quick enough. This was nothing less than a revelation.

Why had it taken me twenty-nine years to unearth this crown jewel of discovery? Then I remembered. I was an asshole. The type who didn't have time for relationships, let alone breakfast in bed. If I wasn't careful, I might just get both in short order, served up on the same silver platter dear Ingrid had been. I watched her from the bed and admired her natural beauty. Lucky for me, I had plenty of experience when it came to ruining a good thing.

I was surprised to find Ingrid a monument to perfectly coiffed femininity. Before flappers, only prostitutes had shaved their armpits and legs. The jazz age ushered in a whole new world of depilation in New York City, and I was amazed we hadn't all been swept away on the resulting sea of cut hair follicles. Ingrid's sculpted muscles and smooth silken skin glowed in the morning light, the very epitome of the modern woman.

Ingrid ordered a smorgasbord from the ship's commissary, and soon the smell of rich drinking chocolate and confectionaries permeated her suite, along with coffee, hard-boiled eggs, sausages, fresh-baked breads, salmon roe and herring. We laid low and spent the morning in her cabin, satiating the enormous appetite we'd worked up during the night. I could have stayed in that bed with her for the rest of the voyage, easy, and was eager to relive some of the previous night's highlights.

A knock at her door delivered my suit cleaned and pressed. Even my tie was straight as an arrow. I marveled at the brown threads like they were a new garment. If this wasn't enough, Ingrid produced a men's shaving kit, complete with lather stone, brush, and blade. My five o'clock shadow had run around the clock for days—maybe weeks—since the last time I'd scraped it off. This morning, however, I found pleasure in shaving. Stood before the mirror in Ingrid's well-lit bathroom, a white beard of warm lather on my face, and shaved around a shit-eating grin. I felt and looked better than I had a right to, all because of a woman. Amazing.

Ingrid had let me into her life so openly and without hesitation that I couldn't help but admire her for it. Did she inherently trust me that much? Should she? Seth the Letch, the sob sisters, the women tabloid reporters, had called me. I gobbled up women's virtue nearly as fast as the bar nuts that had, up until recently, passed for a regular meal. What I felt for Ingrid was, for want of a better term, special. Could a mug like me change overnight in the blink of one woman's eye?

★ ★ ★

After a morning full of playing house in her cabin, Ingrid and I spent the afternoon exploring the ship, the floating metropolis known as the *Athenia*. The noonday sun was high overhead before I realized I hadn't had a drink all morning. I hadn't needed one. With Ingrid on my arm, I felt higher than I ever had before. The buzz from distilled spirits had nothing on what I felt in her presence. She was a much stronger intoxicant and came without the nagging hangover. At least not yet.

We took in the sunset on the Promenade Deck after another round of strenuous lovemaking in her cabin. We held hands while the sun hung above the horizon, suspended just above the water when a corona of rainbow appeared around it.

"What is that?" she said.

"Sun dogs," I said.

"It's beautiful," she said. "I've never seen it before."

"Sunlight is being refracted through ice particles in the atmosphere," I explained. "Makes a halo."

"How do you know so much?"

"I met a guy named Lindbergh once," I said. "He taught me how to fly and a whole bunch of other things about the sky."

I stared at the sun dogs and saw a flash of the Lindbergh Estate in the dead of night. I'd been young and fearless, driving the dark bumpy rural road that snaked through the Sourland Mountains north of Hopewell, New Jersey. I was on a collision course with a story that had changed the world. Changed my life forever.

The memory evaporated. I looked down and saw a massive shadow in the water, approximately four hundred yards off the *Athenia*'s port bow.

"What's that?"

"What?"

I let go of Ingrid's hand and pointed to the spot. A mass of dark water hung just below the surface, in sharp contrast to the sun-dappled surface of the slack tide.

She squinted at the water. "I don't see anything."

"Well, I do."

My eyes may have been blown out from sexual ecstasy, but they could still focus when they needed to, still see what was in front of them. Especially if what I saw didn't jibe with what little I knew of the natural world.

"Maybe it's a whale," Ingrid offered.

It wasn't a whale. Not that I had ever seen a fucking whale in my life. No, by my estimate the whale in question would have to have been half as long as the *Athenia* herself to make that shadow. Moby Dick himself wasn't that big.

I knew the only reasonable explanation for what I saw. Any dope who'd read the papers or listened to the radio would have drawn the same conclusion. The North Atlantic was infested with U-boats, especially the shipping lanes. If this one was checking us out, then why hadn't it surfaced? Why hadn't a periscope or conning tower breached the surface to take a better look? Ingrid turned and gave me a look of concern.

"Maybe the sun is playing tricks."

"Maybe," I said. "Maybe I should have stayed in bed." I looked back out at the ocean. The shadow was gone. I tried not to look alarmed, for Ingrid's sake.

"Seth," she said, "I have to get ready for work.

She took my arm, and we headed into the ship. I turned and took one last look back at the sea. The sun had set and took all its shadows with it. I'd have to let sleeping sun dogs lie, for now.

Something hadn't felt right since we'd gotten back to Ingrid's suite. The shadow I'd seen in the water seemed to hang over us. How could Ingrid not have seen it? Or did she simply not want to? I knew people who refused to see things for what they really were. They were either too stupid or too scared to face reality. Ingrid didn't strike me as either, and that piqued my curiosity even more.

After she changed and left for the salon, I went through her things. It wasn't that I didn't trust her. Just that I felt a compulsion to come up with a solid reason not to. I prided myself on my ability to divorce my emotions from my intellect when needed. Still, I was willing to give Ingrid the benefit of the doubt, instead of my usual doubt of the benefit of trusting anyone. I kept this in mind as I searched for something that would incriminate her.

Ingrid's belongings were compact and utilitarian in design, yet had a style and beauty indicative of their owner. A small cherry jewelry box with gold inlay, silver rings and a wristband from Indonesia hidden inside. A silver hand mirror and comb set with a single strand of long black hair upon it. A black enameled lipstick applicator with green jade egret appliqués. Silk stockings, Ingrid's scent still on them. A Buddhist prayer wheel.

I opened a decorative cedar-wood box from her closet and found family photos and fistfuls of letters addressed to her, care of General Delivery in every major port of call. Apparently, her parents wrote religiously. I imagined they would also most assuredly contain a popular refrain: Pa worried about her traveling the world alone, Ma wondered when she was coming back home to marry and settle down. They all missed her. Ingrid wanted to live life on her own terms. She had champagne taste and a beer pocketbook, Mother Moseley would have said. Good for her, I said.

I walked into the salon, sullied from my dirty work back in Ingrid's suite. The reception I got was nothing like the night before. People who had given me a double take previously now barely glanced at me. I was happy for the cloak of anonymity a clean shave and a pressed suit provided.

I sat down and popped a cigarette into my mouth while I waited for Ingrid to notice me. I hoped I had enough of a poker face left for her not to tell of my trespassing on her personal property. This woman had thrown me a life line when I desperately needed one, and I felt a twinge of guilt when she spotted me from across the salon.

The feeling gave way to excitement when a wink and a smile later, Ingrid stood before my table.

"Something I can get you, sir?"

"A beer and your cabin number."

"You've already got one of them."

"How about a beer in your cabin then," I said. "Away from prying eyes."

"I'm sure that can be arranged." She smiled seductively. "But there's someone I want you to meet first."

"Someone to meet?" I said. "That's a bit of an occupational hazard for me right now."

"Nick is okay," she said. "I'll be right back, and we'll go."

Nick? Who the fuck was Nick, an old family friend? Old Saint Nick? Why hadn't I just said no, like I had with every other dame who had wanted to introduce me to a friend, family member, or dog? It was a terrible thing, feeling myself go soft in the head. Ingrid came back, coat in hand, and I sprung to my feet. At her beck and call.

"I don't even get my suds first?" I said.

"They'll have them there," she said, extending me her hand.

"Where?"

I heard the music before we even entered the Great Hall. The previous night it had been canned melody, blown out of speakers synchronized to Garbo in *Queen Christina*. But tonight, live music from a piano on the stage captivated everyone's attention. White table-clothed rounds illuminated by candles gave the scene an intimate nightclub atmosphere. Ingrid made her way toward the front of the room like she owned the place. I felt like the schmuck who swept up after it closed.

"Isn't he marvelous?" she said, smiling at the gent seated at the piano up on stage.

"Who?" I said, genuinely confused.

I looked up and saw Nick. Somewhere in his mid-thirties, he was a lean, slick, immaculately-coiffed crooner dressed in tails. Dark and handsome, Nick tickled the ivories to some familiar tune while all the women in the audience swooned. I wanted to punch his streetlights out on sight. But why? What in the Sam Hill had gotten into me? I looked over at Ingrid, swooning along with the best of them. There was my answer and my problem, seated right beside me.

Nick finished his little ditty, bowed, and made a hasty retreat while the dinner crowd clapped enthusiastically. The Piano Man made his way over to us. I braced myself for impact.

"Ingrid," he said and gave her a peck on the left cheek. "It's been too long."

I bet.

"Nick," Ingrid said, "this is Seth."

"Hello, old boy. How's business?"

Nick had an American accent. This was unexpected. Made me hate him even more. Now he was more than just a musician on the make. He was an American musician on the make.

"Booming," I cracked.

"I wish I could stay and chat," he said, then waved both hands at the crowd. "But can't let the natives get restless."

"Don't let us keep you." I contemplated shoving his baby grand up his ass. I'm sure the natives hadn't seen that before.

"Grab a table, and I'll show you how it's done." He winked at Ingrid. "Drinks are on me."

Ordinarily, the phrase "drinks are on me" would set my saliva glands to watering. This guy, however, gave me a bad case of cotton mouth. I couldn't wait to get back to Ingrid's suite.

"Thanks," she said.

Hatred can make a guy awful thirsty. Over the next hour, I must have downed five pints. Nick played his set and never broke a sweat. I secreted enough for the both of us. My suit was wet with perspiration by the time he hung his act up and slithered off stage toward us. Ingrid had held my hand during the whole show and only sipped at her Champagne cocktail. She tried to engage me in small talk. But all I could think about was Nicky Baby.

A waiter came out of nowhere and placed an extra chair at our table just in time for Nick to sit down. Had they rehearsed this number?

"Well," he said, "what do you think of my day job?"

"Marvelous," Ingrid gushed. "Perfectly marvelous."

The same waiter arrived out of my peripheral and deposited a Champagne cocktail in front of Nick. He stayed on long enough to produce a light for Nick's cigarette. The waiter's departure gave me an entrance.

I leaned back in my chair. "Does he wipe your ass for you, too?"

"Seth!" Ingrid chided, obviously embarrassed.

Nick looked at me, then Ingrid, then laughed.

"You obviously haven't seen the bathroom in my berth." He waved his cigarette. "Barely big enough for one person."

It was a nice save. But he wasn't done. He was only getting started.

"Not at all like dear Ingrid's." He gave her a wink.

The arrow had hit home. Nick had turned my rapier wit back on itself and drawn blood. He placed himself inside Ingrid's suite, in her bathroom no less. In a masterful economy of words, he had verbally depantsed me and smacked my skinny, white ass. I had to watch my back with this one.

Ingrid laughed. "I knew you two would like each other."

"So, Seth," Nick said. "What brings you aboard our happy home?"

I had a choice here. I could let the liquor speak for me, or I could regroup for Ingrid's sake. She was obviously enjoying our sparring match. And since I had literally nowhere to go, I had all the motivation in the world to dispatch my fellow American, post haste.

"I'm a reporter. On assignment."

"How interesting," he said. "What assignment?"

"I'd tell you. But then I'd have to kill you." I didn't tell him I already wanted to.

"A secret! I love secrets. May I try and guess?"

"As long as you're buying."

Nick snapped his fingers. The ass-wipe waiter brought us all another round.

"I'm guessing you embarked back in New York," he said. I nodded. Pleased with himself, Nick put two fingers to his forehead in mock contemplation. After a moment of silence, he smiled and snapped his fingers. "I've got it!" Nick stared at me as he laid down his cards. "Garbo."

I folded like a cheap tent in the wind. Ingrid looked at me for verification. She could tell by the look on my face he'd hit the jackpot.

"That's amazing," Ingrid said.

"Not really," he said. "It's a small ship. There were a lot of reporters. I just hadn't realized any of them stayed on. You must really think she's aboard."

I was thankful for the rhetorical statement. It gave me more time to drink my beer.

"Care to make a wager?" he said.

"What kind of wager?" I said.

"Whether you can find her," he said, "in the time it takes us to get to Stockholm."

Nick became visibly excited and animated by the prospect. A pitchman putting on an act to exact a sale. I let him have the floor, curious to see where it would lead.

"Life can get so exceedingly boring on these voyages," he said. "As I'm sure Ingrid here has told you."

In fact, she hadn't. But I began to think maybe what we shared last night had been simply a diversion for Ingrid. An amusement, like tonight's male display of colors for her probably was. Nick apparently sensed my dismay and skillfully turned it into an enticement.

"A bet is just the thing to liven this trip up," he said. "Ingrid here will even help you. Won't you, darling?"

"Maybe Seth isn't the gambling type, Nick," she said.

Nick and Ingrid turned to me. I stared at him through the bottom of an empty pint glass.

"What say you, Seth?" he said. "Are you a gambling man?"

For a scam artist to be successful, he has to know his target. It was a bad bet that had gotten me onto this tub, and I was fresh out of collateral to buy my way back into the game. But Nick had no way of knowing that. Just like he had no way of knowing that I was flat broke, flat on my back and most likely headed for the brig once the crew became aware of my ticketless ass. Unless Ingrid was his shill.

"What kind of stakes are we talking about?"

"That's the spirit." Nick rubbed his hands together. The Piano Man wore a gold pinky ring on one hand and an emerald on the other. "Let's call it at a thousand kronor."

"What's that in real money?" I said.

"About $200 US," he said. "But you have to prove Garbo is on board."

"I doubt she'd be up for a duet," I said. "If that's what you're asking."

"That would be grand, but not necessary." Nick laughed a little too hard. "Physical proof will do just fine. Say, an article of clothing? Or maybe a letter with her autograph on it?"

"Don't worry," I said. "I'll come up with something."

"Wonderfully exciting," Nick said. "Let's have another round to celebrate."

The drinks might as well have materialized by themselves for as fast as they came. Nick raised a glass in a toast.

"To adventure on the high seas," he said by way of a cherry smile.

I hoped a rogue wave would come out of nowhere and knock him on his ass. Not likely. I eyeballed Ingrid beside me and downed my pint in one motion. Over the course of the evening it had become impossible for me to read her. To know where her allegiances lay.

Part of me warned I'd fallen for the oldest routine in the book. Attractive young woman provides the bait, then her male counterpart reels me in like the sucker fish I am. Introducing me to Nick had raised me up on my hind legs and had me itching for a fight. But while Nick fit the bill of a con man, I'd be damned if there wasn't something different about Ingrid.

We all produced cigarettes at the same time. Nick lit a match to light his own cigarette, then mine and then motioned to ignite Ingrid's. I instinctively put a hand out to stop him. Ingrid looked on, curious.

"Three on a match," I warned.

"Of course," he said. Nick extinguished the match. "Sorry, my dear."

"For what?" she said.

Nick struck the end of a new match with the tip of his thumbnail and ignited the phosphorous. He extended the flame toward Ingrid. She lit her cigarette, a look of incomprehension illuminated on her face.

Nick nodded toward me. "Your man Seth here is a bit superstitious."

"Not inordinately," I protested.

Ingrid glanced at Nick and then settled on me. "Superstitious about what?"

"During the Great War, soldiers on the front lines were taught to conserve their rations, including matches and cigarettes," I explained. "They would light three cigarettes to a single match. Until the enemy figured out what they were doing."

I turned to Nick and caught his stare. Ingrid turned to him, though he addressed only me like she had ceased to exist.

"The enemy would use the light to target the first soldier," he said. "Verify it was the enemy with the second. Then shoot to kill the third."

"Ever since," I said, "legend has it the third person to light a cigarette off one match is cursed to die a violent death."

Ingrid took my hand under the table and held onto it. I felt a tidal wave of warmth run through my body. She was like a riptide pulling me back out into a sea of love. To drown me?

Meanwhile, above the table on the surface, Nick smiled like a long lost friend. "That was very chivalrous of you, Seth. "My hat is off to you." He lifted an imaginary chapeau off his head with his left hand. I wasn't superstitious or chivalrous by nature, but this guy had brought both out of me in one night. Hat's off to me, all right. Tomorrow it would be his head, if I had anything to say about it.

7. GARBO THE REDEEMER

JAMES

I sat in my hospital bed and contemplated my next move. Sarah, my hot nurse, had to attend to other patients while I listened to Seth's shaggy-dog story about how he got aboard the *Athenia*, was knocked in the head and ended up in a beautiful Swedish barmaid's bathtub. Oh, and saw a mysterious, cloaked woman who may or may not have been Garbo, the movie queen.

Before she left, Sarah had muted the TV monitor on which *Queen Christina* still played. Meanwhile, Seth's Garbo story was turning out to be anything but. Aside from the revelation that he had worked in Los Angeles at MGM, Garbo's studio, we still weren't any closer to placing the movie star on the ill-fated ocean liner. My head ached in the knowledge I had outmaneuvered Martin, my-ex boss, to Norfolk, Connecticut, only to get fired. All on the word of a delusional old man. I had to say something.

"Excuse me," I said, "but where is Garbo in all this?"

Seth looked over at me, both arms in the air, gesticulating about how he had crawled back to life and into Ingrid's willing arms. I knew he knew what I was asking. I gestured to Garbo on the TV.

"Garbo," Seth said.

"Yes. You know, the movie star?"

Seth looked up at the TV and smiled. Garbo was sitting in her courtroom, abdicating her throne for love. I knew the scene by heart. Must have watched the movie over a hundred times with my mother when I was young. The local cable station wore out its copy playing it on the *Late, Late Movie.*

Toward the end of Mom's life, when she was in too much pain to sleep, I'd stay up with her to all hours. I didn't want to waste a precious minute of our time together snoring in the chair beside her bed. We both knew I'd have the rest of my life to catch up on my rest, after she was gone.

"You got somewhere to be?" Seth said.

"Ha ha. That's a good one." I stared at him stone-faced. "You haven't told me one thing. Not one damn thing to prove conclusively Garbo was even on the *Athenia.*"

Seth put his hands down on the bed before him. His face flushed. I looked at him and held my tongue. I wanted to hear what he was going to say. We were stuck together in that room. I had no control over that. But I wasn't going to let him lead me around by the nose anymore.

"Patience," Seth said. "Have a little faith."

"Sorry," I said. "I'm fresh out."

Seth reached over to his night table, grabbed the TV remote that Sarah had left there and turned off the monitor. I looked up in time to see Garbo's face in close-up as she took off her crown, looked straight at Seth and me, then faded to black.

"Hey," I said. "What did you do that for?"

"Why do you even care about my story?" he said and

threw the remote back on the table. "Care about an old movie star who died when you were barely out of diapers."

Without the TV on and Sarah gone, it was like Seth and I were back in his cold, dark apartment. The place had been like a crypt, and the hospital wasn't much better. The twilight from the window beside my bed was the only thing fending off my claustrophobia. Seth was trying to box me in. Pushing me to confess something I didn't want to say. Share feelings I hadn't felt in a long time.

"What does it matter?" I said. "I'm here now, aren't I?"

I'd dodged the question, but for how long? Ironically, it was the same one Martin had asked me when I had to convince him to pony up a ticket to Norfolk, Connecticut, to come see Seth in the first place. But for him I just took a page out of his own playbook and lied. I told myself I needed to lie in order to come and find out the truth. The truth about Garbo.

I had walked into Adversary Productions and told Martin I had the story that would get him his coveted Emmy. I told him he was going to unveil a story on a Hollywood Goddess so sensational, so titillating and revelatory that he would have cable executives eating out of his hand for the next five years.

"What story?" Martin said without looking up from his breakfast burrito.

I hit Martin in the gutter where he lived. I told him Seth had proof of a lesbian romance between Garbo and Marlene Dietrich.

"That's old news," Martin said and laughed. "Rumors of Garbo being a dyke are as old as gospel."

"Rumors," I said. "But never proof."

"What kind of proof?" Martin said, chorizo and scrambled eggs flying from his mouth in a chunky spray.

"What other kind is there?" I suggested boldly.

"You're telling me," he said, "that old man has been sitting on celluloid of Garbo and Dietrich carpet-munching? For the last seventy-five years?"

"Yeah," I lied. Martin hadn't given a damn about Garbo. To him, she was just fair game, famous and dead. Yet another bullshit cable mockumentary by the time he'd be done with it. But I knew better. I knew the world still cared about Garbo, even though they didn't know it yet. And Martin was the dullard I needed to convince to get it out to the world.

Martin prided himself on being able to tell when other people were lying. And in all my years with him, I never had. Until that day. And I couldn't believe how well the whopper of a lie had worked. Martin bought the whale of a tale hook, line, and sinker, and before I could even second-guess myself on what I'd set in motion, he'd authorized two tickets to ride. Unfortunately, I'd sold the idea of a world exclusive so well Martin hadn't trusted me going it alone to get it.

So now I was alone, lying in a hospital bed next to the old man I'd lied through my teeth to see. The old tabloid reporter was insisting I tell the real reason I'd come. I glared at Seth and knew I couldn't fib my way through this. The old man was too sharp. Too smart for me to pull the wool over his eyes. He wanted me to give him something personal to proceed. Something I hadn't told anyone, ever.

"I came," I said finally, "because of my mother."

Seth looked at me and without saying a word, urged me to continue.

"She worshipped Garbo," I said. Mom worshipped Garbo, and I worshipped Mom. "Would've loved to have learned why Garbo forsook the world for a life of isolation."

I told Seth about the day Mom compared Garbo to Christ. It was a rainy fall day, and she had let me play hooky from school to stay home and be with her when she was having a hard time with chemo. We curled up together on the loveseat in our small living room and watched *Mata Hari*, another Garbo classic. During one scene, Garbo stood up and opened her arms straight out to accept her lover. Mom had grabbed the remote and paused the film. Then she'd turned and looked at me with a devilish grin.

Weak as she was, Mom found the strength to get up and walk over to the bookshelf across the darkened room. To stare at the shelf where she kept all her travel books of places she would have loved to visit but would never live to see. Mom brought back a book on Brazil. Opened to a picture of the famous Christ statue that lords over Rio de Janeiro.

"Look," she had said. "They dedicated the statue the same year *Mata Hari* was made. Christ the Redeemer."

I looked at the famous Jesus statue in the book, then back up at Garbo on the screen. I described to Seth how the gestures of statue and actress were exactly the same.

"You think she could have known?" I'd asked Mom as I scrutinized the TV screen.

"I think we're onto her, my love." Then Mom had leaned in and whispered softly out of earshot of Garbo frozen on the screen. "Let's just keep her secret between the two of us. What do you say?"

I'd turned to my mother and smiled back. "Garbo the Redeemer," I whispered and kissed her forehead while

Garbo watched with open arms in my peripheral vision.

Then the silence brought me back into the hospital room, accompanied by a rush of blood to my face. I'd said that stuff out loud? Flushed, I sheepishly looked over at Seth. His eyes were closed, and his chin rested on his chest. Fuck, had the old man expired while I was reminiscing?

"Seth?" I whispered.

"Garbo the Redeemer," Seth intoned. He opened his eyes, raised his head, and I practically jumped out of my bed.

"You got a haunted streak running through you, kid."

Haunted? The idea never entered my head before. Places were haunted, but people were possessed. All I knew was that I spooked easy. Spooked by how easy it was to freak myself out in the presence of this strange old man.

Seth no doubt saw the confusion on my face.

"Doesn't matter," he said. "Makes two of us."

"Enough to tell me her story?"

Seth nodded in silent agreement.

8. OH, THE HUMANITY
SETH

After I'd thrown one too many down the hatch on Nick's dime, my hangover felt like an open head wound. I was lucky I hadn't woken up with two black eyes and broken ribs from the verbal beating I'd taken at the hands of The Piano Man. Usually my mind functioned fine swimming in alcohol, but after being threatened by Toes, stowing away on an ocean liner, a day of sex, ominous shadows, beer, and paranoia, I came down with what the Italian grandmothers in Brooklyn called *morte blanca*. *White death*. A premonition of impending doom. But the *morte blanca* I experienced aboard the *Athenia* that morning was not of my own violent end, but Ingrid's.

The only other time I'd had *morte blanca* was a month after watching the Hindenburg disaster. Later in my apartment in New York City, I dreamt I was aboard the airship when it exploded and became engulfed in flames. I threw myself overboard, an ill-fated phoenix taken flight. I'd awoken alone the next morning, wet with flop sweat, afraid for my life. This morning I awoke beside a beautiful woman I barely knew and feared for hers. If I had any sense at all, I'd be worried about my own skin and not the nude woman's sleeping next to me. It was a solid bet Nick knew I was a stowaway. But Ingrid was the irresistibly sexy siren with perfect breasts and long legs who'd led me to her bed in spite of that fact. Was she a black widow? I still couldn't decide.

Before, I always knew when to cut bait and run. But now, because of her, I was the one caught on the line, fighting whoever was topside reeling me in. On a ship of 400-plus passengers, I wasn't sure I had even seen all the players. For a guy who couldn't swim, navigating these emotional waters was not only going to be tricky but downright dangerous. My bedfellow began to stir.

Ingrid woke up. I hadn't wanted to bombard her with questions the night before. But now that she was conscious, and I was reasonably sober, it seemed like the opportune time.

"Who is this guy, Nick?"

"Just a friend." She wiped the sleep out of her eyes.

"What kind of friend?" My tone was more earnest than intended.

Ingrid sat up. The covers fell down, and her perky breasts rose up like pink balloons toward the sky. The gravity of the situation had no effect on them.

"We never slept together." Her long fingers brushed the hair from her half-opened eyes. "If that's what you're implying."

"Why not?" I said, a little too quickly.

Ingrid looked at me with disdain. I could tell it wasn't the way she wanted to start her day. We were both big fans of morning sex, but I felt I needed to put some questions to her before anything else. It was one of the few instances when the newshound in me trumped the horny toad.

"I decide who I sleep with and don't," she said. "Nicky is just a friend."

"Nicky?"

"Look," she said, her back against the headboard, "I thought you'd like each other. Both being American."

Like each other? I'd found when vying for the attentions of a beautiful young woman, American or not, men were generally fear-biters. Afraid of the competition, we'd sink our teeth into one another first and ask questions later. I was no different.

"Besides," she said, "I wouldn't have introduced you if I'd known you were the jealous type."

"Jealous?" I said. "I'm not jealous."

"Then what's bothering you?"

It was a perfectly reasonable question. What *was* bothering me? I felt a turning point coming on and not just in our nascent relationship. Much as I hated to admit it, Ingrid had struck a nerve I didn't know I had.

"What's bothering me?" I said it more to myself than to her.

"Yes." She said the word like a long-exhaled hiss.

"I juuuust," I stammered. "I just can't stand the thought of you with anyone else."

Where the hell had that come from? I felt like a puppet with a ventriloquist's hand up my ass, putting words in my mouth. Ingrid looked into my wide-open, shocked eyes. I expected the worst, but instead, she smiled.

"Thank you for being honest with me," she said, turned and pressed her glorious, gravity-defying breasts into my chest.

Ingrid gave me a kiss that made me knock-kneed. Good thing we were in bed, because if I'd been standing up, I would have fallen over. Whatever questions about her drained from my head along with all the blood. Ingrid was teaching this salty dog some new tricks, and she put my body and mind in a perpetual tailspin that I didn't have the power to pull out of, even if I'd wanted to. We made love that morning more passionately than I'd ever experienced.

Ingrid left me seeing stars when she went to work that afternoon. But the star I really needed to see was Garbo. Between the bar bet and the news exclusive the scoop would generate, I'd be set. The movie queen would be my salvation. But I'd have to act fast. Over the ship's PA system, the Captain announced that our ocean voyage had officially reached its midpoint. Finding a needle in a haystack as large as an ocean liner wasn't going to be easy. Especially when that needle was named Garbo, and she had made a career of playing hard to get.

The more exposure I had to famous people, the more I realized how much trouble they were. Take Clark Gable, for instance. Gable got juiced one night after Joan Crawford, his equally famous on-again, off-again slam piece, told him where to shove it. Driving his own car down Mulholland, high on sauce, he struck and killed a young woman. Her family cried out for blood. But Gable, valuable MGM property, got a free ride.

Louis B. Mayer, head of the studio, had one of his own executives take the vehicular manslaughter rap. The schmuck did ten years hard time, in exchange for guaranteed life employment. But Garbo made Gable look like a chump. When her two-year studio contract was drawing to an end in 1935, she went to Mayer's office and told him she wanted to go home.

"Six hundred dollars a week is insufficient," she told Mayer. "Especially for a star of my standing."

"What would you consider fair?" Mayer asked, in a paternal tone, no doubt.

"Five thousand dollars a week will do," Garbo said.

According to Hollywood lore, Mayer turned purple and began screaming. The studio mogul who disdained the use of profanity, went on a tirade and called the brightest star in the Metro-Goldwyn-Mayer firmament a bitch.

"Just who the hell do you think you are?" he yelled.

"Greta Garbo," she said and quickly followed with the legendary, "I tank I go home now."

True to her word, Garbo was on the next ship to Sweden. Months passed with no word from the star, and Mayer panicked. He didn't even have her home address. He finally reached her through the U.S. Embassy in Stockholm and offered her $2,000. No response. He doubled it. Nothing. Garbo not only got her $5,000 a week, but the added proviso she would end her workday promptly at 5 pm. News traveled fast in Hollywood and New York: Garbo's balls were bigger than the most powerful man's in Tinseltown.

Garbo always got what Garbo wanted. And the world's most famous and powerful movie star wanted privacy more than anything else. Being a tabloid reporter, I knew that she traveled under several known pseudonyms. I needed a look-see at the ship's passenger list. If I recognized one, it might just be my ticket to a grab-shot. And my ticket to the big time.

I asked Ingrid if she could sweet-talk her way into borrowing a copy of the ship's manifest. She agreed to do it, but said it might take a couple hours. That was fine by me. It afforded me the time I needed to get my head straight. Or at least try.

A walk around the ship would get me my bearings. I stared out at the ocean, half-expecting to see another sinister shadow like the one I'd spied while on the Promenade Deck with Ingrid the day before. Instead, a school of bright blue fish jumped out of the water, racing the ship's bow. I had no idea what the hell they were, until a steward informed a British family down the hall from me. Spinner Dolphins. I couldn't help but watch and smile while my fellow mammals raced the *Athenia* in their natural element.

When I returned to Ingrid's suite, she was waiting for me with the passenger list. I knew I only had to look at the First Class manifest. Garbo wouldn't be traveling any other way. Sure enough, there she was. Not Greta Garbo but Harriet Brown, a more popular travel pseudonym of hers, in suite 437 A.

"Easy as cake." A wave of excitement rushed over me.

"Cake?" Ingrid said.

"Yeah, cake." I reached out for her hand and held it. "You did good, darling."

Ingrid blushed and lowered her head in the way a shy schoolgirl might when being complimented. I still had so much to learn about this beautiful young creature.

"What now?" she asked, the arc of her long eye lashes mimicking her smile.

"Now," I said, "I get to work."

Darkness descended over the North Atlantic, and the floating city glowed with incandescent light. I would wait until night fell completely before engaging Miss Brown. I'd only have one shot at her, maybe two with my Bell and Howell. I practiced switch-loading the flash bulbs in my pocket.

Ingrid worked the Salon floor, and I kept a low profile at the mahogany wraparound bar with plush red velvet seats and bevel-cut mirrors on the walls behind me. I found myself at home in the smoke-filled, crowded room. Nick, now playing the Salon's upright piano, captivated the upper-class patrons as he sang Cole Porter's "You're The Top" from 1934's hit musical *Anything Goes*. I even had a begrudging admiration for Nick, belting out the tune with gusto and getting more than one pretty lady to accompany him. I'd shaken off the *morte blanca* I'd felt that morning, and even Nick's presence couldn't destroy my peace of mind.

After, Nick turned to me at the bar and gave me a wink in time with the last line, the one with *Garbo's sal'ry* in it. It was all in good fun. Or was it? Either way, our little competition would all be over soon. Hopefully, with me coming out on top. Mighty Garbo was mine.

Garbo wouldn't be circulating in the general population. She would be taking all her meals in her suite and fairly used to the comings and goings of the staff. This was my opportunity. She would open the door expecting a porter and a dinner cart. Instead, she'd get yours truly and a flash from my camera.

The element of surprise would be critical, much more so than other celebrities. I was quick on the draw, but I'd seen enough botched candid photographs of Garbo to know she could throw up a hand, coat, hat or any number of objects in front of THE FACE.

I reached in my coat for a pack of smokes. Ingrid appeared and began to wipe the tabletop in front of me.

"I overheard a conversation," she whispered in my ear. The sensation of her sweet breath on my skin made me swoon. "Between an older man and his young mistress. They saw Garbo walking the Promenade Deck."

"Unlikely," I said smugly. The image of the phantom I had seen conversing with the little boy ran contrary to what I had just said. I had either seen Garbo or a ghost on the Promenade Deck. Either way, they were equally elusive to catch sight of.

"What if she isn't in her room when you drop by?"

"She will be," I said with finality. "When does dinner get served around here?"

"In the next half hour," Ingrid said, "you'll start seeing porters coming from the kitchen delivering room service."

A discreet kiss on the ear, and Ingrid went on her way. I bided my time. I was good at biding, especially with a beer in front of me.

A parade of porters in pressed white jackets and slicked-back hair emerged from the double doors of the first-class kitchen, chafing dishes in hand, and white towels hung over flat forearms bent at the elbow. They marched out single file like Emperor penguins. I fell in at the end and looked more like a rabid squirrel in my brown wool suit.

A full moon hung over the ocean as I followed the porters to their assigned destinations. I took a cigarette out of my coat pocket, lit it, and took a deep drag of nicotine. As my eyes adjusted to the moonlight, I noticed a dark shape protrude out of the water. This time it was barely a hundred yards off the port bow. I knew instantly what it was. A U-boat's conning tower. I wanted to run back into the salon and tell Ingrid. But then I would lose my opportunity to shoot Garbo. I hesitated at the railing as long as I dared, then threw my cigarette overboard and ran back in line with the penguins.

We marched to the A-Class Deck as I thought about Ingrid. The presence of the U-boat was unsettling, to be sure. But since we were on a merchant vessel of a neutral country, I felt relatively secure in the knowledge we weren't going to get blown from the water. Still, it gave a guy perspective. As soon as I got this Garbo business over, I'd get to know my barmaid-sidekick a whole lot better. Sweden seemed like it might be a good place to sit out the war. I inserted a flash bulb in my little camera and prepared for the task at hand.

I found myself at the end of a well-lit hallway leading to a row of first-class suites. Several passengers passed me, but I avoided their stares. They were dressed to the nines. I was dressed in my squirrel suit. They probably thought I was lost, and that was fine by me.

I proceeded down the hall until I came to the door marked 437A. No porter had attended to the suite yet, so I was free and in the clear. I took the lens cap off my camera and braced myself. I knocked on the door. From within the room came a woman's voice.

"Who is it?" she asked.

"Room service, ma'am." The nerve endings in my neck twitched, and my palms burst wet with perspiration.

"I haven't ordered any room service," she said.

"Compliments of the captain, ma'am." My stomach sank into my trousers. I always got nervous before a shootout.

There was a momentary silence and more than a possibility Garbo was calling the purser. Notoriously guarded about her privacy, Garbo could easily send me on my way, even if I was legit. Which I wasn't.

"Very well," she said, "come in."

A stroke of luck. I turned the door handle, took a deep breath and entered. Quietly, I shut the door behind me. The cramped outer room of the suite was ornately decorated. I dared to enter the next room. I spied a woman's dress hung over the back of a chair beside the bed. I took a deep breath and turned toward the bathroom.

The door to the bathroom was ajar. Steam escaped. The sound of bath water running accompanied my heart beating in my ears. The movie siren was taking a bath.

"Just leave it on the table," she said from the bathroom.

I readied my camera loaded with a flash bulb and walked over to the door. I pushed open the door and raised my camera up. But there was too much steam to see anything, let alone photograph her.

I rallied all the courage I had on me and walked farther into the bathroom. I waved my free hand in a clumsy attempt to disperse the steam. Garbo began to shriek in a peculiar high-pitched tone.

I clicked off shot after blind shot, filling the fogged room with light. Each time I fired, my subject would produce the same odd scream. Spent flashbulbs shattered on the tile floor like empty shell casings from an automatic weapon. I lowered my camera as the steam dispersed and saw my prey for the first time. With my own eyes. An obese, naked, middle-aged brunette stood up in the tub and belted out a high-pitched wail that made the bathroom black and white tiles rattle.

"Let me guess." The camera hung off my limp arm. "The real Miss Harriett Brown?"

She stared at me, mouth agape in horror. I stared back at her in clenched-ass morbid wonder.

"Oh, the humanity," I said.

Suddenly I had bigger things to have nightmares about than U-boats and exploding dirigibles. Once the fat lady sang, my dreams of making things right would be sunk. I'd be pinched as a stowaway and put under lock and key for the duration of our voyage. Then there'd be no need to worry about Nick anymore.

9. A NIPPLE-GAZER

JAMES

I lay in bed and listened to Seth's voice trail off. His naked-fat-lady-in-a-bathtub recounting made for a great story, but I was still wary. Still suspicious of the old man's motive for confiding in me. The only thing that kept me grounded was the cosmic-carrot of a Garbo exclusive. Until I possessed her, I'd deny my natural flight response, and ignore the voice inside me telling me to rip out my IV and flee.

My feet hit the cold linoleum floor and ached when I applied my full weight. Amazing how weak I had gotten from just lying in bed for twenty-four hours. I shuffled across our hospital room like an old man, holding onto my IV pole for dear life. I walked passed Seth's bed and glanced over at him watching me, an all too knowing smile on his face.

"What are you gawking at?" I growled.

"You look how I feel," he said. "No offense."

"If you mean like shit, then you look like it, too. No offense."

"Chasing after that nurse, no doubt," he said with a laugh. "Tell her from me she can do better."

"Get up and tell her yourself."

"Gravity is my enemy," Seth said. "It's been trying to pull me into the ground for a while now. Already taken several inches off me," he declared. "I used to be five foot eleven."

"When we get out of here," I said, "I'll spring for you to get Rolfed."

"Rolfed?" he said and looked at me like I'd just proffered to pay for an indecent act.

"Therapeutic massage," I rephrased. "People supposedly come out taller."

"Save your money," he said. "No hippy shit is gonna save me now."

Looking at Seth's shriveled-up and veiny visage, I knew I didn't want to end up dying alone. What that meant for my future exactly, I hadn't a clue. I'd never seriously thought about having my own family before. I attributed thoughts like that to adults. I never considered myself an adult because it meant taking responsibility for your own life and the life of others close to you. I had spent a fair share of my time dodging responsibility and keeping everyone's expectations low. Much harder to fail and disappoint people that way. Especially women.

"How are we doing in here?" I turned to see Sarah's smiling face in our doorway. She carried a pink tray full of medicine bottles and pill cups. "I've interrupted something," she said. "I can come back later."

"No," Seth said. "Come on in. I might be dead later."

I stood at attention and made way for Sarah to enter our small room. Her sweet scent grabbed hold of me as she brushed past on her way to Seth's bed. I watched her from behind as she leaned down and placed the tray on the old man's bed corner. Looked back up in time to see Seth smile and give me a wink.

"Guess I'll leave you two to it then." I said.

"Thanks, sport," Seth said and smirked. I waited half a tick to see if Sarah would turn and flash me one of her million-dollar smiles. She didn't. Instead, she focused on administering Seth's medications. So, I made a 180-degree turn and pushed my IV stand into the hallway before Seth could see how easily deflated I'd become.

I walked out into the hallway in a blue funk that matched the color of my thin blue gown. What the hell was happening to me? I'd left the room, jealous of the attention Seth was getting from Sarah. Seth, an old man who was at death's door. Then a wave of guilt washed over me for feeling jealous. He was dying, and I'd become an emotional idiot. Taking a spill on that black ice must have done something to my brain. Maybe my pituitary was knocked sideways, and my hormones were off kilter. I was so mad, I wanted to plow my fist into something. Or cry.

No one expected Seth to ever get out of bed again. I'd heard Dr. Zoom whisper to a colleague about how Seth was circling the drain. His freshness date all but expired. I might have had a concussion, but I hadn't gone deaf. I didn't like hearing him state the obvious.

My mother had died in a hospital surrounded by so-called medical professionals. They were ghouls to me. Their white lab coats a hop, skip, and jump from the black-suited, black-tied undertakers complete with white carnation boutonniere. Except they had a purpose. Disposing of the dead, instead of tormenting the living.

I knew this wasn't a healthy outlook, but then again what did a healthy outlook have to do with being in a hospital? To me, voluntarily working in one meant you had something wrong with you. Like a mental illness. Of course, that was until I met Sarah.

At first glance, Sarah reminded me of my mother. She was a sight for sore eyes, and mine had been bloodshot marbles at the time. She seemed to glow from within like Mom had, and I was attracted to the light. But whatever thoughts ran through my muddled, concussed mind, none were the Oedipal kind. I worshipped my mother in other ways. Her integrity, compassion, and singular intelligence. Everyone did. Sarah radiated with the same intensity. And with a hint of Mom's sense of sarcasm, no less. Though Sarah's seemed to run darker.

I'd asked Sarah earlier in the day if she would talk to Dr. Halverson, my physician, about removing my IV. A saline line connected to a subcutaneous needle that stung like a motherfucker when pulled taut wasn't my idea of a good time. I explained that I'd never liked being tied down to anything since my own umbilical cord had been cut over a quarter century before. I also may have mentioned how being chained to a five-foot steel pole with squeaky wheels was cramping my style.

"It destroys the element of surprise," I said.

The look Sarah gave me withered my resolve in a nanosecond.

"You obviously have a deep fear of commitment," she said. "I think I'll order a psych eval for you."

Then she walked down the hall without another word. All I could do was stand there in my hospital gown and slippers and watch her go. I'd already seen a shrink once before. He said I had an adjustment disorder with mixed features. Whatever the hell that meant.

Halfway down the hall, Sarah looked back and shot me a smile that hit me like a thunderbolt. She turned away, and I found myself appreciating the aesthetic qualities of a nurse's uniform for the second time in as many days. I was crazy, all right. Crazy for her.

I took my time on my little walk and soon Sarah came back down the corridor toward me after finishing her rounds. Her volcanic eyes and full mouth formed a sensual Bermuda triangle and she lit up the dreary hallway. Whereas most men fixated on a woman's breasts, legs, or ass, for me the face was where feminine beauty began and ended. I felt myself being pulled toward her as she drew near.

"Hey," she said. With her hand, she pulled an errant strand of black hair behind her ear.

"Hey," I said and reached up to check my own head-dressing. Why, I had no idea.

"What are you doing still out of bed?" she said.

"I thought I'd make a break for it," I deadpanned and looked down at my hospital gown. Thank god Sarah laughed as she looked me up and down.

"Don't you think it would be a little drafty leaving in that getup in the middle of winter?"

"I didn't say I'd thought it through."

We exchanged smiles. I felt like I was finally on a roll with her.

"How's the rest of your morning been?" I asked.

"Got a nipple-gazer in three."

"Come again?" Did she just say what I thought she'd said?

"Some guy," she said, holding her clipboard at a right angle against her hip, "came in early this morning after he slid off the road. Spent the night freezing his ass off in an embankment. The creep is probably going to lose a couple fingers and toes to frostbite, but he's still got the energy to stare at my rack the entire time I'm checking his vitals. You guys are really amazing."

"Hey, don't go lumping us all together simply on account of the family jewels."

"I saw you checking me out when we first met."

"No way."

"Yes, way," she said. "It's okay when you're not obnoxious about it. Not the leering type, like that schmuck in three."

"I'm glad I pass muster."

"It's not your fault," she said with a sly smirk. "I know I'm hot."

"Now who's being obnoxious?"

"See you later?" she said and put her clipboard behind her back while shrugging her shoulders forward and bowing slightly. She blushed with the ingratiating mannerism. Profoundly adorable.

"I'm not going anywhere." I grabbed my gown with both hands and curtsied. Thank God she laughed again.

"Glad to hear it. I'll come check in on you and Seth on my next break."

Sarah reached out a hand and playfully mussed up my greaseball hair, then continued down the hall. I dutifully checked out her ass as she walked away.

"Now that's the way to do it," she said without even turning around.

My heart raced, knowing that she knew I was checking her out. I had to admit she was right. She was hot.

I thought back to my theory about the source of Sarah's beauty. I thought of her face. Aside from the aesthetic wonderfulness of it, her face made me think of something I hadn't thought of—let alone longed for—in a long time. An emotion old and familiar, but in this context strangely new and unexpected. Sarah's beautiful face had made me think of home. Not so much a physical place, but a feeling. Warm and cozy and safe.

Elated, I turned and walked down the hallway from where Sarah had made her last rounds. Curiosity had gotten the better of me, and I looked furtively into Room Three. What exactly did a nipple-gazer look like? I wasn't disappointed. It was Martin.

10. THE DREAM PRINCESS OF ETERNITY

SETH

It didn't make sense. The queer feeling I had in my gut about my Ingrid. Nick. That fat lady in the tub. The U-boat in the water. None of it. But it didn't matter. When I made up my mind I wanted a story, nothing stopped me. And I wanted Garbo. No matter what the cost. Harriet Brown wasn't Garbo, but I knew the movie star was aboard, and I knew I'd find her.

Then a storm hit without warning. The ocean churned and frothed in cold, wet fury. The horizon line disappeared. The world—top and bottom—was made of water. The only way to tell heaven from hell was whether water was fresh or salty. But then the pelting rain and sea spray mixed so completely the distinction didn't matter.

I had only just gotten my sea legs, and now the Atlantic itself seemed determined to make me toss my cookies. I didn't even have time to turn green before I grabbed the railing on the Promenade Deck and fed my lunch to the fishes. Then I dragged my sodden carcass into the salon.

The dark, dank bar smelled like bourbon and bile. I joined Nick and Ingrid at a table in the corner by a darkened fireplace. They didn't look so hot either. But compared to me, they may as well have been F. Scott and Zelda Fitzgerald.

"Did you get it?" Nick asked. The weather seemed to have temporarily taken the wind out of his sarcastic sails.

"I got it all right," I said, my sail full and ready to rupture.

"How did she look?" he said, curiosity piqued and ears pricked.

"Big."

Ingrid cocked her head toward me like she had back in her cabin. I caught sight of myself in the beveled mirror behind her. Part of me wanted to crawl into her lap, curl my tail between my legs and cry. The other part wanted me to check her for weapons. The fact that she wasn't completely repelled by me made me suddenly realize she couldn't be on the up and up. Unless she had a thing for sewer rats.

"It wasn't her," Ingrid said pointedly. Was this gorgeous woman now able to read minds? "It wasn't Garbo."

"Not unless she's eaten half the crew since being on board." I belched. "The real Harriett Brown is a heifer."

"I guess that's it then," Nick said. "I win."

"The hell you say," I said. "I'm just getting warmed up."

I was bluffing, of course. Without a lead, I was back to square one. Negative one. Once the storm blew over, the entire crew would be called upon to find the freak with a fetish for photographing naked fatties. It was a sure bet the British merchant marine frowned upon such behavior among their paying passengers, let alone stowaways. I'd be in the brig by daybreak.

"You need a disguise," Ingrid said.

Ingrid's complicity made me blush. She must have seen the shock register on my face, because she shot me a sexy smile. Nick, however, wasn't smiling. He was too busy turning green. And not with envy. This amused me. It shouldn't have. I sat right next to him.

"What kind of disguise did you have in mind?" I asked.

Ingrid looked around the bar, for what, I had no idea. She turned back to me, practically a lit light bulb above her head. Inspiration illuminated her features.

"I'll be back." And with that she got up and walked across the room toward the kitchen.

I loved watching Ingrid walk away almost as much as watching her walk toward me. Not that I considered myself an ass man, per se. The sum of Ingrid's parts added up to more than tits and ass in my book. I'd never thought of having a partner in crime before, let alone a dame. She was my intellectual equal, if not smarter. Ingrid made me rethink being solo. This alone made her damn near irresistible. Even if she wasn't on the up and up.

Nick was another story. We stared at each other in nauseated silence. No amount of chin wagging was going to change the contempt I now held for him and I was confident he felt the same for me. Maybe if we talked, however, it would take my mind off my own stomach, which I hadn't been on speaking terms with since the storm blew in.

"Nice weather we're having," I said, ever the sarcastic bastard.

"You said it," Nick managed through clenched teeth.

His entire body clenched. A burst of adrenaline covered my own face in flop sweat. I took a shallow breath, but the storm had sucked all the air out of the room. I looked around, desperate for subject matter. I saw a plaque on the wall behind our table, above the fireplace. Etched in bronze relief was the Latin phrase: "*Si Deus Pro Nobis, Quis Contra Nos.*"

"What's that?" I cocked my head toward the fireplace.

"The ship's motto," was Nick's clipped reply.

I could tell he had other things on his mind at the moment, which was exactly why I asked.

"My Latin's a little rusty," I said.

"If God is with us, who is against us?" he replied without ever turning his head.

Who, indeed? The ship pitched violently to starboard and glassware and furniture went crashing with it. The ship was being tossed around like some sea monster's bath toy. I took up residence in Ingrid's empty seat at the opposite end of the table, the one Nick and I now held on to for dear life. I made my best effort not to look scared. If God was with us on this trip, I'd hate to think of what would happen if He wasn't.

A wave of nausea hit me. In my fevered imagination it was the same massive wave that broadsided the ship. I looked across the room and saw a young porter in a spotless white uniform with a tray of chafing dishes emerging from the kitchen entrance. The kid used the bolted-down tables of the salon to scale the forty-five degree pitch the floor had become. He looked like Buster Keaton silently running up a wall in one of his daring comic skits. I couldn't help but smile at the seemingly gravity-defying act.

"Hey," I said to Nick, "you see that?"

Nick hung above me as if suspended on a seesaw. From his precarious perch he looked like a schoolboy stranded atop a teeter-totter. At first, I thought he was smiling in agreement. Then I realized he was trying desperately not to vomit. His lips curled back at the sides into a menacing grimace. Nick freed a hand to cover his mouth. Ingrid emerged from the kitchen in time to see two streams of bright yellow puke shooting out of his nose right onto my chest.

"Oh my," she said.

"Oh my?" I raised my hands in exasperation. I looked down at the warm bile running down my shirt. "Oh my" didn't even begin to cover it.

A mortified expression formed on Nick's face. He mouthed his condolences to my suit vest. A little late, if you asked me. The ship righted herself, and the pendulum effect left me momentarily catching air above Nick. The combination of motion and putrid smell of Nick's upchuck wafting up my nostrils turned out to be a lethal mixture. Ingrid backed away as I opened my mouth and covered Nick's suit. We looked over at her like twin newborns covered in afterbirth.

"Don't move," she said. "I'll get something to clean—" and disappeared into the kitchen.

Nick and I did as we were told as the ship rocked back into a level pitch. Spent by our little game of you-show-me-your-insides-and-I'll-show-you-mine, I doubt either of us had the energy to spit, let alone navigate out of the room. The storm abated for the moment, but somehow I knew it wasn't finished with us yet. God, Mother Nature, or the Devil himself was having far too much fun watching us mortals squirm to call it quits just yet.

★ ★ ★

Nick retired to his cabin while Ingrid and I went back to hers. I found there was nothing quite like throwing up in front of a woman to destroy the mood. It was just as well. I had other things to attend to before we could once again engage in sexual congress. Ingrid seemed to be fine with this philosophy.

She gave me a reassuring smile while she drew me another hot bath. This time I shed my soiled clothing without having to be told. There was also no argument from me when she rolled up her sleeves and lathered the sponge. I crawled in, the water warm and inviting. The storm outside raged.

Ingrid sent my suit out to be cleaned and pressed. Again. But this time she had more than a robe and a warm bed for me to slither into. I toweled myself off while she proudly presented me with a spotless white, pressed porter's uniform exactly like the one the young man in the salon was wearing.

"What's that?" I pointed at it like a five-year-old.

"What does it look like?" she said, coaxing me like the sexy school teacher every adolescent boy fantasized spending detention with.

"It looks like a porter's uniform," I said, only too happy to state the obvious.

"Then that's what it is," she confirmed and turned the corners of her warm full lips into a sinister little smile.

I had to give her credit. It was ingenious. Ingenious and insane. I was already up to my neck in trouble with the local authorities. Impersonating a crew member would definitely push my head below the surface. One could argue that I was already a goner. Sinking fast into a dark, wet abyss between two continents whose inhabitants would have my head once I reached *terra firma*. Toes and Bernie waited for me on one side of the Atlantic, the Swedish authorities on the other side. I was doomed. So why not go out with a bang?

"Will it fit?" I asked and looked at the shirt collar the same as if it were a hangman's noose.

"Try it on," she said.

The shirt fit, all right. But the pants and jacket came up more than a little short. Ingrid stared at me and tried to suppress a laugh.

"Go ahead and laugh." I looked down at my exposed ankles. "Anything to brighten your day."

I was all dressed up and nowhere to go. But that was the real surprise Ingrid had in store for me. She produced a piece of paper and held it out to me with both hands. Scribbled on the parchment was a Second-Class Suite number, 313B.

"What's this?" I asked.

Ingrid giggled like a little girl with a new puppy. Her high cheekbones glistened in the light, and her eyes squinted with glee. I imagined her in ponytails, standing in front of a blackboard, proudly exhibiting to a classroom of juvenile delinquents a gold star she'd just received. She held her breath and waited.

"You just found out your twin sister is on board," I offered. "And you want me to see who's the better kisser."

Ingrid pursed her lips and shook her head no. She moved the paper closer to me, as if that would jar mental aptitude back into positive numbers. I felt thicker, more sluggish than usual. I squinted at the numbers in mock concentration.

"Sorry, sugar." I stalled. "I got nothing."

Ingrid pouted in disgust. She was tiring of my utter lack of perception. She raised her right eyebrow at me in disapproval. Her come-hither look had turned into a go-wither glare. I'd seen that look once before. A third time and I'd find myself turned out into the storm. So I threw caution to the wind and went for broke.

"You found Garbo," I said, knowing full well I was wrong.

Ingrid jumped up and down with abandon. She let out a laugh and wrapped her arms around me. Squeezed me so hard I felt my eyes bulge. If her exaltation at discovering Garbo's whereabouts aboard ship wasn't enough to bowl me over, jumping into my lap while I was standing up nearly sent us both flying backwards.

"But," I said, while Ingrid clung to me like a double-breasted suit, "how did you find out?"

"The porter, Lars," she gushed. "You know, the one you saw leave the salon. He's been taking our most expensive caviar and Champagne to room 313B all night. To her. In room 313B."

The image of the gravity-defying porter scaling up the wall of the Salon immediately came to mind. That his destination was a second-class cabin intrigued me. But would it be enough to risk another fat lady in a tub? Or, even worse, a fat man? I shuddered at the thought as Ingrid climbed down off of me.

"Did he tell you," I inquired, the journalist in me wanting to verify her source, "it was Garbo?"

"Not exactly," she said. "Swedes know how to keep secrets. But I'm sure of it."

Something didn't sound right. Usually when someone said they were sure of something, it meant they were trying to convince themselves of it as much as you. Also, I hadn't had much experience with Swedes, but was pretty sure they didn't refer to themselves as such. Still, I let it pass. I was running out of time, and my underwear was bunching up very nicely in my butt-crack due to the two-sizes-too-small porter's pants.

"So," I said, "what's the plan?"

Ingrid's peepers opened wide like cat's-eye marbles. The kitty cat was on the hunt and loving it. But catching a tigress like Garbo by the tail was a dangerous proposition. It was good sport, provided you could sneak up on her while her claws were pointed the other way. My experience with the movie star in the men's bathroom taught me to proceed with the utmost caution. Unless I wanted my hair parted with a wrench again, which I didn't.

"Next time she orders something," she said, her index finger brought to her lips in thought, "I'll distract Lars, and you can take it to her."

"That easy, huh?" I was skeptical.

"Why not?" Ingrid's finger pointed at me like a gun.

I didn't have a comeback. Her logic was impeccable. Provided an order did come in and she could distract Lars. Looking at her, I knew that wouldn't be a problem for Ingrid. The kid would have to be dead from the waist down or queer as a three-dollar bill not to respond to her natural charms. She could stop a train in its tracks just by batting her eyelashes.

"There's only one problem," I said.

"What's that?"

"The plan is perfect," I assured her. "But it implicates you directly."

Ingrid considered this wrinkle. She would be aiding and abetting a known pervert. I was already in hot water. She had merely been on the sidelines with soap and sponge, cleaning me up after every inning in this ridiculous game. To move ahead, she'd have to batter up. I knew she knew I was right.

"I've got it," she said. The light bulb above her head shone even brighter this time.

"I'm all ears," I said.

"We don't have to wait for an order." Ingrid struck her teacher pose again. Class was back in session.

"Why?" I asked.

"Because," she explained. "It will be a gift, courtesy of the captain."

I didn't have the heart to tell Ingrid that I had tried this line before, to disastrous effect. Still, it had gotten me in the door, hadn't it? The wrong door, but still a door. Then again, I feared my earlier success, as it were, was due to the very fact Garbo wasn't inside.

The real Garbo would never accept unsolicited gifts, for the very same reason paparazzo like me would hatch such an insipid scheme. Garbo wouldn't have known the term paparazzi or that it literally meant "buzzing insects," for it wouldn't be coined until decades later. Still, she had a sixth sense about us pests and could hear us coming a mile off. There were no flies on Garbo.

"It won't work," I said. "Trust me."

Ingrid looked at me, dejected. She sat down on the settee in her bedroom and pouted like before. She was having too much fun, and I had just poured a gallon of cold seawater on her parade. I would have loved to have sat down next to her and consoled her, but feared my pants would split. As it was, they had stopped circulation to my groin. I feared a couple more hours in them and my ability to father a child would be a non issue.

"That's it," Ingrid said. "That's the answer."

I looked down at her, unsure of what the question was.

"The next time she orders," she explained, "you'll simply beat Lars to her door."

Ingrid smiled with glee. I mimicked her expression. She could tell I wasn't following her. What I perceived as a minor variation made all the difference to her.

"She'll just think it's typical Swedish hospitality," she said. "Fast and courteous service."

"How am I supposed to beat the kid there?" The image of Lars the super-porter Up-Up-and-Awaying in the upended salon played in my mind for a second time.

"Because you'll already be there, silly," she said. "It's just meant to get you in the door. No one's saying the order you bring her has to be right."

"Wow," I said. "That could work."

Ecstatic, Ingrid jumped up and embraced me so hard I thought I was going to pop a button. She had built the plank. Now all I had to do was walk out onto the end of it and jump off.

In hindsight, it made sense that Garbo would have chosen a Second-Class Suite instead of First Class. For the simple reason that idiots like me would never think she'd stoop to traveling any other way but the best. But Garbo had grown up in poverty. Little Greta Gustavsson had helped her family make the rent by working as a lather girl in a barber shop. I couldn't imagine Garbo, even as a child, lathering strange men's faces for their daily shave. But poverty had a way of making you do things you wouldn't ordinarily ever do otherwise.

I contemplated this whole sorry state of affairs while I waited in the shadows of the Second-Class Hallway. The only good thing was that the storm had all but petered out. A semblance of normality had resumed amidships. People once again came out of their cabins and headed off this way and that. And I was dressed up like a clown waiting for my cue to debase myself yet again. I breathed a little easier when a couple emerged from the suite next to Garbo's and walked passed me as if I didn't exist.

Ingrid knew from experience what it took to get noticed, or not. She had been right about disguising me as the help. I adjusted myself in my porter's pants and shook my legs as if in preparation for a footrace. All I needed to do was get into that cabin, photograph the most beautiful woman who ever lived, and get out. All in a day's work. Within the hour, I'd be back in my own trousers, toasting to success with Ingrid. Or lose the pants altogether and do a couple victory rounds in bed instead.

Ingrid appeared at the end of the hallway and gave me the good ole American thumbs up, the prearranged sign to go ahead. As an accomplice, she was aces. I wished I could be so confident of my own abilities. Sure, I'd flown high with Charles Lindbergh as my co-pilot, but Garbo was the hottest star on the planet, and one shot of her would rocket my career into high orbit. It was just a matter of getting the butterflies in my stomach to fly in formation long enough to get the shot.

I swallowed hard and lifted a tray populated by a chilled bottle of Champagne and several chafing dishes, one of which contained my camera. I walked across the hallway to Suite 313B. I told myself, a couple quick flashbulbs blown, and I'd be out in a flash. If I actually ever got into Garbo's suite. The fat lady in the tub screamed in my head. The ludicrousness of our plan truly hit home as I knocked on the door.

"Room service," I said.

I waited, my hand already cramping from holding the tray. I still had time to turn and flee. Then I heard both Ingrid and Nick's voices in my head urging me to stand my ground. But it was the thought of my toes that really stiffened my resolve. Without Garbo's picture, I'd never be able to go wee-wee-wee all the way home ever again. Stand and deliver, Moseley. If not for yourself, do it for your ten little Indians.

"Enter."

The word seeped through the cherrywood door. I couldn't tell whether man or woman had uttered the instruction. Genderless and indistinct in accent as the response was, I'd been given the green light. It was Garbo or bust.

I reached down with my free hand and tried the door handle. It turned clockwise, and the door opened with an audible click. I envisioned the captain and several of his officers lying in wait on the other side. With a net. After all I'd been through to get to this point just seemed too damn easy. Surely there was a catch, and I was all but caught.

I entered a darkened room and shut the door behind me. I could barely make out any features in the room furnishings. The sole illumination came from the porthole, where a silvery sliver of moonlight streamed in, intermittently obstructed by leftover cloud cover blowing by. I imagined the Norse gods were sending me Morse code, signaling, "Get the fuck out while you still can." Of course, I ignored the warning and blindly continued forward.

My eyes slowly adapted to the darkness, and I discerned the outline of a writing table in the corner of the room, opposite a bed. I continued twenty paces to the table and put the tray down without too much fuss. Several empty bottles of Champagne cluttered the corner of the table. I busied myself with untwisting the wire cage that surrounded the cork of the unopened bottle of bubbly I'd brought. The vintage was extra dry, as was my mouth.

I felt a presence on the bed beside the table but dared not look in that direction. Instead, I kept my back to the bed, lifted the chafing dish cover off my camera, then grabbed it from the platter as quietly as possible. I popped the lens cap off and turned toward the bed, pivoting on one heel and soft-shoeing the thin carpet with the other. The outline of a woman's naked figure in repose filled my vision. I took a step closer. I lifted the camera up and prepared myself for taking one shot, maybe two, before all hell broke loose.

Then the cloud cover broke. The full moon shone through the porthole, a beacon of brilliant light. The spotlight it created cast a heavenly glow upon the goddess's nude form atop billowy clouds of silk. Her skin literally shimmered. Garbo herself seemed to be made of light.

She lifted her eyelids, lashes parted like Venus flytraps

about to feed. My heart pounded as if someone had trained a gun sight on my skull. I raised my camera slowly in time with Garbo's breasts rising as she inhaled. Then she locked steel blue eyes the size of twin crescent moons upon the camera lens. I lifted my finger and took aim. Her lips parted ever so slightly in the viewfinder.

I'd heard the legend. Garbo's power to enchant a movie audience paled in comparison to the spell cast upon anyone in her living presence. I'd chalked it up to Hollywood hyperbole. A myth manufactured to reinforce her onscreen persona of the ultimate vamp. I knew the supernatural seductress no one could resist didn't really exist. There was only one problem. Try as I might to click the shutter and capture the image that ensured my future, I found I couldn't move a muscle.

"Come," she commanded an octave barely above the sea waves heard crashing outside, yet loud and clear as a siren's song in my head.

My camera fell out of my hands and hit the floor with a thud. I stood at the foot of the bed, bewitched. Garbo lifted outstretched arms slowly off the bed, open palms and delicate fingers beckoned me to her bosom. I felt my heels then my toes lift off the carpet as I was drawn into her. I entered the silvery light and fell into a dream.

All thought of Ingrid deserted me. Time ceased and the past was forgotten. The face before me was the sole focus of life now. To drink from those lips and drown in those eyes was all I ever hoped for. Nothing else mattered. The "Dream Princess of Eternity," the press had dubbed her. Now I knew why.

11. GORILLA OF MY DREAMS

SETH

I gained consciousness in the dark. The heady, sweet scent of sex and vapors of Chanel perfume were all that covered my nakedness. My body still burned with the heat of our encounter, ears still buzzed with the fading echo of windblown whispers. I felt my way across the bed, ran my fingers over cool silken sheets up to the indent in her pillow where she had rested her head. Garbo was gone, and she had taken the moon with her.

I fought to crawl out from under her influence, but she had left me weak and dim-witted. My mind circled back to suicide cases I had covered in NYC. They tended to strip butt-naked before they jumped to their deaths. I felt literally stuck to the bed like I'd splattered there from a great height.

Garbo had transfixed my entire being. I crawled out of my torpor with the queerest notion that her legs, hips, breasts and lips weren't bathed in moonlight when I'd found her, but emitting starlight. Garbo wasn't of this world. And, in colliding with mine, she'd altered the course of my life forever.

I reached out into the pitch. My hand found the contours of a face waiting in the dark. I jumped and grabbed for the light switch. The stark light illuminated a fat-cheeked, naked cherub glaring at me in mawkish delight, depicted in bronze on the lamp's base. Cupid admiring his aim.

I surveyed the room and saw my porter's costume crumpled in a heap in the corner. But what wasn't visible concerned me most. My camera, my all-important camera was nowhere in sight. I reached a hand under the bed and searched. Maybe the camera had rolled there after being thoughtlessly dropped. I stretched my entire arm beneath her bed but came up empty. Without my camera, I was naked and unarmed. Worse, the love scene of my life was over, and not a single frame of it had been captured on film. No one would believe me that it had ever happened. Ever.

The truth was I had never felt totally alone like I did in that moment. My run-in with The Divine One had done a pretty damn good job of short-circuiting my brain. I couldn't trust my own instincts. I needed time and space to get my head straight. Unscramble my thoughts. I needed a place to hide out and collect myself, away from those incendiary blue eyes of hers.

For the second time in my career, I had broken my own cardinal rule. I had stepped from behind the camera and gotten directly involved with the subject matter. The first time, my actions had led to Lindbergh leaving the country. His faith in me had cost him dearly, and he would never be seen or heard from in the same light again. But this time was different. This time I was the one in over my head. But one thing was clear. I was no match for Garbo head-on and never would be. No man was.

I felt crazed and in no condition to think for myself. Well, I'd been shot at point-blank range with a most potent and primal alchemy. What the hell was I going to say to Ingrid, anyway? Sorry, darling, I got no pictures, but Garbo was one hell of a lay. Shit, I had betrayed the woman who had found Garbo for me in the first place. Sacrificed any future we might have had for one night of unforgettable, carnal ecstasy. But it was more than that, wasn't it? How could I explain to one woman the irresistibility of another one without breaking her heart?

How embarrassing was this? God knows where Garbo had gone, but I had to imagine she was giving me a wide enough berth to scram before she came back. I thought to wait until her return, then do what I'd set out to do in the first place and snap her picture. What did I care if she didn't like it? What was good for the goose, right?

But where to go? The only other person I knew on board beside Ingrid was Nick, who I owed a couple hundred dollars to. Or did I? The bar bet was that I couldn't find Garbo. But find her I did. Hell, I fell into her. Now all I needed was proof. An article of clothing, maybe? Or better yet, something with her name on it. Yes, she owed me that. No woman was going to use and abuse ole Seth Moseley and not pay for the pleasure.

With my head finally clearing, it was time to screw it back on straight, cinch up my trousers, pocket a letter addressed to Garbo on her writing table blotter as proof I'd been with the movie star, then get the hell out of her lair while I still could. And that's exactly what I was doing when a loud banging came at her door.

Then I remembered Lars, the Super-Porter whose place I had taken at the front of the line. He'd probably tried to deliver his order when Garbo and I had been indisposed.

I was probably messing up his perfect track record when it came to customer service, not to mention a healthy tip from the mega star. Too bad, kid. I got to her first.

I didn't open the door. I wasn't that thick-headed. If they—Lars or whoever the hell they were—wanted me, they could damn well come in and get me. Which is exactly what they did. No sooner had I stuffed the folded letter in my pocket, then the door burst inward, and I was surrounded. Surrounded by the largest single creature on two feet I had ever witnessed with my own eyes.

He grabbed me about the neck and shoulders. My first thought was that a gorilla had somehow gotten loose aboard the ocean liner. My next thought was that I was about to be ripped limb from limb. Instead, the thing headlocked me in its mighty left arm, about-faced in one lumbering motion and headed for the hallway.

I squirmed to free my nose and mouth from my captor's smelly, dank leather-clad armpit. I hungrily breathed in its stink through my mouth as I attempted to wriggle free. My heels dragged on the carpet as my fists hammered against a massive torso encased in oily black cowhide.

"Let me go," I said and pounded hard on its back.

No response. Just my luck, it was the strong, silent type. Well, if the monstrosity wasn't going to listen to reason, then I'd have to fight fire with fire.

"Tough guy, huh?" I wheezed and kicked my feet helplessly into the air. "Two can play at that game."

Then King Kong flexed a mighty bicep and squeezed my skull so tight I thought my eyeballs were going to pop out of my head. My mind became thick and sluggish. The onset of unconsciousness grasped me once again. I'd become so strangely accustomed to this feeling in the last forty-eight hours that passing out threatened to become my new vocation. But I decided then and there that there was very little future in it. The pay sucked and the hours were lousy. Normally, such a thought would have made me laugh, if I wasn't so preoccupied with trying to breathe. Breathe and claw my way into a station higher than that of Kong's Raggedy Andy doll.

My heels got some momentary traction on the floor, and I forced my head through the tight hole of my assailant's grip. He sensed my struggle and applied more pressure, like a constrictor. This time around my neck. I was about to mouth my dissent, when he closed off my air passageway. Not good, Moseley.

My eyes closed, and I found myself back in bed with Garbo. She stared up at me, the full moon's reflection echoed in her eyes, her body glowing in my shadow. Several strands of her silvery hair flowed in the electrically charged empty space between us. Floated down and formed cross hairs in front of Garbo's gun sights. And as I lost consciousness, I prayed for my beautiful executioner to put me out of my misery. For good.

My mind connected to reality with an audible snap, or was that my neck? I awoke to see King Kong hovering over me and felt metal grating underneath me. He had deposited me on the floor of some storage hold above the engine room. A single bulb above him illuminated the hulk in a silhouette I didn't care to remember. He must have seen that I was conscious, because he kicked me in the ribs. The loud sucking sound of my burning lungs gasping for air through my mouth confirmed I was back in the real world.

I called him a gorilla for more than his sparkling personality. This guy had a heavily muscled chest and broad shoulders. And with his muscles flexed, the dorsals forced the arms out from his sides and his huge, half-open hands swung out from his body. Add to this a semi-automatic tucked under his left armpit in a shoulder holster and the simian-like stance was complete and I knew I was screwed.

He kicked me in the ribs again, and I knew I had to work up a new angle. I considered my options. Playing dead and wishing the giant would just go away and pick on someone else wasn't going to do the trick.

I had the sudden fear that maybe Kong had mistaken Garbo for Fay Wray and carried her off somewhere as well. But then if he had, why the hell would he be wasting his time with me? Maybe a modicum of cooperation on my part would help keep me intact long enough to find out what in the hell was going on.

"You are an American spy," Kong said with a deep, guttural German accent.

Knowing the current German reputation for intolerance, I decided it prudent to give him the right answer, and knew if I waited too long another kick from the jackboot would be forthcoming. I didn't know spy etiquette, but wasn't there some kind of universal handshake to make sure they only killed their own and not an innocent bystander? Namely, me.

"I'm American, but not a spy," I said with as much equanimity as I could muster. But another swift kick in my ribs left me doubting my own veracity again. Christ, what a week I was having.

Big Monkey reached a paw into his overcoat. Having seen one too many Edward G. Robinson gangster movies, my mind jumped to the inevitable conclusion that the "jig was up." It was curtains for me. I was as sure of my own imminent demise as I was of the sensation of warmth spreading in my porter's pants. Yep, I'd peed myself, all right. The cleaning bill on this get-up was going to be outrageous. Good thing I wasn't going to be around for anyone to collect.

The gorilla pulled out the letter I had snatched from Garbo's suite. He unfolded it and held it out to me in the quasi-darkness of the room. The incandescent bulb from behind him shone through the parchment, and I could make out the letterhead. A stylized eagle with a swastika at the center. Nazis, all right. The body of the letter itself was in German, which I unfortunately hadn't studied in school. But I knew enough to discern that it had been addressed to Garbo and signed A. H. Adolf Hitler?

"If not a spy," he said, "then why were you in Fräulein Garbo's room, stealing this?"

Good question. For a Neanderthal, Big Nazi Monkey had put two and two together. And most likely the truth was going to get me killed. Instead, I'd do what came natural. I'd lie. My time was short anyway. God would surely forgive me one last little lie when I saw him.

"Souvenir," I said and forced the corners of my mouth into a tepid smile. "I'm a big fan."

Another kick in my ribs. Only this time much harder. I writhed in pain as he considered me with a dispassionate stare. He refolded the letter carefully and put it back in his inner breast pocket. Him being a Nazi, I had a feeling I didn't want to see what else he had in his pockets or up his sleeves. And judging from how the conversation had gone so far, I assumed the next thing he pulled out wasn't going to be a lollipop.

"You will tell us the truth," he said and lorded over me in the dark shadows. "Before you die."

And the evening had begun so well. How had sleeping with the girl of my dreams become dying in a storeroom with the gorilla of my nightmares?

Wait a minute. Did he just say "us"?

Of course, he wasn't working alone. Someone had to be behind the scenes, pulling the strings on this oversized puppet. I had known thugs like him before. They never worked alone. Take Toes and Bernie, for instance. They didn't move a muscle unless Johnnie Roses told them to. Someone was in the wings giving the orders to this mug, all right. I could feel them lurking there, just offstage, watching for my next move. Directing the show under a cloak of darkness.

I stared up at the large Nazi and smiled at him. He looked at me and must have thought the tiny American bleeding at his feet had gone stark, raving mad. And then I realized he wasn't so big after all. Physical strength only carried you so far.

Size didn't matter when it came to real power. Prophets, poets, and wise men had known this, and now so did I. Thanks to Garbo. My short time with her had been an education. All of human history in one delectable bite. Or in this case, a kiss and a nibble. What the hell was the line in that Rimbaud poem? The one on childhood? *"It can only be the end of the world ahead."*

Garbo loomed larger in my mind's eye by the second. She was the real gorilla in my dreams. And what she had in store for us all, I imagined, was no monkeyshine. But I had to dispense with Big Nazi Monkey above me before I could catch the rest of her show. Him and his master, that is.

I looked up at the silverback and smiled broadly. Someone had been taking old Moseley for a ride. And I was sick of sitting by and letting them drive unseen. Letting them play me to get whatever the hell they wanted with Garbo. However Garbo figured in this scheme, I had to believe she was innocent. Needed to believe she only used her incredible powers for good. Otherwise, it really could only be the end of the world. Any world I wanted to be part of, anyway.

But why had Garbo chosen me? I'd likely never know the answer to that question. Maybe she didn't either. When she clubbed me over the head in the men's room, I had been a stranger. Then, when she made love to me, I had been a porter. In both instances, it seemed random that I, Seth Moseley, was the recipient of such pain and pleasure. Little reason to believe otherwise. Yet I began to wake up to an awareness that I may not have been chosen at random after all. No, not at random but by design.

When it came to beautiful women, I was a slow learner. But in those quiet, intimate moments with my Big Nazi Monkey, I realized that I had been auditioned, then chosen for a specific role. I had played a part in something much larger and complex than getting a candid snap of a movie star or winning a bar bet. And though I couldn't quite put my finger on it, I knew if I lived long enough, the puzzle pieces would come together, form a pattern and take shape. The better the story, the more the pieces. And this one promised to be a doozy. But why me? What had brought me aboard to connect the dots?

I had to be careful. I had to keep in the forefront of my mind that it wasn't just me anymore. There was Garbo to consider. No, I wasn't a fool. I knew I could never possess the goddess. That would be like trying to possess a moonbeam. Me, I only wanted to preserve that light.

Once I knew what life looked like by the light of the silvery Garbo, I needed to keep it from going out. Because once it was gone, then I knew I really would be alone.

12. STORMING THE CASTLE

JAMES

I sat bolt upright in bed. I'd been listening to Seth talk passionately amidst the beep and wheeze of life-support machines brought in as a precautionary measure. The old man had been animated, filling my head with Garbo and starlight even though he was now surrounded by a mess of tubes and wires. And then, he'd gone quiet.

I turned to see his eyes glaze over as his voice trailed off like some automated fortune teller unplugged mid reading. He'd stopped with Garbo in danger, but from what? My mind raced back to a Garbo biography I'd read, one which had contained a specific quote uttered by the movie star herself about World War II. One that suddenly made all the sense in the world.

I pressed the nurse's call button. Not for Seth but for myself. I had to get to a computer and find that Garbo quote to see if it explained why, in her own words, she would have been on the *Athenia* in the first place. The words that would help me believe that Seth's story about his Nazi run-in onboard the ocean liner was more than an old man's wishful thinking. Garbo's words were the key, the Holy Grail hiding in plain sight. I pressed the call button again.

Sarah hurried into our room and saw Seth asleep, the control to his Stryker pain pump in the open palm of his right hand. Initially resistant to pain killers, Seth had been hitting the juice more and more as his condition worsened. I couldn't imagine what kind of pain would become too much for even an obstinate old fuck like him to ignore.

"What's up?" she said to me while checking his IV line and vitals.

"I need to get on the internet." I knew it sounded stupid the moment I said it. All I needed was to add, "It's a matter of life and death," and I'm sure Sarah would have thrown me out of the hospital herself.

"It can't wait?" she said, her lips pressed together like a ref whose call had been challenged. "Until morning?"

Sarah's temper obviously wasn't a hair-trigger like mine. More of a trip wire that I was on the verge of fouling. But finding the Garbo quote now was an emergency. I had to trespass. I had no choice.

"No." I held my ground. "I need to find something now."

My face flushed under the heat of Sarah's incendiary glare. I wasn't usually this high-maintenance, and I hated how uncomfortable I felt in this new role. I made an excuse of turning away to look at Seth, asleep, surrounded by his machines. I somehow envied the guy, dying there peacefully. How fucked up was that?

"The family resource room is closed," she said in a controlled voice.

Sarah and I hadn't talked since our conversation earlier in the day. There was something there, something growing between us. I knew that at least. Exactly what, I wasn't sure.

But I was sure that even annoyed, Sarah was more beautiful than any woman I'd ever laid eyes on before. I imagined how hot she'd look screaming at me, and didn't think I'd have long to wait.

"Let me see what I can do," she said.

Huh? I looked back up at her in time to see her turn her back and leave the room. "Thanks," I said, but she was already gone.

Women had always been a mystery, but Sarah … well, she was something altogether new. Maybe it was because I was vulnerable. Unemployed. Injured. Hospitalized. Maybe I was seeing things that weren't there, reading into every nuanced movement and glance what I wanted to see. Yes, we'd flirted, and I seemed to get under her skin. But, in reality, I was just another guy checking her out. At least I wasn't a nipple gazer. At least I wasn't an asshole like Martin. And at least it looked like she was taking me seriously. Nobody since my mom had given a shit about what I thought or said, and here this beautiful woman was going out of her way to help me. Lend me a hand. Actually listen to me.

I breathed a sigh of relief. I kidded myself that Sarah and I were simpatico. I wanted us to be thick as thieves. Bonnie and Clyde-style. They were made for each other. Except those two had been shot to death under a hail of bullets by the cops. But who was I to quibble over destiny? At least they had gone out together.

Our room darkened with the setting sun. I looked over and watched the shadows on Seth's face grow and deepen with the failing light. Gone was the natural amber fill-light that had given his flesh some life. His cheekbones grew more pronounced under the fluorescents above his bed. Now he looked like a jaundiced sculpture made of inanimate limestone. Seth appeared more skull and skeleton than skin.

My lungs constricted, and I tried to swallow. I suddenly realized I didn't want Seth to die. And not just because of his Garbo story. No, I was even more craven and selfish than that. I didn't want him to die because I didn't want to be left alone again. I was just awakening to the realization that Seth and I had more in common than just a love of Garbo, and now I didn't want him to walk out on me before Garbo's big scene was over.

I didn't want to be left behind to watch the end alone. Not again.

Garbo had played Mata Hari, the famous World War I German spy who was caught and executed by the French. The film ended with Garbo being led out to a rifle range, though the actual execution was never seen. The mere sound of rifle fire over black was enough to make movie audiences in the early 1930s tremble. Then silence.

Seth's silence was now deafening. Made more so by all the blinking machines surrounding him. I wondered how many other hearts and minds these same machines had monitored, blaring their life-and-death warning signals at the very end like distant rifle fire.

I considered various excuses to make some noise. Wake the old fart up and get on with the story while he still had time and breath. Instead, I summoned the memory of happier times. Wasn't that what you were supposed to do to turn a frown upside down? Fend off the existential angst of aloneness? I could only conjure up two memories.

The first was the ghost of a All Hallow's Eve past. I was five. Encased in a knight's costume fashioned out of empty liter-sized bottles of Pepsi-Cola. Bolted together with brass fasteners. Sprayed with a metallic finish. Mom must have spent a week fabricating the thing. The final effect was amazingly realistic. I admired myself in the hall full-length mirror and saw Mom's proud smile reflected in my armor as we headed hand in hand out the front door.

The second memory was later. More towards the end. Our neighbor had yelled at me for taking our hose and making a pool of their basement. I was terrified the news would be the final blow and kill my mother. Instead, Mom had let out a laugh to wake the dead. The first one heard in our house since she'd been diagnosed with colorectal cancer. Old prune-faced neighbor-lady turned and walked away. There was no intimidating my mother when it came to her son.

"Fuck'em if they can't take a joke," Mom had said. Then she'd hugged me, swatted my behind and told me to go over and apologize to the neighbor lady and help her clean her basement. That was the first and last time I ever heard my mother swear.

"Fuck who?" Seth said.

I looked over at him. Jesus. His eyes were open and trained on me like a hungry raptor just flown in from some far off place. His ability to step in and out of consciousness without any warning really freaked me out.

"What?" I tried not to sound too unstable.

"You said, 'Fuck'em if they can't take a joke,'" Seth repeated. "Who?"

I looked at him with wide-eyed shock. I hadn't spoken out loud, had I? I reached up and felt the bandage on my head. Goddamn concussion had done more damage than I'd thought.

I shrugged by way of a comeback. I didn't want to admit I'd been in my own far-off place, chasing down the past. Some things had to remain secret, or else once-released, their energy would dissipate. Or maybe that was bullshit, and I just didn't want to talk about endings. Not when he and I were stuck in the middle.

"Fine, don't tell me." Seth shifted in his bed and sent a shock wave through the spider web of wires and tubes attached to his limbs. "Where's Sarah? I heard her voice."

"She was in here, but you were out. Or so I thought."

"Just resting my eyes. Plenty of time to sleep later."

Seth turned and scrutinized me in a way that made me feel creepy. Like he had the ability to pull off my face and peer into my skull just by looking at me. I'd made the mistake of letting Martin rent space in my head before, and I wasn't about to have any new tenants. I was all full-up.

Then again, he wasn't Martin. He was much smarter. He could fashion his own key made of words. Pretty much go anywhere he wanted. And I didn't have shit to say about it.

"What's wrong with your pecker?" he said.

"My pecker?" Oh, sweet Mother-of-God, where was he going now?

"Yeah," he said. "You know, your tallywhacker. Your Johnson."

Great. Where was my morphine drip? If I was going to have to suffer through a conversation with Seth focused on my privates, I should at least be as high as he was. Served me right for getting sentimental over the old fuck.

"Why do you ask?" I could feel my eyebrows slanting at right angles like a pissed-off cartoon character.

"What does she have to do?" he said, unfazed. "Throw you over her shoulder and carry you home fireman-style for you to get a clue?"

"What? Who?"

"Sarah, you moron." Seth lifted a hand and smacked his own forehead for emphasis. "You need to make a move while we're all still breathing. God knows I'm not always going to be here to tell you what to do."

Christ. Somehow Seth Moseley as my wingman had never entered my head. And once conjured, the accompanying image of the 747 crashing into the terminal from the movie *Airport* sprung to mind. Except in my version there were flames. Any plane with Seth as co-pilot was destined to crash and burn.

"Assuming that it is any of your business." I felt the sharp burn of acid reflux rise in my throat. "Which, it isn't. I don't hit on every pretty girl that comes within arm's reach."

Seth stared at me, silent and annoyed save for the ever-present rasp of his shallow breath. A machine whined behind him. "Why the hell not?"

Then the thought of Martin popped into my head. Seth had quite a few years on him. But when it came to women, they did sound much the same. Maybe Martin and I could switch beds. Then the two degenerates could swap trade secrets on how to bag chicks, and I could get some peace.

The thought of being alone—away from both of them—was quite pleasant.

"I prefer to take a more chivalrous approach," I declared in my own defense, not quite sure why I bothered. "Now, can we just drop it?"

Seth smiled at me. A big Cheshire grin stretched from ear to wispy-haired ear. It ate me up. I had somehow given him what he wanted. Again. A window on which to perch and peck at my innerworkings. I didn't need—or want—a buzzard like him in my brain. Not now, not ever.

"Oh, I get it," he said. "Okay, Sir Galahad. Just don't come crying to me when some Lancelot storms the castle and makes off with Maid Marian while you're fiddling with your sword."

"It's Guinevere," I said, unable to control myself. "Maid Marian was with Robin Hood, you asshole."

Seth laughed so hard his IV bag jiggled. He wasn't apt to make a literary mistake out of ignorance and laziness. No, he wasn't Martin after all. Seth had purposely provoked me in order to outmaneuver me, then hit me where I lived. If this had been a joust, I'd have already been impaled and my noble steed would've bolted out from under me to the boos and hisses—and laughter—of the unwashed mob.

"Okay, sport," I said. "You've had your fun. Can we get back to Garbo now? Please?"

"Not yet," he said, wagging a scrawny finger at me. "You have to do something for me first."

What in the hell was he bargaining for? Wasn't it enough to humiliate me? I looked at him, then closed my eyes and waited for the kill shot. Seth took his time, too. Savored the moment. He was so quiet, I thought he'd gone back to sleep. And then he fired at will.

"A kiss."

"What?" I opened my eyes. "You want me to kiss you?"

"Not me, jackass," he said. "Her."

The creep factor was off the charts. The morphine was definitely bringing out the pervert in him. Well, he'd have to get his yucks somewhere else. Debasing myself was one thing, but Sarah was off-limits.

"I'm not gonna kiss Sarah in front of you." I flushed with outrage.

"Not in front of me." He hit the button on his morphine pump. "Unless you need me to show you a few pointers."

Seth was having a heigh-ho time pushing my buttons along with the pain pump. Too bad the thing had an automatic shut off before an overdose could occur.

"No," I said, adamant.

"Have to take your word for it then," he said. "Just keep in mind. I can tell if you're lying."

"You're one sick fuck," I said. "You know that?"

"It's just one little kiss. You're making too big a deal out of it."

Too big a deal? Wow. A first kiss was something sacred. Heat spread over my cheeks as I realized I'd already written the whole scene. We were in some kind of meadow situation. In springtime or maybe autumn. Sarah and I would be alone, lounging on a blanket after a picnic I'd planned special for the occasion. Maybe a little drunk off Champagne after toasting to the first time we met.

"Sometime today, Romeo," Seth's voice broke in just as I was leaning in toward Sarah's plump lips.

"I'm not going to ruin things with Sarah," I said. "Just so

you can get your kicks."

"Good thing no one's relying on you to perpetuate the species," he said. Seth lifted his hands up to form a cone through which to bellow. "We'd die out before you got to first base."

"Hey," I said, "keep it to a dull roar."

Seth brought two fingers to his mouth and shhh'd himself. "What makes you think you'd ruin things, anyway?" he whispered.

"It doesn't matter." I pointed a finger at him as if disciplining a dog who'd just stolen a bun off the dinner table. "Because I'm not going to do it. Not now."

"You have no choice," he said with a drug-induced lilt in his voice. "You have to storm the castle if you want Garbo."

Blackmail. Seth knew just how to get what he wanted. If I didn't comply, I wouldn't have anything to offer Sarah by way of my own success. He knew I needed Garbo. But what did he gain from forcing my hand with Sarah? What the hell was he trying to prove exactly?

Sarah walked back into our room. Seth and I both turned to look at her. Seth's pupils had been dilated because of the pain killers. Mine were blown out over my natural attraction to her. Attraction and fear. She gazed steadily from one to the other of us, her own eyes full of suspicion. Had she overheard our conversation?

"Gentleman," she said and rested her hands on her fabulous hips, "you look like two cats sharing a canary. What's going on in here?"

I glared at Seth out of the corner of my eye. Willed him to keep his trap shut. I was ready to launch myself across to his bed and suffocate him if he said anything about the kiss.

Or just about anything else for that matter.

"Oh, nothing," Seth said with glee. "Just telling James here about a girlfriend I had who was allergic to duck semen."

My jaw dropped open. What the hell? "Come again?"

"It was our first date," he said. "We went out to a little private fishing hole I knew, and I talked her into skinny-dipping. The next thing I knew, she was covered in welts. She ran home screaming bloody murder." Seth smiled at me and laughed. "Found out later the pond was full of duck semen. She was allergic to the stuff."

"Let me guess," I said. "And you never saw each other again."

"No. We got married."

I shook my head and quietly questioned my own inner duck. I really didn't know shit about women.

"You were married?"

"You find that surprising?"

Of course, I did. Seth was one of the most annoying people I'd ever met in my entire life. And the thought of a woman willing to be his wife was beyond comprehension. Not that I would ever say that to him. Probably not.

"Where is she now?" Sarah said.

"Helen has been gone five years."

Sarah laid her hand on Seth's and gave it a gentle squeeze. "I'm sorry to hear that."

"I'm glad she passed." He looked up and gave her a small smile. "Before our son."

Seth had a wife and son, both gone. He'd never uttered a word of any of this before. Not that I had asked. Our phone conversations had revolved around famous people. People and events he'd covered for the tabloids. Never anything personal. We were very much alike in that way.

"What did he die of?" I said. "Your son."

"Drugs." Seth looked away. "We'd become strangers long before that. Strangers with the same last name."

I was compelled to say something, anything. Seth getting so personal made me squirm. I wanted to change the subject, anything to ward off an intense feeling in my gut. Stuff back down the emotion I felt rising in my throat. Sarah saved me before I had the chance to do what I usually did in such situations, which was to insert foot into mouth.

"I'm sorry, but will you excuse us, Seth?" Sarah began removing my IV. When she was done, she fished a solitary silver key from her pocket. "James and I have a date in the resource center."

I looked at the sparkly metal object as if hypnotized. Seth giggled, then clapped a hand over his mouth. The game was afoot. I was terrified. Why did women scare me so?

Seth burst out laughing. "Have fun storming the castle."

Sarah looked at me, uncomprehending. I so wanted to counter with a snappy rejoinder. Something smooth and ingratiating like, "How high is this guy, right?" followed by a wink and a nod. Instead, I shrugged and smiled like a fucking idiot. God. Help. Me.

Sarah unlocked the door. The resource room was dark and deserted. We sat in front of the lone computer workstation, and she fired up the old Mac. She wanted to keep the overhead lights off so as not to arouse unwanted attention. I wanted them off so she couldn't tell how much I was sweating.

We didn't speak while we waited for the Internet to come on-line. When the Google homepage popped up, Sarah and I both reached out for the mouse. Our hands touched. I recoiled and let her take the controls.

"Sorry," she said. "You do it."

"No, please," I said too loudly. "You do it."

"Okay," she said. "What are we looking for?"

I told her to type in "Garbo" comma "Hitler." She did and hit the return key. A list of about a gazillion fan sites dedicated to the movie queen came up in the web search.

"That one." I pointed a finger attached to the hand that had my hospital ID tag around the wrist.

My naked forearms had goose bumps running all the way up them. The room was cool, but that wasn't the reason. Sarah was right next to me. My arm hair bristled and stood on end, almost as if it was trying to reach out and touch her.

I watched Sarah move the mouse and click on the link to a website called "GarboForever.com" when a strange sensation overcame me. I felt a heightened awareness to her presence. A sense that I was experiencing something new and exciting, yet oddly familiar. Sarah radiated déjà vu from every pore. We were in this together now.

The sensation lingered. The simplest movement of her bare arm next to mine gave me an adrenaline rush. A glance of her color-contrasted black bra, visible underneath her white scrubs had the same effect. I crossed my legs, highly aware that I wasn't wearing anything under my hospital gown. I had to get a grip.

Her eyes watched the progress bar while the web page slowly loaded. Smokey cool hazel eyes. Sarah's eyes were the star attraction. Making this the only time in my memory I was happy to have a bad internet connection. Time to watch and prepare myself for engagement.

We huddled together in the glow of the computer screen as if for warmth. A strand of Sarah's long black hair danced in the electricity-charged air between us. I moved in to smell her lavender scent, mindful of our reflection in the computer monitor. I didn't want to give away my exact location. Didn't want to give the impression I was ogling and sniffing her like a desperate, amorous hound dog. I stifled a whimper.

The website finally came up. Reluctantly, I dragged my eyeballs back toward the monitor and feigned enough self-control to instruct Sarah to scroll down the fan site's home page to the quotes section. A gorgeous portrait of Garbo came into view and stared back at us. Taken during her silent-film period, the movie star was approximately Sarah's age in the picture. My eyes wandered from one beautiful face to the other. One made of black and white pixels, the other flesh and blood. While Sarah looked for the quote I wanted, I stared at her profile bathed in the light of the computer screen against the darkened room.

"*Hitler was a big fan of mine,*" Sarah read aloud. "*He kept writing and inviting me to come to Germany. And if the war hadn't started when it did, I would have gone, and I would have taken a gun out of my purse and shot him, because I'm the only person who would not have been searched.*"

I watched Sarah while Garbo's words echoed in my mind. Watched her eyes gaze at the screen. Her lips moved while she silently reread the quote.

Now I knew why it was so important when the war had started. Sarah knew it too. It's because Garbo had been on the *Athenia* when Seth said she had been. On the eve of another world war.

"I never knew," Sarah said and turned to me, excitement shining in her eyes, her lips just inches from mine. "Then is what Seth is saying true?"

I looked at Sarah's mouth while the rush of pounding blood filled my ears. My heart pumped faster and faster as my senses cried out for release. A collision was now inevitable. This was no longer about Seth. Or even Garbo. I braced myself for impact. I was going in.

"James?" The word was a whisper and it came to my ears out of sync with those lips, the distance between us closing fast. I was either going to stick the landing or die on impact. My kiss cut Sarah's next words off. Her beautiful lips conformed to mine. Her sweet breath escaped into me. Filled me up. While Garbo stared out at us from the monitor, I kissed Sarah as if my life depended upon it.

Then she pulled away. We stared into each other's eyes. She grabbed my hand. Steadied me. And I closed my eyes and fell back in.

Now Sarah was kissing me back. My ears rang with the sound of castle walls crumbling, freeing me from the claustrophobic weight of my armor, enabling me to hold her with no self-imposed barriers between us.

Sarah led me by the hand to the deserted third floor of Mercy Hospital, but she may as well transported me up the stairway to heaven. I had no idea there was a deserted third floor to the hospital and didn't think to ask what had been there before or why it even existed. I couldn't think of anything at all, except for what was happening in the moment.

We walked down a long hallway, and I looked in one empty room after another. Our hands playfully intertwined, then untwined over and over as we walked. The feeling of walking beside Sarah made me warm with the feeling of belonging. I felt her presence next to me and gazed into the empty rooms and started seeing ghosts. People from my past, the present, and even a few strangers now populated these rooms, staring at me as I passed by. Me and Sarah holding hands.

I found myself in a room looking out a window at a lamppost illuminating a large triangle-shaped beam of falling snow. I couldn't believe how beautiful it was. How peaceful and quiet. Sarah put her arm around my waist and pulled me close. Then she snuggled her head in the nook of my neck, watched the snow with me. My reflection in the window broke out in a shit-eating grin. All of the sudden, I was one lucky bastard.

"I'll bet you're good with the ladies. Bet you're wicked," she whispered. Wow. What a line. The guy in the window winked at me. Some lucky bastard, alright.

As far as wish-fulfillment, this was stacking up to be the best day of my goddamn life. Sarah was gorgeous. The most beautiful woman in the world as far as I was concerned. Her sheer physical attraction was so intense, I could feel it pulling on me. I was in her orbit, for sure.

Suddenly, I couldn't get the original *Sea of Love* song out of my mind. Mom had played the original, 1959 Phil

Phillips' version for me on her old .45 record player to get me to fall asleep. Sarah caught my eye while I stared straight out the window, listening.

"You okay, Romeo?"

I looked over at her, refocused on the cluster of freckles bridging her nose while my internal soundtrack played. I hummed along with the tune while I gazed at her.

"Never better."

Then I pulled away from the window. Backed away and sat on the bed. Stared over at Sarah standing in silhouette in front of the window. I soaked in her essence while she turned to me. The storm raged outside, swirling around her lithe frame from behind. I stared at Sarah intensely, registering her every move. I instinctually knew I would be spending many a daydream in this room and wanted to get every little detail right.

She came to me, her silhouette casting me in shadow while the snow continued its silent descent behind her. I pulled her in by her hips, until they hit me mid-chest. She ran the tips of her fingers through my hair as I looked up at her, her beautiful breasts at eye-level.

"What if someone comes?" I said.

Sarah she pulled back, the light from the lamppost—diffused by the swirling snow—made her nurses' uniform glow around the edges. "That's the entire point, sport."

"I mean, 'somebody'."

"Then you'll just have to contain yourself, won't you. That means no screaming." She kicked off her shoes and slowly pulled off her scrubs, letting them drop to the floor and pool around her ankles. Then she shimmied her cotton panties off and unfastened her lacy, black bra. She stood there for a moment as the lamplight created a halo around her, as if she was a gift from the gods, then she stepped past me, leaving her clothes in a heap on the floor, pulled down the quilt, and slipped into bed. "Remember, No screaming."

She rolled to her side facing me. If she minded me glaring at her, she didn't let on. Instead, she propped her head on one hand and absently ran the other over her bare, curving hips, and across her stomach. The hand finally rested cupping her right breast.

I gulped. "I can't make any promises."

"Your turn." She gestured with the hand atop her breast to lift up my hospital gown.

A feeling of heady, lazy warmth moved through me. I slowly got up off the bed until my shadow overtook the bed, casting her in shades of silver and blue. I reached around to the back of my gown and pulled the knot I had made of the strings. Sarah smiled up at me as I tugged and tugged—but the damn thing wouldn't come undone.

"Uh, I think I'm stuck."

"Turn around," she said with a smile as she got up on her knees. I sucked in my breath and did as I was told.

"Let's see what we've got here."

Her hands caressed my butt while they made their way up to the strings of my hospital gown. My skin sizzled and cracked in the cool air. I stared off into the snow falling outside the window and watched her reflection in the glass.

"Her lover, tall as the town tower clock," Sarah said behind me. "Samson-syrup-gold-maned, whacking thighed and piping hot."

"Who's that?" I said, half-dreaming at the snow.

"Dylan Thomas," she said and pulled the knot out. "You need to read more. But for now, turn around, tiger."

When I did, Sarah pulled off my gown in one quick gesture and I found myself naked before her. Her face a head above mine, she pressed her body into me and everyplace fit tight and true, like two lovemaking peas in a perfect pod.

She leaned down, cast her beautiful face in shadow, as her lips met mine. She kissed me deep. Tantric deep. The snowflakes falling outside the window blurred. I fought to keep my balance on the floor.

Sarah fell back, and I joined her on the hospital bed. She pulled me under the covers and the warmth our bodies made instantly sent electric charges straight to my groin. Sarah had shot any performance anxiety straight out of me in one magical thunderbolt. Something clicked and our bodies began to move together. Effortlessly.

I touched her lightly on the hip and an electric charge jumped between us like one of those lightening machines in a carny funhouse. A smile plastered itself permanently on my face while Sarah played with my chest hairs. I could barely breathe, her touch felt so good.

I stroked the small of her back then came around to the front and flicked my finger tips across her stomach. I had no idea what made me do it, but she shivered in response. We kissed long and sweet and deep. I pressed the length of my body against hers, cupped her buttocks, my dick pressed hard against her thighs.

Sarah groaned, opened her eyes wide in the dark and gave me a blazing stare, straight into me. That was love wasn't it? When someone looks at you and sees you. Sees past all the insecurities and neuroses, all the defenses to the bare, exposed and vulnerable inner-self. I was sure of it.

The next few moments I felt more connected to her than I had to anyone or anything in the last two decades. My nerve endings sizzled with undulating waves of intense pleasure as I slid my hands over her breasts and she arched her back towards me. Then she lay back as I kissed her neck and nipples. Sarah pushed her body against mine, wanting more, but I kept my rhythm. Until it became her own. Until we breathed with the same little gasps.

I was nothing but nerve endings, blazing with urgent energy when she reached down and guided me inside her. A momentary panic came over me, an overstimulation of pleasure, and I felt my consciousness dissolving. Sarah craned her face towards me, hands tight around my head, fingers pressing sharp to my scalp, and then laid her cheek against mine for a mooring. Was she coming undone as well? Breaking apart, shattering into particles, the same waves shuddering through her?

She heaved against me with crazy strength, hips pushing hard against mine, legs wrapping tight around my buttocks while I thrust deeper and deeper inside her. Her breasts pressed into me, mashed against my chest until there was no space left between us.

Then she tightened her grip even more. Crushed me to her tighter, pulling me into her until I felt her body shudder with pleasure. Then the wave washed over me, a riptide that pulled me under and then released me in a thunderous crash of warmth and pulsing release. Soon after, Sarah's strength deserted her and her arms fell back limply on the bed. The fierceness of her lovemaking was spent.

After a time, I rolled onto my side and lay facing her. I gave her little kisses all over her smiling face and closed eyes. Sarah turned over and with the flat of my warm hand, I tracked a route across her shoulders down her back and over the rise of her buttocks. I moved back to the small of her back, a slow circle, my touch never leaving her skin. Traced the route again and again while Sarah let out little giggles.

"That tickles," she said.

"In a bad way?"

"No. In a great way."

I gazed at her face, her beautiful, perfect face and thought of Garbo. Thought of the movie goddess as a real woman for the very first time. I thought of the screen queen giving and receiving carnal pleasure. My hand came to a stop in the small of Sarah's back and lay there.

Sarah opened her eyes and stared up at me.

"You alright, tiger?"

"Yeah," I said. "I was just thinking."

"Thinking about what?"

"About how it might have been with Seth and Garbo aboard the *Athenia*."

Sarah turned toward me and leaned up on an elbow, the white of her eyes glowing in my shadow.

"Don't tell me you're finally starting to believe the old man?"

"Do you believe him?"

"It doesn't matter what I believe," she said, "but what you believe to be true."

"I want to believe." I looked at Sarah, my beautiful Sarah mere inches from me and felt myself pull back. She must have seen the expression on my face because she put a hand out to my cheek. Gently caressed the side of my face while we stared at each other in the snowy twilight.

"What is it?" she said. "What's holding you back?"

I searched for words to explain what was going on inside my mind and heart in that moment. I wanted to tell Sarah how I felt but had no idea where to begin. How to explain away in a few sentences what had taken decades to be created. The quest I had been on for so long, for what I did not know.

"I ... I ..."

"It's okay," she said. "You can tell momma."

I looked into her eyes, caught the reflection of snow falling within her dark pupils like obsidian with snowflake. I was about to speak, when a sound came from outside our door. A dull, thud of a sound but one that startled us both.

Sarah blinked and sat upright. I stared up at her nakedness as she turned her head toward the door to listen. The sound came again, this time a little closer and more distinct. A squishy smack and then a rubbing sound with a squeak mixed in for good measure. Sarah looked back down at me.

"It's Harold," she whispered.

"Who?"

"The night janitor. He must be mopping the floor."

"I thought you said no one comes up here?"

"Almost no one," she said and admonished me with hushes. "We've got to get out of here."

Then she bolted buck naked from our bed and raced silently around to where she'd left her clothes on the floor. Meanwhile, I slid from between the warm cocoon of covers of our secret trysting place and scouted in the shadows for my own sliver of clothing. I never felt more naked in my life.

Minutes later we were both clothed and at the door of the room, listening. Sarah had her back to me as I stood there half-terrified and half-exhilarated. Half of me wanted Harold to catch us in the act. It was the heterosexual male in me, the proud peacock with his tail-feathers sticking out for everyone to see.

We waited until the *swish* and *thwack* of the mop grew fainter, abated. Sarah opened the door a crack and looked out on the dimly-lit hallway. She turned back in the room and looked at me—now all business.

"Okay, I'm going," she said. "You wait here for a minute and then you can go back down to your room."

I stared at Sarah, suddenly lovesick by the notion we'd be separated. She gave me a glare that smacked me back into reality, but quick.

"Are you listening?

"Uh-huh."

Sarah gave me a skeptical look, then turned and opened the door. The next second, she was gone and I was alone. I turned and leaned my back against the door. I stared at the shadowy hospital room, the falling snowflakes outside the window, the bed where Sarah and I had laid naked and entwined mere moments before. The daydream was already playing in my head.

Why couldn't anything beautiful ever last?

13. TO LIVE ONE MORE DAY
SETH

I looked up at Big Nazi Monkey towering over me and knew there wasn't much time. If I was ever going to get to the bottom of how Garbo and I had crossed paths on the *Athenia*, let alone bumped fuzzies, I'd have to stop dancing with the gorilla. But escaping King Kong was going to be a trick. The hardest kind of trick. The kind I had only one shot at pulling off.

I'll admit I'd been slow on the uptick with this one. Kong had caught me unawares when I was still woozy from Garbo's spell. He'd manhandled me into a tough spot, established his physical dominance. But now it was my turn to show off. Show him and his Master watching somewhere off-stage, that Seth Moseley gave as good as he got. And then some.

I'd learned two universal truths working the newsbeat back in the Bronx. First, if it bleeds it leads. Second, money talked and bullshit walked. Thugs were thugs, no matter what team they played for. I had to believe the same held true for the tower of brute power looming above me. Show them something sparkly and watch them go all soft in the head. But first things first. I had to see if Kong responded to verbal commands.

"Hey, you up there," I said. "You got a name?"

A bold gamble but a necessary one. I knew people. Knew how they thought, most of them. Learned from interviewing thousands of them, that everyone liked to be called by their first name. Even the crazies. Especially the crazies. Nevertheless, I braced for another kick in the ribs while Big Nazi Monkey looked down at me.

"Heinrich," he said simply.

He relaxed his mitts from rock-hard fists to rub his palms on the sides of his trousers. A good sign. The giant was bashful after all. I slowly raised up my right hand to Heinrich. He looked at my extended digits with a puzzled expression on his mug.

"Seth Moseley," I said by way of introduction.

I'll be damned if the abominable who had tumbled me like so much dirty laundry didn't reach down and shake my hand. His paw was easily twice the size of mine and felt like it was made of sweaty, cold granite. His handshake wasn't firm, but gentle. Told me I had guessed right. This guy had no personal beef with me. And if I did my job right, I might even elicit some sympathy from him before it was all over. If his master didn't intervene, that is.

Now came the tough part. I never went anywhere without a reserve of silver dollars in my pocket. I knew I had transferred them from my trousers to my constricting porter's pants before I'd embarked on my rendezvous with Garbo. As tight as the porter pants were, I felt naked and ungrounded without some jingle next to the family jewels. Naked and vulnerable like I felt now. I knew Heinrich had lifted my stack of silver while I was under. And that was a good thing.

"You mind if I get up?" I asked.

He didn't answer, not aloud. But when he took a step back without kicking me in the face, I got the impression it was okay. Slowly, I sat, then stood up. My sore bones creaked as I came to stand opposite Heinrich, who was easily a foot taller than me. His nose hair could've used a trim. But I'd see how the evening went before I shared that with him.

We scrutinized each other, and I could tell I'd thrown him for a loop. I was guessing he'd never met an American before. Lucky for me, I knew plenty of Germans, ones that had emigrated to America and made the slums of New York their new home. But even the nice ones had been standoffish. Standoffish yet polite when faced with authority. I figured the new breed wreaking havoc in Europe wasn't much different. To get the upper hand, I had to show confidence, moral and mental superiority. In short, I had to fake it.

"I seem to be missing my coins," I said in the most non-confrontational voice I could muster. Good ole Heinrich, I could tell, instantly knew what I was talking about. But before he got the wrong idea, I put both my open palms up in surrender.

"Not saying you took them." I put on a smile. "Just wondering if you might have come across them."

Further confusion clouded his vision. Heinrich furrowed his brow, looked down at his shoes instead of me. He had momentarily forgotten what his mission had been. Namely, kicking my ass. Now I hoped I had a fighting chance. And here came the kicker.

"I'd sure like the opportunity to win them back."

Heinrich shifted his gaze and then met my eyes. His facial expression wide open. The mug's mug was so wide and flat I imagined you could land a plane on it. Land or take off.

"Win?" he said.

Thanks for playing along, buddy. Now it was up to me to keep the ball rolling. Timing was everything when dealing with primates. Distraction and misdirection kept them off balance and therefore malleable and open to manipulation. I'd saved myself from enough beatings to know that placing an idea in their head was as powerful as landing a punch to the jaw. Put them together, and you were all but invincible.

"Now, if you'd be kind enough to show me some coins," I said, "I'll show you something I guarantee you've never seen before."

Heinrich hesitated. Even if he only got every third word of what I was saying, it had been enough to captivate his imagination. I was breaking new ground for the fella. Talking to him like a human being. Putting on a private show just for him. If he'd been cautioned not to consort with the enemy, his master wasn't around to remind him. Curiosity got the better of good, ol' Heinrich.

I no longer feared for my life when he reached into his trouser pocket. This time he brought out a pile of my silver dollars into the open palm of his massive hand and held them up in the dim light. They sparkled between us while I watched his eyes grow wider watching them.

"May I?" I motioned to pick one up.

Heinrich acquiesced. Nodded his head silently while I carefully selected a coin from the top of the silver pile.

I took the silver dollar and cascaded it down my row of knuckles so it twinkled underneath the incandescent bulb suspended by a wire between us. The coin's large silver surface shimmered in Kong's face. Flashed again and again in his eyes until he was mesmerized.

Heinrich's mouth began to water as if I'd whipped out a bratwurst and waved it around. We all had our appetites in life, and I had whetted his. Big Nazi Monkey wasn't greedy. If he was, he simply would have kept the coins for himself. No, his nature was similar to mine, in that he wanted to win. Be a winner. Who didn't?

"I'm pretty handy with these things." I kept the coin dancing in the light. "I can show you how to do this, too."

While he stood transfixed by the silver piece dancing in my hand, I took note of the door located behind him. Calculated the distance in my head. Kong's arm span was such that I'd never get to the door before he got to me. Not if he was conscious and upright.

"Ever been to America?" I tossed Lady Liberty into the air. I was hedging my bets that it was Kong's identical twin who'd fallen off the Empire State Building and not him.

"Nein," he said.

Yeah, that wasn't hard to figure. But was he a history fan? Only one way to find out.

"Well, this here's what they call a Peace Dollar," I informed him. Heinrich didn't look up. Maybe he didn't know what peace meant in English. Maybe in any language.

True to its name, the back of the 1935 mint read *Peace*, commemorating the end of World War I. An American bald eagle perched majestically above the word. I didn't feel the need to share that the coin was struck as a shining symbol of having beaten their Kraut asses. Plenty of time for Heinrich to read up on the details later. On his time, not mine.

"Let me borrow a few more," I said in a friendly manner, "And we can begin the coin toss."

I caressed Lady Liberty's face in my hand while Heinrich watched. She never failed to bring me luck before. Actually, she'd let me down on numerous occasions, but I was willing to make amends if she was. Heinrich nodded again and smiled. I prayed she'd be right on the money this time.

Heinrich was busy watching my hand while I picked up five more silver pieces from his open hand. Dropped them one-by-one into my open palm. They made a metal popping sound when each reed-edged silver coin struck another. Like a semi-automatic going off in the distance.

Heinrich didn't see me brace myself. Planted my feet firmly on the grated floor beneath us. Put my weight on the balls of my feet and prepared myself to spring into action when needed. All there was left to do was aim high and shoot the devil with a parlor trick I'd previously perfected to win me pints.

"All you do"—I sounded pious as a Sunday morning preacher—"is raise a bent elbow up"—I curled my hand back until the elbow pointed level with monkey's big face before me—"and balance the stack on the flat top of your forearm."

In the blink of an eye, I whipped my bent arm down and out. The coins stayed put, suspended in air for a split second between Heinrich and me, until I snatched the entire stack with the same hand. His eyes fixated around the empty space.

I could tell by the look on his face the precious metal stack was still hanging there in his mind's eye. Heinrich had fallen for the illusion completely. Victory was within the gorilla's grasp. He need only reach out and grab for it.

"Kinder play," he said then looked at me with a broad smile. I surrendered the coins, dropped them back into the pile in his open palm.

The big brute scrunched his furry brow, still staring in concentration at the point in space where the coins used to be. He raised a massive forearm and practiced the move, minus the coins. He might not have had a lot going on upstairs, but he was coordinated for his size. I'd give him that.

I watched while he repeated the movement, this time with the five-stack of coins. In a split second, he had grabbed the entire bundle and burst forth a proud smile. One could even have said he possessed a certain grace when he snapped the coins from the air, though I wouldn't. Heinrich beamed with pride.

"Excellent." I brandished a toothy grin. "But can you handle ten?"

I raised the stakes. I was betting Heinrich and his Nazi buddies hadn't had many poker nights. Didn't hang around smoking cigars, yucking it up over how many people they massacred that day. What did murderers do in their off-hours?

He nodded his consent again. Good boy. I slowly counted out ten silver dollars from his open hand. Stacked those sweet Lady Liberties on the flat surface of my upright elbow and gave good ol' Heinrich a nod.

"Are you watching closely?" I said.

It was time to play my only hand. I wouldn't get another shot at this. My short life flashed before my eyes. They rested on Garbo. She was my jackpot for winning this hand. She was my biggest bet ever, and I was all-in, about to call. Meanwhile, Kong looked lovingly at the remaining coins in his hand. Like gazing at Fay Wray herself.

"Heinrich," I said, now with a stronger intonation than I had ever dared with him before.

"*Jawohl*," he said and snapped to attention.

I needed all eyes forward. Needed him to see how the trick was done. He stared at my forearm with intense concentration. The height of the vertical column of silver on my forearm now equaled the width of my fist, which was exactly the point.

Another dramatic pause. I made it look like I was sweating it for a second. Looked at Heinrich. Gave him a beat to lean his face in closer. Just enough to be in range and ... *POW!* I snapped my arm down, twisted my hand forward, grabbed the flying stack and popped Big Nazi Monkey right in the kisser with a fistful of metal. So hard I felt my own knees buckle. A sickening crunch of cartilage resonated from Big Nazi Monkey's nose.

It all happened so fast, Heinrich barely had time to reach his arms out to me while he fell backward. I avoided his clutches easily. But it was the expression of shock and hurt that played out on his bloodied expanse of face that hit me hard. I felt for him in that moment, even as I opened my bloodied fist and let go of the coins. No time to return them to my skin-tight pants pocket.

The coins fell through the slots of the grated floor. Clinked and clattered as I scrambled for the door and freedom. Heinrich's dead weight hit the floor and shook the entire room. I rode the shockwave while I hotfooted over him, used his belly as a springboard to launch myself clear over his head to the hatch. It was all insult to injury at that point. I hoped Heinrich's master wouldn't hold it against the big fella. We were both playing for keeps, after all.

I reached the door, opened it, and passed into the hallway, then slammed the door behind me, all in virtually one fluid motion. Cut myself off from the trail of carnage I'd left behind me.

I found myself standing in the hallway, surprised I'd pulled off the escape. *Now what?* I hadn't thought through my next move. All I knew was that I had to keep moving. Moving targets were harder to hit.

I wasn't in any shape to go calling on a beautiful lady, but I needed to warn Garbo that in addition to one besotted tabloid reporter, her stable of onboard fans now included one supremely pissed-off Nazi the size of a gorilla. And I couldn't forget the aforementioned gorilla's mysterious master.

I needed dear Ingrid's help now more than ever. Would she excuse my betrayal of her with Garbo or would I be up shit's creek without a paddle? Hard to know, but I was determined to live one more day and find out.

14. EYE OF THE STORM OF THE CENTURY

SETH

First, I ran to Garbo's suite and rattled the handle. The door had been secured since my good friend Heinrich had dragged me through it. I leaned in to listen, no sound emanated from within. I couldn't afford to loiter. I'd have to find Garbo another time, another way.

Next up, Ingrid. I stuck to the early morning shadows en route to her room, praying that she'd let me in. I didn't want to imagine what would happen to me if she didn't. Couldn't blame her if she wouldn't. I'd no doubt broken her heart. But I'd feel shitty about it later, once my adrenaline slowed down. If I wasn't murdered first.

"Who is it?" Ingrid said from the other side of the door after I'd given it a couple of soft raps.

"Me," I said. Rotten traitor Seth Moseley.

Ingrid unlocked and opened the door quickly. I barely had time to offer up a pathetic-looking smile before she reached out a gorgeous hand and grasped my collar. She dragged me inside like so much dead weight, shut and locked the door behind me.

I was a traitor. By rights I should have been in the ninth circle of hell, waiting my turn while Satan's three faces chewed on Judas, Brutus and Cassius. Instead, I was in the bedroom of a beautiful Swede who didn't deserve to hear the painful truth I was about to tell her. Poor kid. Did Swedes read Dante?

"Listen, my sweet Ingrid." I started. "There's something I need to explain."

Dressed only in a robe, Ingrid let it drop and stood in front of me completely naked. I stared at her beautiful body as she attacked my porter's uniform, unbuttoning my vest. This was going to be a lot harder than I'd thought.

"I was with Garbo," I blurted out and put my hands up in surrender.

Ingrid kept unbuttoning my vest. Hadn't the girl heard what I said?

"Did you hear me?"

Ingrid looked up with an almost maniacal look on her face as she ripped the unbuttoned vest off my body.

"Don't just stand there," she ordered. "Help me get your clothes off."

What the hell? This wasn't the reception I'd expected. Ingrid worked frantically on the buttons to undo my trousers while I stared down at her in horrified fascination. She took rejection a lot harder than I had imagined. She pulled me towards her bed while she manhandled me.

"Ingrid," I said. "I'm sorry, but, but … I don't love you. I love her."

"We'll discuss it later," she said and stripped me of my pants. "Now get your arse on the bed if you want to live."

Arse? Either that Nazi gorilla had knocked me harder than I'd thought, or Ingrid's voice now was laced with a distinctly British accent. She popped my shirt open like a sugar-starved kid opening a bag of hard candy. Buttons flew everywhere.

"Down," she commanded and threw my naked arse onto the bed, jumped on top, and straddled me. She took my hands, one of which was still bleeding from smashing Heinrich's nose, and placed them on her shapely buttocks. Then she leaned forward, put her ample breasts in my face and started grinding away. I was afraid to tell her that, not only was this seduction not going to work, it was disturbing.

"When they come through the door," she instructed in a low octave, "act like you're enjoying yourself, for God's sake."

What? My mind spun. Who was coming through the door? Was this the best position to receive guests? I started to struggle out from under her when loud banging sounded on her door, and my anxiety went through the roof.

"Who?" I said, trapped underneath her sexy death grip.

"Who do you think?" she whispered and kissed my neck with all the sensuality of a starving vampire. Ingrid worked her way up to my ear and growled. "Moan, damn it."

Ingrid moaned in my ear. Loudly. I wanted to buck her off. Get the fuck away from her. But she dug her claws into me like a crazed hellcat. Then she pinched me on the side. Hard. I let out a yelp. She moaned even louder.

The door exploded inward, and Heinrich goose-stepped into the room, then stopped short as if he'd seen a ghost. I could only see part of him as Ingrid's bobbing breasts were squished against my face. But I caught enough of a glimpse of his bloodied mug, my handiwork, to see that whatever penny dreadful we'd been cast in, he was just as shocked as I was at the turn in the plot. It's not every day one walks in on the sight of a naked woman going to town on a prostrate man.

Honestly, part of me wanted him to come over and rip me out from under the crazy woman's embrace like a sheet of paper from an Underwood typewriter. Instead, Heinrich unceremoniously retreated. He exited, stage left as if ordered by an irate off-Broadway director. Even shut the door behind him. What a gentleman.

"What in the hell just happened?" I said up on my elbows and shaking with fear.

"Nazis are prudes," Ingrid said as she sat up and pushed her hair out of her eyes. "They're under strict orders not to ever interrupt a couple making love."

"Orders from who?"

"Who else?" Ingrid said, her beautiful breasts gleaming with the sweat of her labor. "Hitler."

"Holy fuck-a-moley." I stared up at the lovely woman poised above me. A woman I thought I knew. "Who the hell are you, and why do you have a British accent?"

"That's not important," Ingrid said, a creepy little smile forming on her face. "What is important is that you never speak of what you have seen."

Ingrid put her right hand down to rest on my chest. My heart raced under her touch. Was she going to push her talons through my ribcage and rip my ticker out for an encore? That would be the surest way of making sure I didn't talk, wouldn't it?

"Never. Speak. Of Garbo."

That British accent again. My mind reeled. I looked around the perfect stranger's room in a feeble attempt for clues to her true identity. Anything to help me unravel the beautiful enigma perched atop me.

Dear God. It hit me that Ingrid had been holding the reins the entire time we had been together. She'd steered me this way and that. Had known how I'd respond before I did. True, Ingrid obviously had secret knowledge I didn't currently possess. But how did she know which buttons to push? And how long had I been part of the plan? A plan that must have been created long before I ever stepped onboard.

Had Ingrid's plan included putting me out to stud with Garbo? Were the two vixens in cahoots with one another? A secret league of femme fatales sharpening their fangs on me while en route to God knows where? What cockamamie cat-and-mouse game had I gotten myself into? Or had I just gone plain crazy?

I found my answer, or at least one big-ass clue, behind her, just over her bare shoulder. On her shelf across the room, placed in plain sight among her other phony possessions like it had always belonged there, sat my Bell & Howell camera case. Everything snapped into sharper focus for me in that moment. I looked back at the woman formerly known to me as Ingrid, the beautiful, innocent Swedish barmaid. She stared back, straddled unabashedly naked on top of me. She had me dead to rights.

"So, you knew about me and Garbo?" I said.

Ingrid didn't answer. Didn't have to. It was a rhetorical question. I just had to say it out loud to make it real. Hear with my own ears her silent admission that I was and had always been, merely a factotum for her. An unwitting servant in service to a purpose still unknown—unknown to me, at least. A servant I now imagined had outlived his usefulness. Ingrid had stripped me to the bone. She'd taken everything from me, including my camera.

We stared at one another as the door to her suite once again exploded inward. This time I didn't take my eyes off her to see who was crashing the party. Yeah, I was a dumb horse, but not a stupid one.

"Let me guess," I said as multiple shadows loomed wraithlike. This time they didn't stop at a respectful distance but descended upon me. They grabbed my arms and legs in the tunnel vision surrounding Ingrid's visage. "British officers aren't prudes."

Under different circumstances, I imagined she might have laughed at my comment. But there wasn't anything funny about what had just transpired. Or would be in the near future, I feared. Not really.

Ingrid grabbed her robe, slipped it back on, and watched as the British First Officers draped me in a sheet, confiscated my stolen porter's uniform—one would assume as tangible evidence of my myriad transgressions—and dragged me away.

Ingrid was a smooth operator, all right. Bloodless. Or so my vanity wanted me to believe. Thinking her a monster was easier on my psyche in that moment. But I could tell she was engaged in some serious business. The kind professionals practice their entire careers. Yes, heroine or villainess, my beautiful faux barmaid had a job to do, and it wasn't shilling drinks at the onboard drinking hole where she'd picked me up. Picked me up, bathed me, then dropped me back in hot water the second I was no longer needed.

★ ★ ★

When my British escorts and I reached the outer deck, sea and sky were calm. But a storm was brewing, all right. One that couldn't be seen even as I found myself in the eye of it. An all-seeing eye that had been watching me from the start, waiting patiently to make a move. Waiting for the right time to show itself and all hell would break loose. I'd flown through a sucker hole—what pilots called otherwise serene skies—into a deadly maelstrom of cat and mouse all swirling aboard the *Athenia*.

Truly, I wanted back in the game. But to even have a chance of survival, I'd have to be patient and await my turn. Slow down, watch, then seize any opportunity quickly and without hesitation. I knew I had to figure out what I brought to the table first. Figure out how and why Ingrid had chosen me. What there was about me and my history that warranted bringing a non-professional into the mix in the first place. Only when I figured out how I fit into this crazy puzzle could I use that knowledge to escape what was shaping up to be the storm of the century.

In hindsight, escaping Heinrich had been easy. Too easy. No, I had to consider that I had been played for a patsy up to this very moment. Maybe was still being played. By Ingrid. By Heinrich's hidden master. Even Garbo.

Garbo. What the hell was a movie star doing mixed up in all this intrigue? I had to believe she and I were the outsiders. The amateurs, out of our depth and in deep, open water. Or was I fooling myself yet again? Maybe for Garbo, movie stardom was her avocation. Maybe she really belonged in the shadowy cloak-and-dagger world of spies and counterspies, and I was the one truly alone.

If that were true, then why did I feel such a strong connection with her? I knew that behind her illusion was still a woman made of flesh and blood. A real woman I'd fallen hard for and not just because we had slept together. Why did I feel so compelled to look after her well-being, even though there was a very real possibility she couldn't care less about mine?

I'd fucked up often enough to know you eventually have to pay the consequences. And I always had. But now everything was different. Exponentially harder. Once Garbo entered the picture, I knew there was more at stake than just my own neck. No, it wasn't just me anymore. I wasn't alone in this. And if I played my cards right, I hoped I'd never to be alone again.

15. A KISS TO BUILD A DREAM ON

JAMES

I listened while Seth recounted his great escape from Heinrich, only to be betrayed by Ingrid, the Swedish-cum-British seductress. Meanwhile, I couldn't wait to get back to my own raven-haired beauty. Sarah's shift didn't start until 8:00 a.m.

Garbo's words had echoed in my head while Sarah and I embraced and kissed in the dark of the resource room and made love on the abandoned third floor. Echoed even while I felt the young nurse's heart beat against my chest, tasted the warm wetness of her lips and tongue. Held the small arch of her back with my fingertips. She had been hot to the touch. Yet there was Garbo, watching over us from a respectful distance the whole time. Whispering her secret in between my ears. Keeping me from losing myself in Sarah completely.

Now both Sarah and Garbo were gone, and I was back in my hospital bed listening to Seth. He hadn't said a word when I came back from my "date." Didn't ask how I'd fared with the beautiful nurse. But then again, I guess he didn't need to. My face, flushed with pleasure, probably said it all.

Still, I expected him to gloat. I had been too chicken shit to make a move on my own. Only Seth's threat to cut me off from Garbo had given me the nerve to lock lips and hips with Sarah. Maybe both of us were off our game. Seth was dying, after all. And I was falling for Sarah. Hard.

"I never saw it coming," Seth said, staring forward.

He was twisting his top sheet in both hands. White knuckling his covers and sweating through his hospital gown. He was sans morphine, and it showed. Taken himself off painkillers in order to be more lucid. For me. For a price.

"Seth." I shifted my body toward him, ready to jump if needed. "Are you all right?"

I don't know how, but the old man saw me motion for the nurse's call button without looking over at me.

"No," he said. "They've done all they can do."

Then Seth grabbed for the pink basin beside his bed, the one stationed beside all our beds, and dry-heaved into it. Quick and violent, his face became closed like a fist, and he puked once more into the bucket.

Seth barely made his night table with the basin and leaned back in bed covered in flop sweat. I stayed quiet, monitoring his shallow breathing. Making sure his chest rose and fell in a semi-consistent rhythm. I knew he wouldn't allow himself to be put on a respirator.

"No heroic measures," I'd overheard Seth say to Doctor Moonbeam. That was Seth's new nickname for Dr. Zoom. No, once Seth's lungs gave out, that was all she wrote.

"Seth," I started.

"Save it," he said, his breath short. "It's just the morphine. Stomach never could—"

Maybe he was having a bad reaction to the morphine. But there was something in his raspy, labored breath that made me afraid. Afraid he'd go down hard. Suffer.

"Anyway, you need me compos mentis," he said and turned to give me a scowl. "Gotta finish." He took another breath. "Can't croak before the story ends."

I had to keep it together. For Seth. Christ, for myself. I had to fucking think of something, anything to say.

"You'll get no argument from me." I channeled Martin, my asshole of an ex-boss. "Walk it off, old man." Seth smiled, thank God. He relaxed the death grip he had on his sheets. I knew he was scared. Hell, I was fucking terrified, and I wasn't the one dying. I wanted nothing more than for his pain to end. But until then, he'd stay focused on the story. Take his mind off what was happening to his body. Off what inevitably came after he was done.

"Where was I?" he asked and blinked.

"You were describing how the British officers dragged you away while a beautiful, naked Ingrid looked on," I said.

"Right. That's right. Give me a second," he said and closed his eyes, "to catch my breath."

I was happy to. Watching the old man suffer had brought back memories of being with my mother when her own end was close. I'd play the fool to get my sick mother to laugh. Being only ten, I had a limited range of stories and antics with which to distract and try to comfort her. So, slapstick it was. That it came naturally seemed an added bonus at the time.

Before Mom went into the hospital for the last time, I had put on a spontaneous afternoon vaudeville act in the backyard. She'd watched from her second-story balcony seat while I set the stage. A late January snowfall provided a perfect backdrop.

Both big fans of *The Six Million Dollar Man*, one of Mom's favorites that she'd got me hooked on when it was in reruns, I assumed my best impersonation of a dour Lee Majors, a.k.a Steve Austin. He was always dour. Then, with a serious, constipated expression I would run in slow, exaggerated motion back and forth. Again and again, across the white expanse.

The neighbors must have thought I was nuts. Especially old prune-faced neighbor lady, but I didn't care. Looking up to see my mother's silhouette fogging panes of glass with gales of silent laughter was enough to keep me doing encores all day.

Now, from my bed, I hawkeyed Seth dozing and remembered how much Mom had slept toward the very end. Like I had done with her, I imagined Seth the healthy, twenty-nine-year old, vibrant and obnoxious tabloid reporter. The one who'd headlined his own story aboard the ill-fated *Athenia*. I mentally erased the wrinkles of his heavily lined face and added forty pounds to his lanky, gaunt frame.

My mental makeover made me smile. Young Seth was a handsome man in an arrogant way. He had an ever-present smug expression I would have disliked on sight in anyone else. But this guy grew on me quickly. Yeah, the Young Seth I conjured was everything I imagined he would be. Everything I needed him to be. Complete with black fedora and a lit cigarette hanging from his lower lip.

Since meeting the two Seths, Garbo had become three-dimensional and taken on incredible detail in my mind's eye.

More complex than I could ever have imagined by myself. I saw her the way Young Seth must have seen her through those analytical blue eyes of his. Even more amazing, I felt Garbo's steel-blue gaze trained on me.

I'd searched for Garbo's ghost ever since I'd moved to Los Angeles. I should have known I'd never find her there. Garbo hated every minute she'd spent in L.A. during her reign in golden-age Hollywood. That was well documented. But who in their right mind would have guessed I'd find her ghost in Norfolk, Connecticut, haunting an old tabloid reporter?

Garbo. Mom. And now Sarah. Three beautiful, mysterious women. Three sphinxes, each enigmatic in her own way. Garbo, alive beyond the screen, elusive and remote even while whispering secrets. Mom, alive in spirit and dreams, yet obscured behind panes of glass stained with the fog of time. And Sarah, my beautiful Sarah, alive, interested and apparently available. The greatest mystery of all.

And Sarah had kissed me. After I'd offered up my lame-ass version of a smooch, Sarah leaned her lithe, soft, and strong body into mine and laid one on me. A knockout punch of a kiss, right in the kisser. The kind of kiss, I had to believe, that made kissing catch on in the first place. A kiss to build a dream on.

16. IS THE JUICE WORTH THE SQUEEZE?

SETH

I'd never been on the bridge of a ship before. The view from the *Athenia's* was awe-inspiring. A one-hundred-and-eighty-degree panoramic view of the Atlantic Ocean. Nothing but water and sky. I could even see the curvature of the earth. A massive blue ball of water that we sat on the tippy-top of.

In short, I was scared shitless.

Two stewards escorted me into the room while Captain James Cook conferred with his first officer. The captain was a massive man himself, and from behind, dressed in formal whites, he reminded me of Moby Dick. I had no desire to piss the leviathan off and waited patiently—which was against my nature—for him to turn around.

While I was waiting to get my ass chewed out by the captain, Lars the porter appeared and stepped onto the bridge. I smiled at him, but he didn't smile back. Then I realized he wasn't there to take the crew order for high tea. Rather, he stood across from me and looked with disdain at my stained and stolen porter's outfit. Lars was there to add fuel to the fire. The one the captain would light to burn me at the stake.

Captain Cook finally turned around, gave me a stare and sized me up with one big scowl. Moby was even scarier from the front. I tried to keep my cool, but dressed as I was, an impostor, that is, I felt compelled to speak first. Not my first mistake since I joined the *Athenia* back in the Port of New York. Obviously not my last, either.

"Captain," I said, "something strange is going on aboard your ship."

"Hold your tongue," he said. I held it.

Then Captain Cook took a giant step closer to me. I resisted the urge to jump back. He was as tall and wide as Heinrich, but with his captain's hat and white beard, his head looked even bigger. He reached out a massive hand and grasped my porter's vest. Then tightened and twisted his sausage-sized fingers into a fist. My entire upper body and a generous portion of my chest hair caught in his vice-like grip. I prayed I wouldn't piss myself.

"Why is this man dressed as a porter?" he bellowed.

"He's a stowaway, Captain." The first officer said from behind the captain. "Porter Lars here spotted him entering a passenger's cabin earlier this morning."

Captain Cook turned and considered Lars while keeping his grip on me. I could tell Lars was almost as nervous as I was. He lowered his eyes and put his hands behind his back to bow. The captain grimaced at the crown of the young man's head.

"Report, Porter," the Captain said. "When did you first catch sight of this scofflaw?"

Lars lifted his head and stared scared into the Captain's huge face. He took a big swallow before talking. "Back in port, sir. He boarded with the reporters." He turned and looked at me. "He looked ill, so I let him into a men's room off the Promenade Deck."

"Why didn't you report him then?" the Captain said.

"I thought he was a paying passenger, sir."

"Then what?"

"Then I saw him again. He was fraternizing with a stewardess and the American entertainer in the Main Salon. I assumed he was just another passenger."

"Get on with it," the captain snapped.

"But the next time I saw him, he was entering a lady's suite," Lars said. "A very special lady's suite, dressed as ... well, dressed as he is now."

"What is the passenger's name?" the Captain said.

Lars hesitated. All the color drained from his face and he looked more scared than before, if that were possible. Paradoxically, Captain Cook became even scarier looking, all but having lost his patience with both of us. I closed my eyes and braced for impact.

"Garbo, sir." Lars said just above a whisper. "The lady's name is Greta Garbo."

I didn't need my eyes open to know Captain Cook was now glaring at me. I could feel the intensity on my face and in my chest. His grip became even tighter. I winced and opened my eyes, afraid they were going to pop out of my head for the second time in one day. The first having been in Heinrich's smelly armpit.

"Who are you?" he said to me. "What are you doing on my ship?"

"Seth Moseley," I said. "I'm an American reporter. I can explain everything, Captain."

"Silence," he commanded. "You speak when I tell you to."

Then the room got smaller and ten times hotter. Sweat rolled down my cheeks under the glare of everyone's contemptuous stare. They all waited to see just how the captain was going to eviscerate me. Every muscle in my body contracted, adrenaline pumping through my veins in anticipation of his first verbal blow. I was about to be hung out to dry and knew it.

"First Officer," the Captain said.

The first officer materialized from behind the captain. He was tall and thin as a reed or appeared so in contrast to the white whale. The young officer came to attention.

"Yes, sir."

"I want this man taken to the brig where he is to remain in isolation for the duration of our voyage."

"Very good, sir."

"And get him out of that uniform."

"Yes, sir. Very good, sir."

Then Captain Cook let go of me and turned away. I couldn't believe it. That was it? My face flushed once again, this time out of indignation. He hadn't asked me anything. Not one damn thing. I straightened my bloodied vest and threw my chin out. This was by no means over.

"Captain," I said. "It might interest you to know that there are Nazi agents aboard your ship."

Everyone froze, including the Captain. Obviously, I had broken every rule in the book by speaking out of turn, again. But honestly, how much hotter could the water I was already up to my neck in get? The Captain turned back around.

"One more word out of you," he said and raised a sausage finger to wag at me, "and I'll have you flogged."

"But, Captain—"

"Get him out of my sight!"

Then the first officer, the stewards, even Lars swarmed around me. All hands on deck pushed me back, out, and off the bridge while the white whale watched. That's when I caught a glimmer of recognition in his eye. The faintest tell that I hadn't said anything he didn't already know. And that's when I really exploded.

"You have a duty, Captain," I said as his crew manhandled me away, "to see to the safety of every passenger aboard your ship." That included me, of course.

The captain turned away while I bucked and weaved to break free. They almost had me through the door, when I braced myself at the threshold and held fast.

"This isn't over," I screamed back at the captain. "You're making a big mistake—"

Then a fist came out of nowhere and hit me in the gut. I wheezed and fought for air while folding like a cheap tent in the crew's arms. They whisked me away, but I managed to twist and contort back to catch sight of the captain staring after me through the glass window. Now his look of rigid anger had been replaced by rigid fear. I hoped it was the bug I'd put in his ear about the Nazi scum on his ship. Hoped at the end of the day he was one of the good guys, but I was fast learning I couldn't tell who was who or what was what anymore.

Nothing had been business as usual from the moment I stepped on the *Athenia*. And as I was being carted away, I realized that I might not live to see land ever again. That the big blue ball I spied from the bridge was where I might spend my last remaining moments on earth. So, I swore, then and there, come hell or high water, that I'd squeeze every last second I had left to try to see Garbo again.

Garbo had been the tall glass of water I'd been thirsty for my entire life but didn't know it until fate joined us. It sounded idiotic, but I'd never understood what people said when they said they were in love before. Now, with Garbo—I got it. She was the juice that made my life worth living. And I needed one last drink.

17. THE FOURTH ESTATE MEETS THE FIFTH COLUMN

SETH

I woke up in the dark alone. Again. This time, however, it wasn't after a rapturous night with Garbo. No. Now I was in the dark, dank hold of the ship where powerful turbines hummed in my ears. I rubbed my eyes and sat up. I needed to consider my options.

First, I needed to get a sense of my little prison. I felt around the best I could until I realized that the door to my cell didn't have bars, a window, or even a fucking knob on the inside. The only light in the room was a thin, dim shaft that seeped in through an inch gap between floor and door. The space had, no doubt, been designed to let in air and, in my panicked and vivid imagination, water. Seawater.

The mental image of drowning hit me like a wave. Water cold and thick as blood rushed in and quickly filled my dark crypt. I imagined that's how my end would come. That and hearing the powerful giant engines beneath me falling silent. Choked to death by salt water mere seconds before I was. Or maybe they'd explode when engulfed, like mega-ton cherry bombs blowing me to bits. In that case, at least I wouldn't drown.

Back in '34, I'd covered the shipboard fire that killed 134 people and set the *SS Morro Castle* adrift off the New Jersey coast. I'd seen first-hand the carnage fire on the water caused. Human bodies burned beyond recognition, washing ashore or drifting as barbequed fish food for hungry sharks. Fodder for nightmares and a hatred of the sea ever since.

I sat back against some sort of wall and concentrated on that slice of light. I didn't need to see the whole room to know things weren't looking so good for me. Captain Cook, master of the *Athenia*, apparently didn't care that Nazis were aboard. That didn't bode well for anybody.

Jesus, was I losing my grip or what? Left unabated, my brain would turn on itself and make me a gibbering idiot. I needed to take action. But what action could I take? I was alone. Helpless. No one could have described what solitary confinement felt like before that day in Davy Jones' lockup. That the ship might sink, and I'd drown in the drink was just the paranoid cherry on top of an already generous slice of psychological hell.

I had to embrace the darkness of my situation or be consumed by it. I escaped into the recent past. Thought of my Ingrid, the beautiful duplicitous bitch who'd landed me in here. How sweet she had smelled as the British officers pulled me out from under her. Honeysuckle, wasn't it? Honeysuckle and betrayal.

Anger was good. I focused my gaze squarely upon that one-inch gap between door and floor. Saw a miniaturized, naked Garbo reclining in the light. At least I could congratulate myself on having had her. After all, how many guys could truthfully say they'd made time with The Divine One? Figment or not, she turned to me and gave me a disapproving stare. Even in my imagination, I couldn't catch a break.

I knew I'd stumbled onto something never before seen or heard. I knew Garbo had reached out to me, beckoned me to her bosom, but had I just been a tool? Had the whole thing been staged? Now that I thought about it, had she acted resigned as I made love to her? Was she remote even as I held her in my arms? Whatever was going on had to do with Ingrid. My camera sitting on Ingrid's shelf was proof enough of that.

I wished I'd been able to read the Nazi fan letter I'd seen in Garbo's room before it was so rudely taken away by my good friend Heinrich. Obviously, Hitler was in love with Garbo, obsessed just like the rest of the schmucks of the world. But did the despot actually think she'd drop everything and join him? Was that why she was onboard in the first place? Had I been Garbo's last fling before she joined up with her number-one fascist fan?

Garbo had seduced me, but why? Had she known I was a reporter? No, she definitely wouldn't have slept with me if she had. She hated the paparazzi. To her I was just a hapless waiter. But then again, why bang the help when you could have anyone in the world? It's as if she'd reached out to me in the dark in desperation. Needed to make contact with someone, anyone.

I couldn't sit still. I crawled forward on all fours and sniffed the gap in the door. Maybe I could will myself through it. Collapse my ribcage like a rat and squeeze through the tight spot I'd found myself in. Rats never gave up when they were trapped. They died trying to escape. I admired their tenacity. Their mindlessness became an advantage in the face of certain death. Rodents didn't weigh the odds, they just acted. Went for it. I started to slip my finger under the door when two high-shined men's shoe tips reflecting a far-off light appeared.

"Moseley," the shoes said. "You in there?"

Was I imagining this, too? Was I so pathetic as to have lost my marbles in only a matter of hours? I scooted closer to the shoes, dared to reach a single finger out and press against one. They were real, all right. I scurried back into the dark as if the shoes would see me in my diminished state and run away.

"Yeah," I said to the size tens. "Do I know you?"

"It's me," they said in unison. "Nick."

Nick? The last time I'd seen The Piano Man he'd been busy tossing his cookies into my crotch back in the ship's bar. A warmth in my groin accompanied the memory. That just wasn't right.

"Nick." I smiled in the dark as if he could see me. "How've you been?"

"Can't complain," he said. "But I didn't come down here on a social visit."

I wanted to ask him how he'd come to know I was where I was. Had the news made it all over the ship already? Or were he and Ingrid in cahoots all along like I'd first thought? Then again, what the hell did I have to lose at this point? I knew it couldn't possibly be a shakedown because I had nothing left to offer anyone. Or maybe I did?

"What's the angle, Nick?" I said to his shoes and tried to sound indifferent.

"I can get you out of there," he whispered as I raised myself up to stand against the door. "You interested?"

"Go on," I said.

Does a bear shit in the woods? I wasn't exactly in any position to negotiate but knew it never hurt to hear the details before you sold your soul to the devil.

"I'm assuming," he said, "you've guessed by now that Ingrid is not a Swedish barmaid?

"The thought had crossed my mind."

"She's a British secret agent," he said. "She used you to throw the Nazi agents off her scent."

The mere mention of the word scent conjured a whiff of Ingrid's intoxicating honeysuckle. I crossed my arms in the frigid darkness. British agent, huh? She could have been the Queen Mum for all I cared. Wouldn't stop me from cleaning her clock once I got back on the outside. But first things first. I turned my attention back to The Piano Man's shoes.

"Whose side are you on?" I asked with more than a hint of suspicion. "And please don't tell me you're neutral."

I heard Nick shuffle his feet on the other side of the door. He didn't have to bluff. He was holding all the cards.

"Let's just say," he said, "I represent the interests of one very important, very powerful individual."

Well, that narrowed it down, didn't it? Could have been me, for Christ's sake, except for the important and powerful part. Nick wasn't telling me much. I'd try a different tactic.

"Okay, I give," I said. "What do you want me to do?"

There was silence on the other side of the door. I looked down and saw Nick's shoes turn and walk away. Heard their footsteps become faint as he soft-shoed down the hallway that led to the stairs and topside. Had I said something to offend him, my one chance at freedom?

"Nick?" I whispered as loud as I dared. "Are you still there?"

Nothing. My nerve endings twitched. It must have been five, maybe ten minutes before I heard footsteps heading back toward my door. I knelt on the floor of my cell. Sure enough, Nick's shoes appeared in front of me again. My heart sped up with the ray of hope they reflected into my cell. I stood back up to receive my sentence.

"I have the key," Nick said.

"Great," I said in a hushed yell. "Let me out."

"Only after you swear allegiance."

What was this, kindergarten? I hadn't sworn an oath to anything in my life, other than the pursuit of my own happiness. Who the hell did this guy think he was, Uncle Sam?

"To whom?" I said to the shoes.

"To me."

Wow. Was this guy off his rocker or what? Still, what would be the harm? It wasn't like he could hold me to anything. Once I got on the other side of that door, all bets were off. I'd be a free man. Given the circumstances, it was the only choice.

"Ok, sure. I swear."

Again, silence on the other side of the door. I broke out in a cold sweat. Shit. He was onto me. Either that or he was really good at turning the screws on people.

Then I heard a key inserted into the lock. The metallic scraping sound was music to my ears, and I stepped ever closer to the door, determined to be out of that little box as soon as humanly possible.

The door opened and a blast of light stopped me short. A bare incandescent bulb hanging in the hallway all but blinded me. I raised my hands up and squinted, only able to discern blown-out shapes of color.

One of the shapes I made out right off was Nick's face sporting a wide grin. I was never so happy to see another guy in my life. Nick was turning out to be an okay guy, something in rare supply aboard the *Athenia*. I took a step out of my cage and breathed a deep breath of freedom.

"Thanks," I said. "You got me out of a tight spot."

Nick smiled. "I'll be your Huckleberry."

Huckleberry? At first, I thought Finn, and then realized the reference was to the Arthurian legend. In more chivalrous times, a damsel in distress presented her knight in shining armor with a garland made of the sweet, black berries. Her pledge and gratitude all in one token. Nick was turning out to be full of surprises. Either he was the most well-read music man I'd ever met or a swish. I didn't particularly care which. I was free.

"What now?" he said.

Nick backed up so I could step into the confined hallway. My eyesight limited, I could nevertheless see that he was dressed all in black. Quite a switch from the white coat and black bow-tie getup he wore the first time we met. Nick had been tickling the ivories in the Grand Salon while Ingrid was busy reeling me in. What a sucker I'd been.

"Now?" I rubbed my eyes trying to force them to refocus. "Now I find out what the hell's going on on this tub."

That wasn't going to be easy. My profile had risen considerably aboard ship since the first go-round. Ingrid, the British staff, Captain Courageous and, lest we forget, Heinrich the Nazi Monkey. They'd all be taking turns gunning for me now.

"No offense," he said. "But what makes you think Garbo will even talk to you now?" Nick's smile widened. He looked at me like the proverbial cat who'd eaten the canary.

"We have a special connection," I said and gave him a wink in the half-light of the bare bulb above our heads.

"You don't say?" he said, thoroughly amused.

I had a nice, juicy rejoinder for him. Instead, I turned and led the way down the tiny hallway in the direction of the stairs, which led to the top deck. I couldn't tell what time of day it was, but I hoped for darkness and not broad daylight. I was beginning to see the virtue of working under cover of night. That is, in light of everyone onboard seemingly determined to keep me in the dark.

"Oh, and I should tell you," Nick said from behind. "There's been a recent development since you've been down here."

"Do tell," I said.

My newshound's sixth sense began to tingle in anticipation. I feared what earth-shattering event had occurred in the past ten hours of my incarceration.

"England and France," Nick said slowly and deliberately from behind me, "have declared war on Germany."

An alarm bell went off in my head. A loud, blaring siren warning of imminent danger. Who was this guy, a Fifth Columnist? A secret-society type who knew things a beat before everyone else? As a member of the fourth estate, I didn't appreciate how coy Nick was being. Then again, I didn't have much of a choice in the matter. I needed all the friends I could get, even fair-weather ones—if I was going to get back to Garbo.

But how long did I have left? With world war a sudden reality, there would be no stopping the Nazis from getting what they wanted. It was only a matter of hours, maybe less before we'd be surrounded. And what could one man, or woman, even in love, do against those odds?

18. WHORES OF A DIFFERENT COLOR

JAMES

Sarah barged into the hospital room and startled both of us back from the *Athenia*. I landed back in a world of hospital corners and orange-scented disinfectant to find Sarah visibly shaken. She came to stand between our beds, fidgety with nervous energy.

"I just called security on that asshole in three," she said.

I looked from Sarah to Seth, then back. And then my brain cleared. Martin. Martin was the asshole in three.

"What?" I stammered. "What did he do?"

"An underhanded grope," she said and wrung her hands. "While I was checking his IV line."

"I'll kill him," I blurted.

The immediacy of the statement took Sarah off guard. Seth recovered, returned to earth and cocked a skeptical eye at me. He wriggled his nose. The newshound in him sensed something was up. Like he smelled a rat. "Kill who?"

"Just some creep down the hall," Sarah said.

I felt my face blush while Seth watched my reaction. I cast my eyes down to my hands pressed into my lap. I couldn't look at either of them. The inevitable look of disappointment coming my way.

"Tell us about him," Seth said.

Was he talking to me? I looked up and saw that Seth was still watching me.

"What's he in for?"

No, he was asking Sarah. While looking for my reaction.

A rush of fever enveloped my skull, blood thumping in my ears. I felt an imaginary spotlight on me. Again. The energy in the room had shifted violently. I pressed my fingernails into my lap until my knuckles turned white. I forced myself to become rigid, braced for impact. I was a ship in heavy seas.

"Just some guy who ran off the road yesterday," Sarah said, and crossed her arms.

Seth reached out a hand for Sarah. She took his hand in her own. He drew her to his bed until she sat down on it. My hands became fists. All I could do was watch.

"Is his name Martin, Sarah?" he said.

"How did you know?" she said with a look of astonishment.

Seth wasn't looking into the past anymore. Now I felt sure old Scrooge was visiting my future. Had seen through my thin visage, knew that I didn't have the balls to kill Martin. That instead I had fallen back in league with him. Seen that I wasn't worthy of having the Garbo story. Foretold I was not deserving of the beautiful woman who sat next to him and held his hand. Seth had seen all my darkest fears about myself come to pass.

"What's going on?" Sarah said.

I looked up into her hazel eyes and saw that the beautiful woman had been unglued by her experience with my ex-boss. That I'd already failed her before we'd even had a chance to get to know one another. Establish trust. Then I looked at Seth.

A moment of silent recognition passed between me and the old man. He could tell I'd known Martin was on the premises and had kept mum to both him and Sarah. I was fully exposed now.

I opened my mouth. My jaw hung on its hinges for a full second before any sound came out. I felt like the old TV in our room, warming up before an image materialized.

"Sarah," I said meekly.

"James," she said, her eyes narrowing.

"The guy who groped you," I said. "I know him."

Sarah's face went completely blank. No judgment. No questioning expression. My imagination had suspended her in the moment. She was a freeze-frame of ripe, red-lipped lust and vulnerability interwoven in my mind in one perfect image.

My idleness had to be over. A new era of ownership and responsibility was being forced upon me. The next words out of my mouth must be testimony. Testimony that I had changed. Could change. Or at least had the potential to if given the chance. If it wasn't too late.

"He's my boss. Or, at least he was before he fired me."

Sarah's eyes opened wider, turned to Seth in incomprehension. He met her stare. Then they both blinked and turned back to me.

"Your boss?" she said. "Why didn't you say anything?"

"I didn't want either of you to know"—I swallowed—"what kind of asshole I'd associated myself with. I'm sorry."

The moment hung there between the three of us as Sarah took in the information Seth had obviously already processed. He reached up his left hand to Sarah. Patted her on the shoulder. While all I could do was pray. I prayed that my lack of faith in myself wasn't contagious.

Sarah looked at me with a vacant stare. Like she didn't know what to think about me now. I filled in the beautiful, empty canvas with my own deepest fear. God, had I lost her already?

Martin hadn't shared my love for Garbo. She didn't make his nipples hard, he'd said. Nor did he worship women in general. Where I thought I had to cure cancer to bed a woman, Martin caused cancer and didn't think twice about *bumping nasties* with the first young, unwitting victim to stray his way. Shit, what movies had his mother taken him to as a child? Apparently, she hadn't realized what a horse's ass he'd turn into as an adult. Otherwise, she would have surely smothered him in his crib and saved me all this trouble.

Martin was a shark in the Hollywood cesspool of self-proclaimed players. He preyed on unsuspecting young women who'd stepped off the bus fresh from Paducah. Martin would invite them to industry parties. Then when they were a little drunk and blinded by stars in their eyes, he'd circle and bump his prey to gauge their resistance. More aspiring actresses had bruises from Martin hitting on them at parties than ever taking their lumps on the stage or screen. Few gave into the mouth breather, but those who did usually left for home the next day, thoroughly disgusted with Tinseltown.

In his own reprehensible way, Martin saved many women from wasting their lives in Los Angeles, pursuing dreams of stardom that would never happen. I imagined they led happy, normal lives somewhere off the Hollywood radar. If Martin hadn't permanently scarred them with a sexually transmitted disease, that is.

Martin had said he made an exception when he met me. For what I lacked in tits and ass, I made up for in brains. The fact that I'd been flattered by that statement should've indicated otherwise. But the stars in my own eyes had been so blinding, I couldn't see the bill of goods he'd sold me. Five years of indentured servitude later, I was scared I might not have a happily-ever-after of my own. Afraid I'd labored under the false assumption that Martin, my mentor, wouldn't fuck me, too. Fuck me over, that is. Only for it to come true in Norfolk, Connecticut.

Now all I had to do was go into the room marked *Three* and say, "Martin, fuck off." In theory it seemed so simple. Something I had dreamed about doing for years. And now I had my chance. But I suddenly felt sick to my stomach. My body's way of telling me it wasn't going to be as easy as all that. Thankfully, the wave of nausea passed as quickly as it had come.

A large hospital security officer was visiting Martin when I arrived outside his door, the one Sarah had unleashed on Martin's ass after her first exposure to him. I wanted to hear what they were saying. I quietly stepped into the room behind the officer while he lectured my asshole ex-boss.

"We take our staff's personal safety seriously here, Mr. Hinkle," the officer said. "If it happens again, I'll have to call in the local authorities."

"I understand, Officer," Martin responded in a sweet, honey-dripped voice. "My bad. It'll never happen again. I promise."

Of course, this was Martin-code for "go fuck yourself, you hick." But it satisfied the rent-a-cop. The officer turned, saw me, stared into my eyes for a second then left the room.

Then Martin looked up at me, seeming relieved to see a familiar face. But then he must have remembered who led him here in the first place, and a veil of faux-indifference descended over him. Martin turned away from me.

"Martin," I said.

The neutral tone in my voice was intended to stop a verbal firestorm before it got started. But I could see by the look on Martin's face, he already had match in hand ready to strike.

"Well," he said, "if it isn't a prodigal son darkening my doorstep."

"I was here before you," I said. "You drove off and left me, remember?"

Ah, Martin. I could always depend on him to get everything ass-backward. It was a particular skill that he possessed. He got things wrong like other people painted or sculpted masterpieces. The Maestro of Mistakes was at the top of his game.

"Oh, sure," he said. "Blame everything on me. If you haven't noticed, I'm in a fucking hospital bed."

Mouth open and speechless, I stood in my hospital gown, hand grasped around the handle of a hospital cane to keep me steady. I turned to go, my ass crack exposed to the asshole in the bed. I made it as far as the threshold.

Pierced the imaginary plane into the hallway with the cane before Martin spoke.

"James," he called from behind. "Wait."

I could have kept going. Never turned around again. Left Martin for dead like he had me. But I wanted something. Part of me wanted him dead for disrespecting Sarah. Wanted him on his knees, begging for his life. That was the part of me that turned around. The part of me that wanted to draw blood.

"Make it quick. Whatever you have to say, say it quick."

"I made a mistake," he said, then quickly looked down at his feet. Contemplated his frostbitten toes, covered in white gauze at the foot of the bed.

"Go on," I said.

Martin looked up again. I knew it was near impossible for so arrogant a man as Martin to admit he'd been wrong to someone he considered beneath him. Remorse was not part of the man's DNA. On the other hand, he needed me and wasn't above groveling when he needed something. I'd make him confess his sins, full well knowing it was killing him inside.

"I should never have left you behind," he said in a little-boy voice, looking in self-pity back to his toes.

Fascinating. My attention was riveted. I couldn't wait to see what a guy with no genuine emotions other than fear and hate was about to say next.

"And?" I nudged him ever so slightly toward the cliff edge of total humiliation.

"*Aaaannnnddd*," he said. "I. Feel. Badly."

Ah, now we were getting somewhere. Sure, the grammar was all fucked up. Martin had incorrectly applied the adverb to describe what he felt. Instead, he had quite aptly described how his dysfunctional emotional self operated. He was not good at feeling. Martin felt emotions badly. It was the biggest truth he had ever laid on me. And he never even realized it.

"What about the nurse?"

Martin looked up, genuinely surprised. Eyebrows arched back as if ready to sling arrows. He hadn't seen this one coming.

"What nurse?"

"The nurse you groped," I said. "I heard what you said to the security officer, but you didn't mean it, did you?"

Martin glared at me. Confession time was over. As much as he knew he needed me, he loathed having to answer to me. Martin looked at his toes again. He wouldn't stand for it. I imagined he weighed how many of his little piggies he'd be willing to sacrifice to keep his pride. But knowing Martin the way I did, it was a stall tactic to front a new mode of attack.

"You like her," he said, then looked up at me with open, bottomless contempt. "That's what this is all about to you? Some girl's honor?"

"Not all," I said. "But it's good for starters."

"Name your price," he said, trying to contain an ever-growing rage from entering his voice.

"Apologize," I instructed.

"I'm sorry," he mouthed.

"Not to me," I said. "To her."

Barely in control, Martin tried to burn a hole through my head with his eyes. This wasn't a wild guess on my part. I knew how the man thought. He was that immature.

"What's in it for me?" he said, self-restraint all but exhausted.

"Redemption." I was innocent as a choir boy.

He was good and steamed now. Almost ready to jump out of the bed and throttle me. Almost ready to lose any chance he had at controlling the situation and me ever again.

"Fuck redemption," he said, his voice cold.

I had him. As long as I stayed calm and made no sudden movements, I had the fuck dead to rights. And it felt good. But I had to be careful. Martin was more dangerous than an injured animal. I could never turn my back on him. Never let him smell my fear for a second. All would be lost.

"You think you've got the balls to play with the big boys, huh?" he said. "You better be sure."

"You left the party early," I said.

Martin cocked his head like a dog trying to figure out what the hell it was looking at. In redirecting him, I now had his full and undivided attention.

"The old man," I said, "he gave up the ghost."

Martin's eyes widened. Our little game relied upon knowledge and perception. I had introduced a new element that he hadn't figured on. I'd shown him the river card and immediately anted up.

"The old man," he said. "He's still alive?"

"Just down the hall." I indicated with a nod of my head. "We're sharing the same room."

I'd never realized what leverage I had over Martin until now. Until I realized why I had come to Norfolk, Connecticut, with Martin in the first place. I smiled and let his brain catch up. Martin had an important decision to make. Hold 'em or fold 'em.

"In the same room, huh? That's excellent work, James."

Martin gave me a creepy little smile. He actually thought I'd orchestrated my own head injury in order to bunk down with the old man? Good. Let him. There was no reason to disabuse him of the notion. Not when we were engaged in mortal combat.

"The Garbo story," he asked, "is it juicy?"

"Better," I said. "It's a solid."

Martin smile turned into a shit-eating grin. I smiled back while I felt bile rise in my throat.

"I see it now," he said. "You and me, Jimmy. We're whores of a different color."

"You mean birds of a feather," I said. "And it's *horse* of a different color, not *whores*."

"Whatever," he said and dismissed the malapropisms with a flick of a gauzed hand. "And to think all these years I thought you were a schmuck."

I stared at Martin as he congratulated himself on my apparent duplicity. I knew it was all a ruse on his part as much as mine. The difference was his sleight of hand was showing. Mine I'd keep close to the vest because I knew the second I let him, Martin would try to fuck me. He'd take the project and credit for everything and leave me out in the cold. Again.

"Louie," he said as if he could ever be Bogart. "I think this is the beginning of a beautiful friendship."

Friendship? The only thing Martin and I had in common was neither one of us had any friends. I'd learned from him long ago not to trust anyone and had kept everyone at arms length since. We were about as friendly as a Mexican standoff.

"I'll take a co-producer credit this time," I said, calling his bluff. I had Martin at my mercy, for the moment. But now I had to commit to seeing things through. Failure was no longer an option. I needed to make the most of the leverage I had over him. Stall for enough time to rope-a-dope him like Seth had.

"Sure, kid," he said. "What are friends for?"

Martin forced his lips into a quivering smile. I stood by his bed and bared my teeth right back at him. We were skull to skull, locked in battle, and in my mind's eye, the cane I held turned into a scythe. We were whores of a different color. And mine, I imagined, was pale.

19. FAIL TO PLAN, PLAN TO FLAIL

SETH

Since I'd been aboard the *Athenia*, I'd been beaten, manhandled, molested and held at gunpoint. I'd also made love to the greatest beauty of our time. Of any time. My time with Garbo may have been brief, but her star had become my true north. Her memory my guiding light, even in the darkest hours of my captivity.

Nick and I had made our way to the top of the stairs and faced a small corridor not twenty paces in length. A door on the other end shone with a bright, chest-high yellow-white disk. I guessed the sun had been up for a while because its energy pulsed through the door's porthole which acted as a lens, focusing and concentrating the light.

We were halfway down the hallway when Nick stopped and tugged my sleeve. "What's your plan?" he whispered.

I turned back to give him a reassuring grin. "It's simple. I find Garbo and find out what she's up to."

"But ... how will you ... what if—?"

For someone who'd just made me pledge fealty to him, Nick was sure acting all hibbity-jibbity. I wondered what was on the other side of that door at the end of the hall. Whatever it was, I needed little Nicky on my side and I needed him to go at my pace while I worked the angles. Angles? Who the hell was I kidding? Now that the world was at war, any angles I tried to work and any battles I tried to wage were most likely doomed to failure. Much larger forces were at work now and likely had been way before this voyage began. Whatever I did now wouldn't matter a whit in the larger scheme of things. But I wasn't going to tell Nick that.

I glanced back at the sun-catcher porthole, and said, "Hey, I've got an idea. Why don't we switch clothes?"

I was at least half a foot taller than Nick. He stood in my shadow as my back blocked the intense light from reaching his beady eyes. His pupils grew large in the shadows. I could tell by the expression on his darkened puss my proposition wasn't to his liking. Not one bit.

"Why?" he said.

"I'm a tad conspicuous in these duds." I looked down at the jumpsuit I'd somehow acquired, courtesy of the gracious Captain Cook and his merchant marines.

I was fairly certain I wouldn't last long among the paying customers dressed like a ... well, dressed like a fugitive. Or a poor slob who'd wandered away from the engine room. Either way, I'd accrued a rogue's gallery of enemies and parading around in clothes that announced I wasn't supposed to be parading around at all just wouldn't do.

"Give me your duds, or our bet is off."

"Okay," he huffed. "No need to get hot under the collar."

Nick and I emerged onto the Promenade Deck not long after, me dressed in burglar black and him in fugitive blue. The sun's glare off the high shine of wooden deck temporarily blinded me, and I moved gingerly along the metal outer wall until my eyes adjusted. Nick followed close behind.

Everyone aboard had taken cover. Like there was anywhere to hide on a sitting duck. I felt like the guy without a country from the Edward Everett Hale tale. Except now I looked more like the new sheriff in town—or the new bad guy. Meanwhile, my deputy raised a hand and pointed toward the horizon.

"Look." I raised a hand to my eyes to cut the glare and looked off into the watery distance. And there it was, a long, black shadow growing beneath the rising sun. An inky blot darkening the horizon and spreading larger as it made its way toward us. Some kind of military ship. Black as the depths of the sea.

"What is it?" Nick said.

"It's not the good ship Lollipop."

I had to find Garbo. Before it was too late. Find Garbo and find out what she was up to. And whatever it was, I'd make it my business and no one else's. I wasn't going to let anything come between us anymore. I'd fry first. I'd fry as sure as the inkblot on the horizon was a Nazi pocket battleship. The kind I'd seen pictures of in my own paper, *The Journal*. State-of-the-art Nazi warcraft not a mile off the *Athenia's* port bow and closing in fast.

But I couldn't go straight for Garbo. Not yet. That would be like playing Marco Polo in a shark tank. I had had the right idea but the wrong execution. No, if my instincts proved out, Garbo was being watched. My money, if I'd had any, was on locating sweet, deadly Ingrid. Her, I would find. Her, I'd put questions to in such a way I'd finally get some fucking answers. Yeah, good ol' British Ingrid would be square with me for a change.

Nick and I made our way onto A-Deck, the First-Class Passengers Suites just off the Promenade Deck. I was wondering what I was going to do with my newfound sidekick, right about the time I spied Lars, the porter who had snitched on me. Or rather, he spied me.

Lars was pushing an empty service cart in our direction down the hallway. I imagined, room service had become a premium since war had been declared, and the kid was probably getting the best tips of his short life now that hostilities had officially begun. Then he caught sight of me, and from his expression I could tell I had officially ruined his day.

"Lars," I said, "long time no see."

The kid tried to backtrack, but I was on him before he could even think of running. Nick followed my lead and pushed Lars's cart to the side of the hallway. Lars started a healthy scream, cut short by my hand over his mouth. No time to get caught and thrown in the brig again. This time we'd play things my way.

"Now, now," I said. "No need to upset the passengers."

I turned to Nick. Whispered into his ear the part Lars had played in my incarceration. Nick loved every minute of our little intrigue. He nodded and seemed to know intuitively what I was asking of him before I asked it. Nick was immune to the implied danger of being my accomplice. He probably assumed, quite rightly, nobody gave a fuck what we did now. Of course, unless we got caught.

"I need you to stay low with Lars," I said. "You think you can do that?"

"No problem," he said. "We'll wait for you in A-Deck men's room. Won't we, Lars?"

I turned back to Lars, whose mouth I still covered with my hand. He stared back at the two of us, wide-eyed. We must have looked half-insane to the kid. Nick didn't know it, but A-Deck men's room had special meaning for Lars and me. It was where this little merry-go-round had begun for the two of us. Lars nodded.

"Good boy," I said and handed him over to Nick. We were all in this together now, along for the ride until someone told us we could jump off. I turned from the boys and ran.

★　★　★

I beat it through the silent ship's empty corridors, Nick's size tens pounding a metallic drum roll to Ingrid's doorstep. I stopped and caught my breath. Then stuck out my chin, set my jaw a la James Cagney in *Public Enemy* and rapped my knuckles hard on her door.

"No more games, doll," I whispered with all the menace I could muster. "Open up."

But Ingrid didn't answer. I knocked again. Nothing. I tried the door and found it was unlocked. So, I struck my best tough-guy pose and let myself in.

The bad-guy shtick drained out of me as soon as I saw her lying face-up on her bed. This time she wasn't striking a seductive pose, wasn't half-naked, enticing me to go another round of rub-a-dub-dub all hands in the tub. I drew closer. Someone had given her the once-over twice. The poor kid was all mashed up. Ingrid, the breathtaking beauty, was now barely breathing.

"Hey." I knelt down beside her.

Ingrid turned her beaten and bloodied head to look at me. She peered out through swollen, half open eyes. Her pupils were completely black, solid-red where the whites should've been. I wasn't any doctor, but I had been around the block enough to know that wasn't a good sign.

"Seth," she said with quiet effort. "Shouldn't be here. He'll … come back."

"Who?" I put a hand on Ingrid's right arm. The only place on her body that wasn't black and blue and red. The urge to run and get help filled me. Fat chance of anyone believing me, but I felt I had to try. Ingrid may have been barely conscious, but she could read my mind.

"No time. " She skipped ahead, always a few steps in front of me ever since the beginning. "Must get to Garbo."

"Ingrid," I whispered, "what do the Nazis want with Garbo?"

I couldn't stand to see her this way. Couldn't stand to think of anyone having done this to her. Felt guilty that I had ever contemplated being a tough guy with her.

"Not N—" Ingrid said and closed her eyes.

"Nazis?" I said.

I leaned my face in, close to hers. Kissed her temple. I needed her to tell me what she knew, but I couldn't get past the horror of seeing her this way. This was Ingrid, for Christ's sake. The sweet innocent Swedish barmaid. The devious resourceful British agent. The first woman I knew to give as good as she got and then some. How could this have happened to her?

"Who then?" I said as quietly as I could. "What the hell is going on?"

Ingrid opened her eyes again. Then she opened her mouth, but nothing came out. I put my ear above her red, still beautiful lips.

"Please, sweetheart." I said, tears welling up in my eyes. "Please try."

Ingrid forced breath through those lips. I caught the slightest sounds of speech. Rising like a stir of echoes from deep within a vertical cave.

"Love," she whispered. Then she gasped, her chest rising in convulsion. She grasped with her left hand for mine. I held it fast as her chest fell, her last breath escaped through her swollen, red lips. "Love is listening."

Then Ingrid was gone.

Deep sobs welled up in me as I closed Ingrid's eyelids with my fingers. I let myself cry over her body. Kissed her lips closed with my own. Covered her face up with the bed sheet. Said a prayer, then lifted up off my knees.

Love is listening. Her last words played over and over in my head, but what did they mean? I had to get a grip for the second time in one day. I sat on Ingrid's bed beside her now-still body and composed myself. What chance did I have, really? Against a stone-cold killer who would beat a woman to her death for knowing too much. Knowing and not telling. Only that love is listening.

Must have been Nazis. Who else could have done such an unspeakable evil act? Whose name was behind Ingrid's tongue-twisting cryptic message, "Love is listening," when she exhaled her last breath? Who was I looking for? Heinrich? I couldn't even imagine Big Nazi Monkey had it in him to do this. Not to my Ingrid. And what the hell did that have to do with love or listening?

Then again, what the hell did I know what people were and weren't capable of? I barely had a handle on my own abilities. If Ingrid was in a life-and-death battle, then she knew the dangers. Knew she might very well end up paying with her life. She fought until the bitter end, for whatever it was she believed in. I couldn't imagine the level of personal strength it took to stay true to your beliefs in the face of certain death. Such singular devotion beyond saving one's own neck was foreign to me.

Then I remembered what Father O'Keefe had said to me back at Amherst, my alma mater: "If you fail to plan, Moseley, you plan to fail." Except his Irish accent had been so thick, I thought he'd said, "plan to flail." The good priest had been my guidance counselor and the first to suggest journalism as a career. He'd wanted me to plan, not fail or flail. I wondered what would he make of Ingrid's last words?

Flail. That's what I planned to do now, all right. Flail and fail under a hail of bullets. How alliterative I could be when scared out of my wits. That had to count for something, right, Father O'Keefe? Seth Moseley, smart aleck to the very end.

Then I remembered the dead girl under the bed sheet. No doubt in my mind Ingrid had taken the beating meant for me. She'd saved me with her brains and her body. I loved her for that. Felt I owed her now. I must finish what she started. Even if the only thing that came of it was that she hadn't died in vain. And I met my own death with all the nobility I could possibly muster.

Survive, Moseley. That was the key. Stay alive long enough to find out who killed Ingrid and why. Long enough to find Garbo and what *love is listening* meant. Finally fit all the pieces together and get the bigger picture. The only one that really mattered now.

Picture. I looked over and up at the now empty shelf where my camera case had been. Ingrid's murderer had taken the time to confiscate my personal property. Why? What was a photograph worth compared to a human life? Yeah, I'd come aboard to photograph Garbo only to find out I wasn't the only one looking to frame the movie star.

A shiver ran through me. I looked back down at Ingrid's body, a tiny speck of blood now showing through her bed sheet shroud. A beautiful woman cut down in her prime. I feared whoever was now lurking behind my stolen camera wanted to shoot the same ending for Garbo. The same way most of her motion pictures ended. In a dramatic death scene.

20. LOVE IS LISTENING

SETH

From Ingrid's cabin I went directly to A-Deck men's room, Ingrid's blood literally on my hands, I had to wash up and get my bearings. But when I got there, Nick and Lars were nowhere to be found. They had disappeared into thin air, and I was left alone to stare into the same mirror I'd stared into when I first realized the *Athenia* was my new temporary home. Enough. Time was running out.

I ran out to the Promenade Deck. Looked for any sign of Nick and Lars. Wishful thinking. A handful of A-Class passengers stood in their whites like ghosts, sipping cocktails while their privileged offspring played shuffleboard. I could have remained on the darkening Promenade Deck of the S.S. *Athenia* and sipped sidecars with the swells. God knows the Old Seth would have. But I had to see my beloved again. I had to get back to Garbo.

So I beat it through the *Athenia*'s mahogany-lined corridors to Garbo's suite. I had no real expectation that the screen goddess would be there. I put an ear to her door and listened. Nothing. I knocked. Still nothing. Had the Nazis already gotten to her? Were they inside keeping her mum? Time was a wasting. I'd already bested one of the gorillas, and I told myself I could do it again. So I crossed the empty hallway, then made a run for the door. I was going in no matter what.

No sooner had I busted through the door of the curtain-drawn cabin, than a shot rang out. THWAK! The hardwood molding of the doorframe beside my face exploded. Fine, sharp wood fragments smacked into the left side of my face and neck. Sure as shit, whoever was on the other end of that bullet was readjusting his aim. I was a goner.

"Don't," a feminine silhouette from within the darkened room warned, "move."

I did as I was told. The side of my face burned like I'd been set afire, but I didn't so much as twitch.

"Drop your weapon," Garbo said in her distinctive low contralto voice.

Weapon? I held out my open palms, red with Ingrid's blood. Garbo, in all her enigmatic glory, rose from the bed and closed the short distance between us in a few silent steps. The .9mm semi-automatic gun in her right hand pointed at my racing heart. Never taking her huge eyes or the .9mm off me.

"Seth," she said.

This was the first time we'd been vertical together, and Garbo was taller than me by a couple inches. I stared her straight in the nostrils, not daring to make eye contact. Her schnozzle was perfectly proportioned, as was all five-feet, nine-odd inches of her.

"I nearly killed you."

"I know," I mouthed. The left side of my face felt like it was melting. A warm trickle of wetness ran down the left side of my neck. My blood was on the run. Garbo embraced me. Pressed her beautiful breasts into my chest and both the pain in my neck and my questions temporarily evaporated. Lust was nature's anesthetic.

"Nazis" I whispered. I still didn't dare look her straight in her baby blues.

"I know," she said and rested her head on my shoulder. Then she pushed back and looked at me with a perplexed expression shimmered across her magnificent face. "Why are you here? This wasn't part of the plan."

Plan? I let myself look up into Garbo's eyes. Her glowing-white-hot-from-within porch lights were so intense, I squinted under their glare. I had dreamed of being this close to her again. But suddenly her full attention became more than I could bear. I wanted to run, shrink away from her spotlights, they were so intense.

"What plan?" I said and felt light-headed. Now there were two beautiful Garbos before me.

"Seth?" she said.

My knees weakened, then buckled underneath me. I fell forward and Garbo dropped her gun and caught me in her arms. She held me while I looked up at her, my double vision reunited into one. The woman the entire world had fallen for was holding me up.

"Seth," she said, her famously long lashes fanning my face. "Are you all right, my love?"

Then the sound and vibration of the *Athenia's* engines cut out. Full Stop. Replaced by ghostly metallic sounds of lashing ropes, scraping hooks and urgent voices speaking German. Then I blacked out.

★   ★   ★

When I came to, I was on Garbo's bed squinting against the sun. She had opened the curtains to let in enough light to work by. I gazed at her face while she concentrated on the task at hand. She applied a wet washcloth to my wounded face, then rinsed it with fresh water in a basin on the night table. Her expression had softened from before. The storm in her eyes temporarily abated, the electric charge in the atmosphere dissipated.

"Looks like you've lost a lot of blood," she said matter of factly. Then she took my left hand and washed the dried blood off of my digits. Her simple act of kindness toward me was enough for me to pledge my allegiance to her anew.

"Not mine," I heard myself say as if from deep within a cave. I reached to retrieve recent events, however fuzzy in my aching memory. "Ingrid's."

Garbo stopped. Concern darkened her eyes. She looked down at the palm of my hand.

"Is she hurt?" she said, a slight tremor in her voice now.

Not, "What are you talking about?" Not, "Who is Ingrid?" But, "Is she hurt?" Garbo and Ingrid had known each other, all right. And by the expression on Garbo's face it had been more than a passing acquaintance. I'd already figured as much.

"Ingrid is dead."

Then Garbo's huge glacier-blue pools covered in mist. She wiped the same spot on my hand over and over with that bloody washcloth. Like a leopard methodically scraping the same patch of earth, searching for a telltale scent. A whiff of honeysuckle?

Everything stopped in that moment. Garbo, who had dominion over the hearts and minds of legions of men and women worldwide, stopped time to grieve. Nothing dared interrupt her as she lowered her gaze to the blood that now stained her own hands. Ingrid's blood.

"Why?" was all she said.

The question, I had to believe, was not directed at me. But I tried to answer anyhow. I found my voice and told her everything I knew. How I had met Ingrid. Met Nick. Met Heinrich, the Nazi gorilla, after meeting her. Then escaped King Kong and led him directly back to Ingrid. How she had spared me long enough for the *Athenia's* authorities to come.

Garbo took it all in. Her gaze never wavered from her red-painted hands. I didn't attempt to read her thoughts. A child shooting rubber bands at the moon stood a better chance of reaching them. Instead, I stared up at Garbo while she stared down. Her strawberry-blonde tresses hung down between us, suspended just above my chest.

"This world is darker than I ever imagined," she uttered in her low contralto voice.

I tried to breathe. Tried not to black out again from the injury to my face. I needed to focus my thoughts on where I was and what to do next. That's when a verse popped out of nowhere and filled my aching head. A long-ago lullaby, recited by my mother as she'd rocked me to sleep one summer night.

"*Lavender blue and rosemary green,*" I sang. Garbo sank her head lower. "*When I am king you shall be queen.*" I reached with my clean hand to the base of her neck and gently pulled her down to me, brought her forehead to rest on my chest. "*Call up my maids at four o'clock. Some to the wheel and some to the rock.*"

Garbo's shoulders quaked and shook. Her lips pressed into my shirt, stifling a scream, even as her slowly setting eyes spilled, soaked my suit vest with tears.

"*Some to make hay and some to shear corn,*" I singsonged softly, rocking her back and forth. "*And you and I will keep the bed warm.*"

I kissed the crown of her head, and we stayed like that for a moment. Then another. Then she startled. Garbo looked up as if she had been summoned by a far-off silent bell, rung out especially for her.

Then, close as we were to each other, Garbo stared into me with those penetrating blue eyes. The ones I'd fallen for so long before back in Los Angeles on a studio lot. A flicker of bright blue flame grew large in each one. Her pilot lights had come back on. Her engines were ready to ignite with me in their line of fire. Blast off.

Garbo got up off the bed and methodically cleaned herself up. She cleaned her hands, then took the basin filled with blood and water to the bathroom. I heard her pouring it down the tub drain.

I had to be wise and choose my words carefully. I had to behold her when I spoke. Wanted to show her I could be trusted yet not provoke her. But time was running out. I had told her what I knew. Now I needed some information. I waited until Garbo came back out of the bathroom.

"Whoever killed Ingrid"—I hit her with everything I had—"didn't want to be exposed."

Garbo looked at me, distracted again.

"I have no time for this," she said.

A smart tactical move on her part. Garbo wasn't taking any chances. She had obviously been taught not to trust anyone. To suspect everyone. Had that been Ingrid's teach-ings or her own baser instinct, honed over a lifetime of being watched, wanted? Hunted?

"Don't you?" I held my breath.

It might have been a trick of light from the porthole or maybe my own imagination. But I thought I saw despair on her patrician face. Was Garbo despondent over being all alone? Burdened in the knowledge there was no one who knew the truth now? Her truth.

Then, quick as the emotion had surfaced, it was gone from her face. Retreated back into her where no one could see. Fathoms beneath her cool exterior.

She came over, sat down on the bed and faced me. She crossed her hands, one atop the other. Her perfect posture didn't give anything away. She was good, all right. She deserved her reputation as the best actress in the world.

"You must compose yourself and leave," she said. "They will be here soon."

I stared at her beautiful face. Tried to imagine what she was feeling. But she had already closed me out. Closed everyone out. Garbo had started the clock again, and there was no time to waste. Still, I wasn't finished.

"The letter." I reached out a hand to close the space between us. To connect. I had intended to rest my hand on top of hers, but Garbo pulled back before I could make physical contact.

"It was signed A.H.," I continued. "Adolf Hitler wrote you."

Garbo turned and got up from the bed. I thought I glimpsed another expression. Either she couldn't turn away fast enough or thought she was safely hidden behind her strawberry blonde mane. This time, I thought I saw an expression of relief.

"That." Her lips formed a smirk. Then she turned back to the porthole. "Is none of your affair."

I had to pull myself together. My face still throbbed, but Garbo nursing me had taken the sting out of being shot at, even by her. She had come to my aid, even as the hour of her own departure drew near. Even as a harsh new reality beckoned to her. I rose up from the bed.

"That's why you have a gun," I said.

To be fair, everyone on board seemed to have a gun. Except me. But somehow, Garbo having a gun seemed out of place. Incongruent with my image of her. Why would someone as powerful as she even need one.

Then it all clicked, snapped sharply into focus.

"You're going to kill him," I said.

Garbo looked at me, mirrored my own surprise reaction. The letter. The gun. The look in her eyes. All of it now added up, made sense. Sense in a mad-scientist sort of way. She raised a perfectly manicured finger and pointed passed me.

"You must go, Seth" she said. "Before it is too late."

I looked back over my shoulder and spied the fat-cherub lamp I so hated. Cupid the little fuck had gotten me good. I'd fallen head over heels for the most beautiful woman God had ever created, and now I had to be the messenger of bad tidings. Give her the worst news possible.

"Haven't you heard?" I said. "The war has already started. You're too late."

But Garbo wasn't listening to me anymore. She moved toward the porthole, the dimming light fired her pupils now a purple-blue. I could see she was receding far inside herself. She was sinking somewhere unreachable. I knew there was no reason to try and convince her to alter her present course. But I'd have her answer one last question, Goddamnit. One last question before she was lost to me forever.

"I have to ask." I took my first tentative step since having passed out at her feet, shivered as I got my footing. "Why did you sleep with me?"

Garbo turned from the porthole. She crossed her arms in front of her bosom and scrutinized me. She was so calm and collected—the illusion fully restored—that I had the false sense I was living a dream again. Then she raised two fingers to her lips.

"Have you a cigarette?" she asked.

I patted my breast pocket and found that I had. A pack courtesy of dear old Nick down in the gallows. I produced one for Garbo and searched Nick's pockets for a match. I pulled a book of them out of his borrowed trouser pocket. They were from the *Athenia's* Grand Salon. A raised image of the ship embossed in gold leaf on the matchbook's cover. I did up the honors. Lit the end of Garbo's cigarette held between those famous pouty lips. She inhaled deeply. The ember end of the cigarette burned brightly as I waved out the match.

"Thank you," she said and exhaled. "At first, it was Ingrid's idea."

I recoiled with shock. Garbo smoked tentatively and watched my reaction. Then a muted noise from outside the ship diverted her attention. She turned to look out the porthole and became animated.

"They're boarding," she said. "Please, hurry."

I had intended to leave. I really had. But my feet stuck in place. Try as I might, I just couldn't leave without knowing.

"But why?" I said.

Though I already felt like yesterday's news, I couldn't let the issue be. What was I to her? To Garbo. The compulsion to know was beyond my control.

"Please," I begged. "I've got to know."

Garbo came charging from around the bed. I thought for a second she was going to clock me. Instead, she put out her cigarette in an ashtray adjacent to the night table. I swiveled to face her in time to see her open the night table drawer and produce the same handgun she had used to pepper my face with splinters. A warning shot I would not get again.

"If I tell you," she said, "will you go?"

"Yeah," I said. "Sure, I'll go."

Garbo turned to me. She pursed her lips and closed her eyes. Another sound came from outside the porthole. Then she opened her peepers and glared at me. I braced myself for impact.

"The Nazis," she said. "They've been suspicious of me."

"Suspicious?" I repeated, thick-headed as ever.

Garbo grimaced. She put her gun in her purse and snapped the latch shut, threw it on the bed. Then she reached up and grabbed me by my arms, turned me toward the door.

"Men," Garbo said. "I needed to show I enjoyed their company."

Whoa. The night we had spent together. Our mystical transcendental union, had all been for show? I'd been a sexual shill. Put out to stud for the almighty mission.

A flimflam orchestrated by Ingrid for the sake of Nazi stooges waiting in the wings. And I'd bought it hook, line and sinker.

"So," I said, hurt like a love-stricken puppy dog. "Our night together … it was all for show?"

"What does it matter now?"

I swung around to face Garbo. She backed away from me as if I'd gone bonkers. Yet not quick enough to evade me. I grabbed the Goddess in my arms. Pulled her to me and planted a kiss on those beautiful lips before she even knew what was happening. Then I pulled away and looked directly into her eyes.

"I love you," I said. "I've loved you ever since I laid eyes on you, the very first time, back in Los Angeles."

I looked into her eyes and for a second the flame in them wavered, like a wind had passed over them. Garbo pursed those full, red lips again. Lowered her chin and cast down her true blues. Just like she had the first time I'd seen her. Not that she'd remember, even though I had every reason in the world to.

"Love fades," she said her magnificent eyelashes fanning downward in slow motion.

"Not mine," I said.

Garbo lifted her chin and opened her eyes wide open. Her expression registered surprise. Then a tiny smile came to her lips. We kissed again. This time she was right there with me. My face no longer hurt. As if her lips had the power to heal, I felt like a brand-new man. A man willing to do anything to keep her safe and out of harm's way.

We embraced, and I felt Garbo's body melt into mine. Her strong, lean physique against me made me weak all over again. I put my chin on her shoulder and stared at her cupid lamp with a dumb grin spread from ear to ear across my face. He smiled back at me, as if to say "I told you so." Score another victory for the little guy. For love.

Then Ingrid's face, her beautiful, beaten face flashed in front of my eyes. In front of Cupid.

"Love was listening," Ingrid had whispered.

I pushed Garbo back. She looked up at me, tears in her uncomprehending eyes.

"What, Seth?" she said.

I put my index finger up to her luscious lips to shush her. Then I went around her to the night table. I reached down and grabbed the lamp. Lifted Cupid up to eye-level and scrutinized him. He stared back at me with that stupid, shellacked smile plastered on his fat face.

"Love is listening," I said aloud, then with both hands, smashed the lamp down on the night table. He broke into several large pieces. I inspected Cupid's insides as Garbo came to my side. Found a foreign object glued to the inside of his chest. A metal object with numerous holes bore into its surface, wires leading out of it down into the central electrical cord. I yanked and snapped the wires.

"What is it?" Garbo whispered as I held the thing up.

"An electronic listening device," I said and pocketed the thingamajig. "They've been listening to our conversation all along. I've got to get you out of here."

We got to the door, and no sooner had I opened it than Heinrich was there, filling up the damaged door frame. Garbo stared up into the mug of the swollen, broken-nosed brute. I could tell she was startled by the sight. No doubt taken aback by the man's sheer massiveness. Garbo had been absent when Big Monkey and me mixed it up in her digs the first time round. Now my stomach soured at the thought of an encore performance of King Kong beats up the chump.

"Heinrich." I said. He smiled back at me as if we were old friends. Heinrich reached out for me, but I evaded his grasp. Before King Kong had me back in his hairy mitts, before I was dragged away kicking and screaming, I was going to cast a spell of my own for once. I improvised, reared back then threw a punch at Heinrich's head. Caught him square in his twisted snout.

Heinrich yelped, reached up with both hands to his honker and winced in pain. I pushed the brute out of the way, grabbed Garbo by the hand and made for the hallway.

Then a huge hand grabbed me from behind. Pulled me by the neck and yanked me forcefully away from her. Only when Heinrich plucked me from Garbo's grasp did I realize how hard she'd been holding onto me. Had held me tight in her embrace like only a true lover would. With all her might.

But it was not enough. Garbo held her arms out to me as Heinrich manhandled me back down the hallway. Whatever they did to me didn't matter now. I lived only to try and save the woman I loved. The woman I had inadvertently put in harm's way, before piecing together what poor Ingrid had tried to warn me about. About love listening.

The *Athenia* was rigged. Ingrid knew the entire ship was riddled with eavesdropping devices. Knew Cupid had ears in Garbo's suite. Now I had to assume whoever was pulling the strings knew everything about me, Garbo, and Ingrid.

Had heard every conversation, every last word. Every tender whisper between lovers. There were no more secrets.

Garbo's plan to kill Hitler was out in the open. Thanks to me, she was in more danger than ever before. But instead of fear, I felt an energy of purpose re-enter my life and limbs. I knew what I had to do, even though it sounded insane. I had to do the impossible, while there was still time.

21. SPELLBOUND

JAMES

"Well?" Sarah asked, her eyes riveted on Seth's face.

"Well what?" Seth loved the attention the raven-haired nurse gave him. So did I. Who the hell wouldn't?

"You purposely left out the most important part," she said, her tone of voice full of feigned annoyance. She turned to enlist me in making her point.

I kept my gaze squarely on Seth. I didn't want to give myself away as I already felt I was oozing puppy love through my pores. Plus, I was too busy enjoying the electricity our touching forearms was generating throughout my entire body. My nerve endings were on fire. My upper lip wet with perspiration from the contact high.

"Garbo," Sarah said, turning back to Seth. "When you kissed her, did she kiss you back?"

Excellent question. When a kiss was all you had, was it enough to go on? Had to be, right? One kiss had made me fall for Sarah. One kiss could tell an entire tale all on its own.

"Kiss and tell?" Seth smiled at Sarah. "I figured you'd be opposed to such rude behavior?"

I scrutinized Seth, propped up in his bed on a wedge of fluffy pillows. He was winded and in pain, but his eyes were alert and animated as he gazed upon Sarah. He knew a good thing when he saw it. Thank God he'd forced me to open my eyes, too. Before it was too late.

When Sarah had arrived in the room, in the middle of Seth's latest chapter, she'd checked my pulse, listened to my heart, and taken my blood pressure and temperature. I felt shaky from her touch and shaken from hearing Seth's whale of a tale. Then Sarah had dropped the bombshell—I'd been given my walking papers. I was being discharged from the hospital, and in a couple of hours, my status would change from patient to visitor. But I pitied the fool who tried to separate me from my newfound friends. Not after I had just met them. Not after I'd just fallen for Sarah.

It was true that Sarah and I didn't even know each other. I didn't even know her last name. Had only just made love the night before. Met the first time the day before that. But I was sure what I felt was the genuine article. I'd been infected, for certain. For the very first time, I had a textbook case of being bitten by the love bug.

Now off-duty, Sarah sat vigil with me, listening to Seth's story. He was up to his old tricks, toying with us. Not giving anything away. The fucking guy was on his deathbed and still enforced a quid pro quo. I had to admire that, even though I dreaded where he was going next. Sarah shifted in her seat, breaking our physical connection. Immediately I felt my body begin to cool.

"Excuse me," a female voice said from the doorway. We all looked over in unison to an older nurse poking her head into the room. "Mr. Main, you've got a visitor in the lobby."

Thank god I had remembered Video Guy had given me his card the last time we saw each other, back in the snow storm where Martin abandoned me. God, that seemed like such a long time ago. Now the card that I'd fished out of my pants pocket was the ace up my sleeve. And I had bet my future on his help.

"Thank you," I said, and the nurse was gone. I looked at Sarah and Seth. Both gazed at me expectantly. Walking out on the most important part of a conversation wasn't my idea of fun. Especially, when I was a featured attraction.

"Hurry," Sarah said and nodded toward the door. "Conduct your business, Mr. Main. Seth and I'll be fine 'til you get back."

"No way," I said, "am I leaving you two alone."

"Why?" Seth said and added some teeth to his smile. "Don't you trust us?"

I bit my lower lip. Seth knew how to squeeze every last drop of enjoyment out of watching me squirm. But I had a schedule to keep. He knew I had someplace to be.

"Of course, James trusts us," Sarah said, leaned in and planted a peck on my cheek. A lightning bolt traveled through my wires. I blushed then blushed again at Seth's approving look. That hospital room could be such a fucking tough room sometimes. Tough and wonderful.

I got up from the bed and walked toward the door. I wanted to turn back and ask some innocuous question just to forestall my departure. I used to do the same thing to my mother when bedtime came in the middle of an exceptionally good episode of *Who's The Boss*. Took a pair of pliers and screwed the toothpaste cap on real tight. Steal another ten minutes of Alyssa Milano while my mom pried it off. She knew I had a little thing for Alyssa, but she never said a word.

"Go," Sarah said before I could even turn my head. Just the way Mom had. Tough room, for sure.

I walked down the hallway toward the lobby, quickly passing Martin's room. He was either too busy masturbating, on the phone, or both to notice me. Thank goodness. I wanted to keep our contact to a minimum until I had everything I needed squared away.

I hurried into the little hospital lobby, scanned the waiting area, and found my gentle giant. When I'd called him earlier that morning, it was obvious he was surprised to hear from me. Especially when I told him where I was. And that I needed him to come to the hospital as fast as he could and bring his equipment.

"What the hell happened to you?" he said as he got up from his chair and stared me up and down. I didn't realize how bad I looked until I saw Video Guy's face as he took in my pale blue hospital gown decorated with yellow baby ducks.

I recounted the highlights of my life since I'd seen him last. Skipped over some of the uglier (and more personal) details and cut to the third-act climax of Seth and me landing up in the same hospital room.

"So, the reason I called you," I started, then decided to lower my voice.

Video Guy leaned in, but still stayed far enough away to not catch the lunacy-inducing whatever-the-fuck disease I had obviously contracted. He cocked an ear from a respectful distance.

"Listen, the reason I called you," I started again in a whisper, "is that I need you to finish shooting Seth's story. Without Martin knowing."

"Your asshole boss?"

"Asshole *ex*-boss,"

Then I remembered I'd forgotten to mention Martin was in the hospital too, only three doors down from Seth and my room. Video Guy's face showed surprise as I connected the dots for him.

"Okay," he said, obviously game for my subterfuge. "So how do you wanna go about this thing?"

"You can pass your stuff into me through our window," I said. I explained how Martin seeing him walking down the main corridor with his camera equipment would probably be a dead giveaway. "Then I'll help you crawl in. Sound good?"

"Okay. But how will I know which window is yours?"

I put a grateful hand up to his shoulder and felt a breeze on my backside. I smiled. Video Guy was willing to help me cover my ass on this one. The one time it really counted. In return, I'd make certain I never turned my back on the big guy like Martin had turned his back on me. Especially when my butt was still hanging out for everyone and their brother to see.

"There's a broken picnic table just outside our window," I said. "Trust me, you can't miss it."

Sarah had agreed to do whatever it took to help Seth and me. In return, I wanted to bring it into the end zone and do a little victory dance. But most of all, I wanted to make a connection. I'd always felt on the outside of society. Watched while other people got together and made things happen for themselves and for each other. Now I was in the thick of things, thriving for the first time I could ever remember. And it felt good.

I'd asked Seth to bequeath his life rights to Sarah on camera. Remove any cloud on the chain of title to his Garbo story. That was a fancy way of saying Martin couldn't steal the story and not give me my co-producer credit. She had no role in our production and possessing soul rights to Seth's story would finally make Martin negotiate in good faith. I'd forced his hand with the one ol' Seth had left behind for me.

When I went back to my room, I stood just outside the doorway for a minute and watched Sarah and Seth talking. Couldn't hear what was being said but I didn't care. I was too caught up in watching them together. Watching her profile while she laughed at something he said. Watched the old man bask in her glow even as he himself was fading.

The same starburst special effect went off in my head every time I saw Sarah. My eyes tracked her the same way they had fireflies, when I had chased them as a kid on a dark, hot summer night. So earnest to grab a hold of the light, I'd fallen down an embankment, sprained my ankle and freaked my mother out. Unless I wanted to do that again, I'd have to find a way to keep my eye on Sarah and where I was going at the same time.

I knocked on my own hospital room door, announced my entrance. Sarah turned to me and smiled, then rose from my bed. Seth was smiling too, though he wasn't about to get up.

"Everything okay?" she said.

"Yup." I looked at both of them, mums-the-word expressions all around. "How about in here?"

"We're good," she said. "Guess it's my turn now."

Sarah was referring to the part of the plan where she went to Martin's room and distracted him while Video Guy waded through the frozen ocean of snow to our room. Odds were good Martin would never look out the window anyway. But I wasn't taking any chances now. Except for exposing Sarah to LA's number one menace when it came to a young woman's virtue. But I was confident she could hold her own.

Still, I was having second thoughts when Sarah motioned toward the door. I gently caught her arm by the elbow and stopped her. I needed her to know that what she was about to do was voluntary. Voluntary and disagreeable, though greatly appreciated.

"You don't have to do this if you don't want." I gave her my best stern stare. "If we get caught—"

I already knew from my days back in L.A. that camera equipment entering a hospital was against HIPPA regulations. But when I told Sarah of my plan to shoot the rest of Seth's story, she'd agreed to help, without hesitation. She was going out on a big limb for me. A limb that could break off at any moment and land us both in hot water.

Sarah brought two fingers up to my lips. On contact, her fingertips sent a thunderbolt of adrenaline through my body. How did she do that? Sweet Sarah the Spellcaster. I was at her mercy.

"I want to do it," she said. "Anyway, you need me."

Hell, yes. In more ways than one. Sarah looked over my shoulder, shared a smile with Seth. Then she turned and left the room, closing the door behind her. I stared at the door for a solemn moment. Then I turned around.

Seth looked up at me, his slight frame reclined deep into the mash of white pillows behind him. He scrutinized me with a crinkled brow. His chest rose and fell with shallow breaths. A seriousness overtook him.

"You got this?" he said and leaned his head back in exhaustion.

"I got this," I confirmed and walked up to the foot of his bed. Seth's eyelids lowered until his eyes were all red, horizontal slits. "You just hold on. I'll do the rest."

A couple minutes later, Video Guy appeared outside our window. Covered in snow, a suitcase in each hand. He'd obviously taken a fall or two wading in the deep snow to get to us. He looked like the Abominable Snowman gone on vacation.

I opened the window, and he handed each case in to me. Next he climbed in. Seth looked over at him and gave a weak smile while Video Guy cleaned the snow off his jeans and out of his red beard.

"The gang's all here," Seth said. His breath was visible as a fine mist, like it had been back in his cold apartment. But our hospital room wasn't cold. Seth was.

I helped Video Guy set up his equipment as Sarah returned to our little production. I introduced her to Video Guy, and she smiled at him. He wasn't expecting a nurse—a beautiful woman at that—to be in on our little shell game. He gave me a conspicuous wink, letting me know he approved.

"How did it go?" I asked her, scrutinizing Sarah for any signs of telltale damage.

"Fine," she said with a nod.

"Do you think Martin saw anything?" I said. "Does he suspect?"

"No." Her voice had dropped an octave.

"Well, what did you two talk about?" I said.

"Talk?" Sarah shot me a look as if to say grow up already. Shut up and let it be.

"To keep him preoccupied," I went on. "You know, while Video Guy ... while Tom passed by his window. What did you say?"

"Really, James." Sarah shook her head. "I didn't have to say anything. I just flashed him my tits."

Sarah stared straight at me to nail her point home. I didn't say anything. I didn't have to. Sarah knew I was mortified. I was all for misdirection. But I wasn't too sure I'd signed on for this. I mean, *Goddamnit!* Martin the fucker had gotten to see those beauties, too? Was nothing sacred?

Then I heard a short, sharp hissing noise behind me and instinctively turned to Seth. For a second I thought his tank was leaking oxygen, and we were all about to be blown to kingdom come. Yet his eyes were open, and he was smiling. I turned further and saw that it wasn't Seth, but Video Guy hissing. He was trying his best not to bust a gut.

"Sorry, James," he said.

The big guy finally gave up and let out a thunderous belly laugh. Then Sarah and Seth joined him, laughing while I stood there.

"Martin." I shook my head. "What an asshole."

Then I laughed, too. The kind of laughter that brought tears to my eyes. Tears and relief surrounded by my little family of conspirators. I shared a moment of closeness that I hadn't felt with anyone since my mother and I sat in a darkened movie theater telling each other fart jokes and cracking one another up. A long, long time ago.

★   ★   ★

Video Guy mounted his camera on a tripod at the foot of Seth's bed while Sarah helped with the cables. Meanwhile, I set up and turned on the two light stands placed on either side of Seth's bed. I stood back in the relative darkness of the room and stared at a glowing Seth in the center of the scene.

My mind reeled back to a scene in *Queen Christina*, where Garbo silently walks around the large room she shares with her Spanish envoy lover over the course of that three-day snowstorm. Enraptured, her lover, lying in front of the fire where they had been together only a moment before, watches her.

"What are you doing?" he asks while she lightly touches a spinning wheel, looks in a mirror above a bureau back at him, then ends up on their bed staring down on him in a magnificent close-up. Garbo's voluminous eyes reflected the fire and the man before her. Reflected her man with love in her eyes.

"I have been memorizing this room," Garbo says, her glorious face taking up the entire, forty-foot-long by twenty-foot-high movie screen. *"In the future—in my memory—I shall live a great time in this room."* My mother's favorite Garbo line of all time. The one that always made her cry.

Then my mother's hospital room flashed in my mind. Mom was always there in her bed waiting for me. Always with a smile. Details of furniture, pictures, life-support machines burned in three dimensions into my memory so vivid that they had remained unchanged over time. We'd spent a lot of time in that room ever since she'd died. I revisited her there thousands of times over the years. Visiting hours were never over.

"Honey Buckets of Love," she would say. That's what she called me whenever I dropped in. Like true love, honey never went bad, she had said. Honey, like her love, was forever.

"Hi, Mom," I'd always answer and smile back at her.

"You go get 'em, tiger," she'd say and let out a soft laugh. "You hear me?"

"Yeah," I said. "I hear you now."

Video Guy nudged me back into this hospital room, back into reality. Everyone was waiting for me to call the shot. I looked at Seth from beside the camera. He moved his head up to meet my gaze.

"You ready, buddy?" I said.

"Yeah," Seth said out of breath. "Let's do this."

Sarah came up beside me and put her hand in the small of my back. Then she reached down while no one was looking and cupped my bare-ass cheek. My entire body flushed. Sarah had my back.

"Camera," I said.

"Rolling," Video Guy said and pushed his camera controls.

I stared at Seth as the two lights bathed him in a warm, yellow-white glow. Seth's face became younger in my mind's eye. He was Young Seth again lying there before me, awaiting my command. Spellbound.

Seth had done what I asked. Had held up his part of the bargain and was holding on. He was going to recount his story for Video Guy just like he'd told us, and then take us all along as it veered toward its fateful climax. Seth was finally ready for his close-up. Ready, because now I was too.

"And," I said, my face pointed forward, eyes always forward from now on. "Action!"

22. TERRA INCOGNITA

SETH

I'd woken up gasping for breath, bathed in a hazy, amber-colored shaft of light that emanated from a porthole to my right. I was lashed with ropes to a metal crossbeam, part of a clockwork consisting of large gears and girders. My old buddy Heinrich, now armed, stood as a dark sentry in front of the metal door to the steel-reinforced room.

Four load-bearing walls told me I was being held captive underneath something heavy. Somewhere I hadn't known existed. Something on the *Athenia* I hadn't seen before. I was in a pickle, all right.

Garbo's starlight had attracted some pretty evil customers. Now I sensed they were crawling all over the ship, looking for her. That they took the form of Nazis with guns made them only more ominous. They were playing for keeps. But so was I.

I turned to my right and saw Lars, the porter, sitting in the shadowed corner of the hold.

"Hey," I said. "Is that you, Lars?"

Lars looked up, then stood up and walked over to me. He didn't say a word as he came straight up to my face.

"What have you gotten me into?"

"You?" I said. "I'm the one all tied up in knots."

I took a gander around the rest of the room, then my eyes came back and set on Lars unenlightened face.

"Where's Nick?"

Lars scrutinized me and scowled. He seemed to be having some kind of internal struggle. I waited for him to come to a conclusion.

"You mean," he said, "you don't know?"

"Know what?" I said.

"You really don't know?"

"No," I griped. "I really don't know."

Lars took a step back. The column of light coming from port side of the ship caught him and lit up the left side of his face. He looked genuinely confused at my answer. Probably as confused-looking as I did to him.

Then the door to the hold opened, and Heinrich made way for a dark visitor, standing still and silent at the threshold. I had been expecting Heinrich's unseen Master. Knew the megillah wasn't aboard alone, calling his own shots. The silverback probably couldn't take a leak without asking for permission. Lars turned and we both stared at the lean shadow framed in the open doorway. My mind filled in the silhouette with detail even before he opened his mouth.

"Am I intruding?" he said and stepped forward.

"Not at all," I said in resignation. "Nick."

Nick stepped into the fading daylight of the porthole. It was The Piano Man, all right, dressed in a Nazi uniform complete with Colonel's cap. He came to stand next to Lars, not five feet away, and gawked at me, strapped to the crossbeam. I had been right about Nick. Thank God, I was finally right about something.

"Hello, Moseley," he said and smirked. "Surprised to see me?"

"Not exactly."

I was telling the truth. Ever since I'd set foot on the *Athenia*, I'd learned nothing was what it seemed. Everyone had played a role, including me. But Nick was the master at role-playing. He may have been the latest in a long line of broken illusions, but his had been carefully and indelibly crafted from the start. I wouldn't underestimate him again.

"The outfit is a nice touch," I said.

Nick turned back to Heinrich, dismissed him with a wave of his hand. The lug turned and exited stage left. The metal door slammed shut. Nick, Lars, and I were alone, staring at one another in silence.

"That's better." Nick turned to me and produced a silver cigarette case from his breast pocket. "Cigarette?"

"I quit," I said. "Those things'll kill you."

Nick laughed as he lit up. I wanted him to laugh. Laugh it up while I worked slack into my ropes. The flop sweat my body generated helped me squirm ever looser in my restraints.

"You know Lars," Nick took a deep drag off the cigarette while he stepped closer to scrutinize me. "I admire this man, Moseley." The ember end of Nick's cig burned ever closer to my face.

"Why's that?" I said. "Nazi pig."

This made Nick smile even wider. Lars, on the other hand, looked grim. He watched from behind Nick while the Nazi closed the gap between us. I peered into the black of Nick's pupils. They were lifeless like a doll's eyes.

"I've obviously anticipated your every move," he said.

"Ever since you came aboard. And still you struggle, trying to escape. Such tenacity."

It was true. The *Athenia* had served as a floating mousetrap, designed by one big rat. Nick. I hadn't figured he was a mastermind when I first met him. Didn't think he was capable of duping me the way he had. But then again, I'd had blinders on. Ingrid had turned my head with her body and then the Garbo setup. And now we were all paying the price for our ignorance. First Ingrid. Then Lars and me. Next, Garbo.

"So Nicky." I tried to regain my footing on the situation, even as I stood tied to a metal girder. "What now?"

Nick stared at me with those charcoal-black eyes. Not a hair out of place nor blemish on his face. He was the picture of healthy, well-tended evil.

"Now, my journey continues" he said. "And yours, well, *cursom perficio*."

Ah, more Latin. A subject I'd unfortunately neglected back in school. Along with learning the virtue of staying on dry land even if that meant avoiding Toes to keep my toes. Ah, Toes. I was downright nostalgic for such an honest form of brutality.

"Come again?" I said.

"Your journey is over, my friend." Nick said.

I stole a glance at Lars. The kid was coming apart at the seams with fear. I liked Lars. Wished he hadn't been dragged into this mess. But there wasn't anything I could do about that now. And I was afraid life was only going to get scarier for the porter from now on.

"Tell me," I said, "did you kill Ingrid, too? Or did your big errand boy do your dirty work for you?"

Lars eyes went wide with fear and shock while Nick calmly took another drag off his cigarette.

"Ingrid the barmaid?" Lars said. "She's dead?"

"I'm afraid so, Lars," I said. "Thanks to Nick here."

Lars turned to Nick, who took a step closer to me. Our faces were now a mere six inches apart. I could see the deep pores on his face. Smelled the sweat and cigarette smoke embedded in his uniform. I fought in my restraints while Nick leaned in to whisper in my left ear. I thought about biting him right in his five o'clock shadow, but I already had a bitter taste in my mouth.

"I like you Moseley," he whispered. "That's the only reason you and the boy are still alive."

Then Nick pulled back and extinguished the cigarette on my chest. Hot, seering pain reignited my rage and I writhed in my restraints while Nick looked on, amused.

"Let's cut to the chase," Nick said, back in his normal voice.

He swiveled his head down and away from me like an automaton. Reached in the right side pocket of his jacket and pulled out what appeared to be a black button with a long tail of wires attached to it. Two fingers dangled the doo-hickey before my eyes.

"Do you know what this is?"

"Your butt plug?" I replied and continued to work on the ropes behind my back. I wasn't going to give him the satisfaction of letting him know how stupid I had been.

Nick turned to address Lars, who had stepped back into the shadow of the wall where I had first spied him.

"How about you, young Lars?" Nick said.

"No," Lars said.

"It's called a bug," he said, unfazed. "An electronic listening device. They're the latest thing."

A cold sweat broke out all over my body. I stopped twisting and stared up at the thingamajig Nick dangled in front of me. Identical to the one I'd pulled out of Cupid. I knew what he was going to say next. Still, I willed him not to. Didn't want to hear it.

"I heard everything you and Garbo said." Nick smiled. "And everything you did."

Lars and I exchanged a glance. The kid was getting an earful. Probably thought even less of me now that there was definitive proof I had defiled Garbo. We both turned back to Nick.

"Where was it?" I asked.

"Inside the cherub lamp," he said, gloating. "On her night table."

Nick mugged while I played along. I wanted him to think I was beaten. I lowered my head and pretended the news was taking its toll on me. Taking its toll on me instead of restoring my resolve to fight. Fight on to the bitter end.

"Now I know Fräulein Garbo's true intentions," he said and smiled. "Thanks to you."

Nicky was good. Really good. I could tell he was someone who practiced torture. Had studied and mastered it like an art form. He was a natural at inflicting pain. A born Nazi.

"Ingrid was another story," he said, twisting the verbal dagger into me ever deeper. "She wouldn't betray Garbo, no matter how persuasive my methods. But I knew I could depend on you, Moseley. And in the end you betrayed Garbo, however unwittingly, just like I knew you would."

Nick pocketed the electronic bug. I felt a crackling energy coming off him. Some kind of dark vapor trail of evil surrounded him, tugged at me in an unnatural, ghostly way. Like a shadow that didn't rely upon light to be cast. Nick was at his diabolical best.

"What's going to happen to her?" I said.

"Fräulein Garbo?" Nick mocked me. "She will continue her journey to Germany."

"But why?" I said. "When Hitler finds out—"

"Herr Fuhrer believes Garbo is a goddess," Nick said. His eyes lit up, his facial muscles animated. "A goddess of Aryan perfection. The Mother of his Master Race."

"A mother who wants to kill him," I chimed in.

Nick moved in quickly. He reached in his breast pocket and produced a penknife. Then he pointed it at my heart, just below where he'd burned me while extinguishing his cigarette.

"He believes she is immortal," Nick said and pushed the knife into my skin short of puncturing it. "He believes that anyone who mates with an immortal—impregnates a deity—will become immortal."

I stared at Nick more in wonderment than hatred. He was addressing me, but I could tell was talking more to himself. The thought of Hitler having his way with Garbo made me sick to my stomach. If I was lucky, maybe I'd get to vomit all over Nick before he moved away. One more projectile spew for old time's sake.

"How much would you pay, Moseley," he said, "to be immortal?"

Nick removed the offending penknife from my chest and laughed. Put it back in his breast pocket as a spot of blood formed on my shirt. Appeared as black wetness on the black shirt fabric. Nick had nicked me, after all.

"You're insane," I said. "You think you can hold Garbo for ransom?"

"I don't think anything," he said. "I've spent two years planning this mission. Right down to the very second England and France declared war on Germany. Hitler needs Garbo, now more than ever. He's obsessed with her. He'll pay, all right."

I couldn't help but register shock at the audacity of Nick's confidence. Was this some cruel joke to extract as much anguish out of me as possible before finishing me off? Nick had absolutely no reason to bluff, but there was still something about this whole mess that didn't quite add up.

"You'll never get away with it," I said. "We're surrounded by Nazis. As soon as they realize—"

"Realize what?" he said. "This whole mission is top secret. Only a select few know Garbo is even aboard. And after tonight, even fewer.

I turned to Lars. The boy had sunk down to the ground and was hugging his knees. He probably had guessed he was doomed, but Nick's verbal confirmation of the fact was all too much for him. I looked back at Nick, glared at him. He had planned all along to sink the *Athenia* with everyone aboard.

"You really are sick," I said. "You know that?"

"I've been watching you a long time, Moseley," Nick said in a calm, even voice. "Ever since the Lindbergh baby kidnapping. The world felt poor Charles's agony and cried along with him—especially in Germany—when his infant son was found dead. Then you exposed him as a so-called Nazi sympathizer. Why?"

Nick and I locked eyes. He knew he'd hit me below the belt. I had to admit, for dramatic effect it was a nice touch. If you were into sadistic improvisation, that is. He took out another cigarette and lit it. Took a deep drag and blew a smoke ring toward the porthole over Lars's head. Caught in the light column, the undulating grey-white ribbon glistened like diamond dust, then dissipated into nothingness.

"You betrayed a great hero and friend of Der Führer's." Nick had a penchant for theatricality. He was eating the scenery while playing to an unseen audience. "I ask you again. Why? Was it for money? Fame? A woman? What?"

Yeah, I'd sold out Lindbergh to save my own skin. He was going down in flames with all the pro-Nazi, America First babble anyway. I saw no reason to go down with him. But did I have to be the one to nail him to the wall? Write an exposé in *The Journal* chronicling his downfall as an American Hero. I had betrayed Lindbergh for money. Told myself that I was a journalist with a responsibility to report the news. Even if it cost me a dear friend.

"Sure," I said to him. "All of the above. Why do you care?"

"Because," Nick said in a vacant, expressionless tone, "it proves you're no better than I am. You see, we're both opportunists. We make the most of the cards we are dealt."

Nick dropped his cigarette and extinguished it under the crush of his jackboot. Then he walked to the porthole and stared out. No doubt admiring a scene unfolding of his own creation. Beyond his own sick, greedy imagination.

Then Nick turned back toward me, the purple-reddish glow of a fading sun illuminating one side of his face, the other side hidden in shadow. Reminded me of my own scarred face. Of a two-faced mercenary.

"I just happen to have all the aces," he said with a burning glare, "and you have nothing."

"At least," I said, "let the boy go."

The faintest glimmer of a smirk formed in the corner of his mouth. He looked down at Lars, seated beneath him.

"But then," he said, "who would keep you company?"

The look of recognition in Nick's face gave me shudders. Everything I had experienced in the last seventy-two hours was coming into sharp focus for the first time. Garbo had thought she was going to Germany to kill Hitler. But she was the one being drawn inexorably to the slaughter. After being sold to the highest bidder, like so much chattel.

Nick brought his forearm up to his face and looked at his wristwatch. I could tell he was doing everything for show now, relishing his role. The one he'd written and cast himself in the lead. A film noir where the bad guy wins.

"Look at the time," he said. "Have to be going."

Nick turned and made haste for the door. I bit my tongue. Felt my own warm, salty blood flow. What more was there to say? Nick rapped on the door twice with a leather-gloved hand.

"One more thing," I said in a purposefully loud voice.

Nick turned around. He looked at me with concern. Like I'd strayed off the script that played in his head. I let him stay that way for another beat.

"You owe me a thousand kronor." I smiled.

Nick's facial features eased into a shit-eating, toothy grin. "Never let it be said—" the Nazi turned on a dime as Heinrich opened the door—"that I welched on a bet."

I stared at the back of Nick's head while he and Heinrich communicated in hushed German. Nick was a smooth operator, all right. He had communicated to me that he was going to hold Garbo for ransom. He also made it known in no uncertain terms that he knew me to be a self-serving newshound, willing to sell out anyone for a story. But he didn't know everything about me.

"But I'll take my camera back," I said. "Instead."

Both Nick, Lars and even Heinrich looked at me now. I heard the gears in Nick's head grinding away on that one. Asking for my camera back was like a drowning man asking for a drink of seawater. And I saw by the expression on the faces of the three men surrounding me that they concurred.

"Sure," Nick said. "I'm no kibitzer. I'll make sure you get your precious property back."

And then he was gone, the door locked and bolted behind him. Just me and Lars remained. The young porter looked over at me, incredulous.

"What was that all about?" he said.

"We're going to get out of this, Lars," I said. "And when we do, I want proof of what happened here."

I could tell Lars thought I was nuts just by the look of renewed disgust on his face. He lowered his head again, shook it back and forth silently. I didn't blame him. I probably was nuts. But I was a nutcase on a mission.

Garbo was *terra incognita*—unknown territory—for me. But once having discovered her, I found I was no longer a man without a country. I belonged to her, much like a subject belonged to his Queen. But when push came to shove, could I be counted on to make the ultimate sacrifice for crown and country?

I prayed I'd become a man willing to die to protect her sovereignty. No longer the mouse that had betrayed Lindbergh, a friend who had trusted me. Nick seemed to know. Me, I wasn't sure.

23. BACK IN THE SADDLE AGAIN

SETH

Lindbergh had been a hero by twenty feet. That's by how much *The Spirit of Saint Louis* cleared telephone wires as the plane lifted off the end of the runway at Roosevelt Field on Long Island, New York at 7:52 a.m. on Monday, May 20, 1927. Just two hundred and forty inches shorter on liftoff, and Charles Augustus Lindbergh's historic transatlantic flight would have ended in instant incineration on the tarmac with him trapped within an exploding fuselage jam packed with 450 gallons of fuel.

"It shouldn't have worked," Lucky Lindy had told me years after. "By rights I should have been blown to smithereens."

Instead, Lindbergh attained instant immortality exactly thirty-three hours, thirty minutes and 29.8 seconds later, when his plane touched down at Le Bourget Aerodrome in Paris, France. Time and space had been on Lindbergh's side. In return, he won the admiration of the entire world. Even the nascent Nazi party and their young fuckup of a leader, Adolf Hitler, had taken notice.

Since Nick had left us alone, Lars had told me about the contraption I had been tied to was a catapult. An overgrown slingshot for launching a small plane with pontoons into the air. I had seen one taxiing up the Narrows back in the port of New York and yet another suspended from a hoist, waiting to be loaded back onto … the *Athenia*. The very same one that must have been suspended above us now.

While Lars helped me free myself from my bonds, I told myself that nothing was a coincidence anymore. Me being on the *Athenia*, meeting Ingrid, Garbo, and now Lars. Somehow the fates had decreed that I was the right man for the moment. But right for exactly what, I still had no idea.

Hitler's obsession with the occult was common knowledge. What was news, however, was the connection to Garbo. Even in my own scandal sheet, *The Journal,* we had reported that all the occult leaders of the world were in agreement: Garbo's attraction was supernatural. Now the leader of the Fifth Column had chimed in. Hitler the madman wanted Garbo the Goddess for her otherworldly power. Did he intend on somehow turning her into a secret weapon? Hadn't the Allies, if in fact they were the ones behind her mission, tried the same thing? Sent her to mesmerize and kill him?

I stood in the middle of the metal room and stretched my wings over my head. I was free. Free, yet bound in the knowledge that time was almost up. I crossed my arms, shook with a shiver. Garbo's life was more in peril than ever, and I was stuck down here, helpless to aid her.

Nick had been good to his word. Heinrich had entered the metal room and shut the door behind him. At first he gave me and Lars a wide berth. Then he produced my camera case and held it out to me. Heinrich hesitated before passing the camera into my hands. I could tell by looking in the big galoot's eyes he wasn't entirely on board with his boss' instructions. He handed me the camera case like he was handing over a loaded gun. The case that I'd last seen in Ingrid's suite when she was still alive. Still in the game. Then the big ape left without saying a word.

I opened the case, took out the camera, grabbed the flash, attached it to the side of the camera's housing and snapped it into place. Everything seemed to be in working order. I only had seven flashbulbs left. Too bad about the bulbs I'd blown shooting Harriet Brown, the Garbo alias who had turned out to be a fat woman in a tub. Back then things had been simpler. Back then Ingrid was still alive.

I caught Lars eyeballing my camera with an infantile curiosity. He was just a kid after all. Maybe nobody had played with him as a child. I whipped the lens cap off my camera with a dramatic flip of my hand. The porter was instantly amused.

"This is a seventy millimeter lens." I pointed to it for added effect.

I put my hand around the lens shaft and racked focus. I pointed it directly at Lars so he could see inside the mechanism. I slowly rotated the outside of the lens to open the aperture inside. Lars's face lit up like a kid with his very own box of jawbreakers.

"Do you see?" I said. "Opens up like a metal tulip."

Lars caught sight of his own reflection in the lens. Smiled and let out a snort of amusement, fogged my lens.

"Sorry," he said.

"It's okay." I produced a cloth from the case to wipe the lens clean. "No harm done."

We exchanged a quick glance. Then I turned and headed for the porthole. Lars came in tow like a little obedient circus animal trained to walk on its hind legs. The kid was definitely growing on me while we both walked into the light.

"Let's see what we've got here." I turned my lens out the opened porthole.

The deep red sun hung low against the darkly purple sky, and bright blue Venus had begun its rise. I lowered my eyes. The Nazi pocket battleship was less than a quarter-mile off the *Athenia's* port bow. Black as tar, the ominous vessel had the word *Vaterland* emblazoned in white lettering on her port bow. She was small for a battleship—fast, lean and lethal-looking, cutting through the surface of the water like a knife or a dark dorsal fin.

The warship's full complement had turned out to enjoy the show. Some two hundred Nazi seaman dotted her top deck, standing shoulder to shoulder. Turned out to see Garbo? Were they all Nick's accomplices? Or were they simply clueless tin soldiers along for the ride, taking the sea air?

I felt completely impotent for the first time in my professional career. For the first time, I didn't want to know what was going to happen next. Worse, I wanted to get involved and change the game. I needed to make a move, but what?

I leaned in closer to the porthole and forced myself to look down at the Lido Deck, located directly beneath me. I spied Captain Cook, Master of the *Athenia*, and Colonel Nick, my pal. They were standing amid a contingency of Cook's officers dressed in their formal white uniforms, surrounded by a much larger armed contingent of Nick's Nazi soldiers, wearing black.

I wore Nick's borrowed black suit. To look at me, I was in league with the bad guys. Yet white or black, things got harder and darker the deeper you went. The same was true for black and white film. I knew the truth of the scene being played out before my camera would never be captured. I'd only capture the light reflected on the surface. But the truth was much farther down, where light couldn't penetrate. Played out in the darkest depths of men's hearts. Men like Nick. And men like me who allowed it to be.

I raised my camera, looked through the viewfinder and zoomed in on both Captain Cook and Nick. The Captain didn't look pleased. He stood stone-faced as Nick addressed him. I was out of earshot, but I imagined Nick gave the orders. Was Captain Cook upset by The Piano Man's sudden rise in ranking? To the Captain, Nick must have represented an affront to his supreme authority on the sea. To me, Nick was an affront to humanity.

I caught Nick in the crosshairs of my viewfinder. Stuck my lens out the porthole as far as I could, opened the aperture to let in as much light as possible—too far away to use a precious flash—and snapped the Captain and Nick's portrait. The requisite mechanical click of the camera used to be music to my ears. The sound of history, captured forever. Not now. Now the sound was as hollow and empty as if I had pulled the trigger of a gun.

The mass of black and white uniformed men on the Lido deck parted like the Red Sea. I could tell by the look on their faces just who they were making room for. A visual wave ran through the crowd as every officer snapped to attention. Even Captain Cook and Nick. Garbo was making her grand entrance.

Lars was right beside me. He must have sensed he was missing the show. I graciously moved aside and let him take a look-see through my camera's viewfinder. Without a word, he accepted my offer and gingerly held the Bell & Howell in his hands.

I knew Lars was fascinated watching Garbo, along with everyone else. For even with the power of the sun waning, she shone bright. She stepped onto the deck like it was a stage, glowed self-illuminated under the ever-darkening skies. I could swear I heard thunder off in the distance.

"Take a shot," I whispered and startled Lars.

I took his right paw and put it up to the shutter release. He turned and looked at me with uncertainty. I gave him a reassuring nod. He looked back through the viewfinder, giddy with anticipation.

"Get her in the crosshairs," I instructed and watched him steady himself. "Ready. Aim. And fire."

Lars depressed the shutter release like a dutiful camera assistant. That metallic CLICK came again, and by the expression on Lars's face, he may as well have been in porter heaven. A bitter taste formed again in my mouth. The same one I had had when Nick had been in the room.

"I'm sorry I got you into this," I said.

Lars looked at me with genuine surprise. Then he looked down at the camera in his hands, fiddled with the aperture.

"I was angry at first," he admitted. "But now I know you were only trying to protect Garbo."

Lars gave me back my camera. I looked through the viewfinder but only made a show of trying to get another shot. Instead, I concentrated on Lars next to me. The little guy was acting brave, even though I knew he was scared shitless.

"Why are you here, Lars?" I took another snapshot out the porthole. "Working on the *Athenia*?"

I turned and looked him straight in the eyes. Lars looked quizzically at me. He motioned back to the porthole, pantomiming with his mitts to turn the attention back outside. Not inside on him.

"My mother and father are both dead," he said. "I joined the merchant marine. The *Athenia* has been my home ever since."

I put a hand up on Lars's shoulder. The kid was all alone. This ship was his entire world, the crew his entire family. And then I stepped on board and all hell broke loose, or so it must have seemed to him.

"You're a good porter," I said. "The best."

Lars blushed as he characteristically lowered his head to avoid my stare. I glanced up behind him, and that's when I spied a hatch in the upper-most corner of the metal room.

"What's that?" I said.

"What?" Lars said and looked up at me.

"It's a hatch," I said, excited. "A door out of here."

I put the strap of my camera over my shoulder and ran over to stand just underneath the hatch. The ceiling was easily twelve feet off the ground.

"Help me fashion a makeshift ladder," I said.

I started to stack crates, boxes, whatever I could find underneath the hatch. Then I realized Lars wasn't helping me. I turned around and saw him frozen with fear in front of the porthole.

"Lars," I said. "What are you doing?"

"I don't want to die," he said.

"I don't want to die, either," I said.

"If they see us up there," he said, "they'll shoot us."

I took a step toward Lars. He backed away from me and stepped out of the light. I smiled and shrugged at him.

"Listen, kid," I said. "All I know is that I can't let them take Garbo without doing something. Anything. But that's me. You don't have to do anything you don't want to do. Okay?"

Lars was silent for a moment. Then a muscle in his jaw clenched, and he nodded. He walked toward me, grabbing a box on his way.

"Let's get out of here," he said and helped me stack boxes higher and higher toward the metal hatch.

24. DRAWING DOWN THE GODDESS

SETH

Lars and I emerged onto an open deck between the *Athenia*'s two smokestacks, and I saw a set of stairs leading up immediately to the right. I took the stairs in twos. Lars followed close behind. The night air was chilly and darkening with every passing moment.

The voice I'd heard in my head, the one that had told me to kiss Garbo back in her suite, now told me I had to pull out all the stops. And boy, was I listening. I turned and bounded up those stairs in a flash. Came to a stop at the top in front of a chain strung across the handrails with a sign hanging from it that read *Stay Out*!

I knew what the sign meant. I was entering forbidden territory. But I had to move on. I was out of my depth. Dealing with forces way beyond my control. There was nothing I could hope to do now but antagonize Nick and his mission to abscond with Hitler's coveted prize. But that was good enough for me now.

I climbed over the chain and the warning sign. Stepped onto the landing at the top of the stairs. My head spun, and I quickly assessed the situation. A large white tarp spanned the fifty-foot transom between the *Athenia*'s two smoke stacks. I looked underneath the canvas and found what I was looking for—a small, two-seat, fixed-wing seaplane with pontoons resting in a slingshot catapult. My heart jumped several beats. The point of no return. I was going to have to fly.

I knew the essentials. A single-prop engine with cantilevered wing. Passenger seat located in front of the pilot seat. I had this. Lindbergh had been a great tutor. But what he hadn't covered in my short introduction to aeronautical education was the catapult. My mind raced to make up ground as my hands worked to unfasten the lines to the tarpaulin. By hook or by crook, I was getting airborne in front of a capacity crowd of armed Nazis. What could possibly go wrong?

Lars instinctively helped me unfasten the tarp. He busied himself while I looked down over the edge of the transom at the Lido Deck below. All eyes were still fixed on Garbo being led by Nazi escorts into one of the *Athenia's* lifeboats. The lifeboat would be lowered over the side down to the ocean's surface to an awaiting Nazi transport boat.

I turned back to the newly exposed seaplane and sank to my knees. Garbo and I appeared to be headed on separate journeys now. She was to be sold like a beautiful slave to the highest bidder. I was the schmuck who was going to try and go out in a blaze of futile glory and take a few Nazi thugs with me. One moment in Garbo's arms, the next, gone like quicksilver. Life was so fucking strange.

I hurried back to the seaplane, inspected the machine. The little puddle-jumper was designed to be flown ahead and bring the mail into port. Then the seaplane would be refueled, new cargo loaded, and it would stand ready to be hoisted back into the catapult when the mother ship arrived in port. All hunky-dory, except for the fact I wasn't going to be landing in port. Or on land, for that matter.

Lars gave me a boost as I got into the cockpit of the plane, strapped my camera above the dash, just behind the tiny windshield. I stared at the instrument panel. The fuel gauge read full. Check. Thank God. Then I looked up at the single-prop engine in front of me. *Was I out of my fucking mind?* Check. I turned the ignition switch. Her engine came to life, but then I remembered the propeller needed to be turned over. Shit.

I looked down at my little friend, Lars. He looked up at me and gave a solemn smile. I indicated with hand gestures what I needed him to do. He nodded at me and dutifully walked around the front of the plane toward the prop. The kid was turning out to be the best friend I ever had. The best friend I would ever have.

While the seaplane's engine idled, my mind raced back to the singular issue of landing. Taking off was relatively easy. Landing was something else. And landing on water was something else beyond that. I'd heard enough stories of water landings to know the margin of error was next to nil. Water plus velocity equaled a hard, unpredictable surface, which on impact could knock you unconscious, swallow and drown you. A pilot who hit water at the wrong angle became hamburger in a can. A can that could explode in flames at any second. Not exactly my idea of fun.

Then again, what the hell was I worried about? The Nazis would blow me out of the sky once I took off. They'd take care of my landing for me. One less thing for me to focus on. I was destined to crash and burn, so why not just go with it.

I watched as Lars grabbed the prop with both hands and was about to pull her down, when I heard the report of rifle fire. Aimed our way. The Nazis had found us out and opened season on our asses.

"Holy fuck," I said.

To his credit, Lars stood his ground and pulled harder on the propeller. The prop turned over, then stopped. Another crack of rifle fire came from below. This time, we both looked down, saw they weren't shooting at us at all but at a ship's officer fool enough to try and rescue Garbo. A Nazi sniper on the Nazi battleship shot at the First Officer of the *Athenia* twice, the second time hitting him in the head. He fell off the side of the ship and hit the water, dead.

Lars turned and grabbed hold of the prop again. This time he pushed up clockwise, before wrenching down counterclockwise. The propeller turned over and revved up, generating a pillar of wind. Lars shielded his face and ran back over to stand below me in the cockpit. I looked down at the seaplane's control panel and grabbed the throttle.

"Thank you, Lars." I screamed over the engine noise.

Lars had his hands over his ears when he smiled. Then he removed one of them to give me the thumbs up. Sweet kid.

The catapult release on the seaplane's dash was clearly marked. I grabbed hold of the lever and said a Hail Mary. How long had it been since I'd done that? I pulled on the catapult lever.

Before I knew what the fuck was happening, me and two thousand pounds of metal were thrust airborne. I cleared the *Athenia*, instinctively pulled back on the stick and revved the throttle. The responsive little plane ascended into the sky in a near-vertical trajectory, like a rocket. Great way to stall an engine, Moseley. She stalled all right. I leveled her off and pulled on the choke again. She sputtered back to life as soon as I refreshed her engine's oxygen supply. Too close for comfort.

I looked down and saw everyone looking up at me. Saw Lars between the two smokestacks waving a hand. I must have been putting on quite the aerial acrobatics show. Even Garbo was attuned to me. She sat perfectly still beside Nick, watching me from the open-air transport boat as it navigated the waves from the *Athenia* to the awaiting Nazi battleship. I managed to take several aerial shots of the transport boat with my camera. At least, I thought I did, blindly clicking off shots while my eyes where solely fixated on Garbo. Watched while she turned away.

I had what I needed. I could turn, fly away and live to fight another day. And maybe that was for the best. Maybe telling Garbo's story of bravery would rally a movie-loving world to viciously attack Hitler, force him and Nick to return her unscathed. Then we could be together again. Together forever. It was worth a shot, wasn't it? Better than what I currently had planned. Better than failure and certain death. Maybe even get my beloved killed in the bargain.

I banked the little plane to the right and began my journey away from Garbo. This was it. The moment I knew was inevitable yet wished never to come to. The right decision was to go and get reinforcements. The moment when fantasy collided with harsh reality. I had been given an out, and now I had to take it. Seth Moseley, scumbag tabloid reporter, lives on to tell the story yet again. Hurray for scumbags everywhere.

I plotted my course with the compass affixed to my plane's control panel. Heading was north by northwest. I'd fly to the horizon, then take a right. It would be night soon. I'd be flying blind with only my self-hatred and the little dashboard light to guide my way. I was exhausted but knew the moment I fell asleep, I'd be dead.

What was so bad about dying, anyway? Whatever waited for me on the other side couldn't be worse than what I'd experienced so far here on earth. So much human misery. A fair share of it caused by yours truly. The porter Lars's face flashed before my eyes. It would be a relief when it was all over. Still, I never thought it would end this way. End with me flying away from Garbo.

I headed toward a Sucker Hole. What pilots called a glimpse of blue sky through the clouds. They called them that because there was usually a storm brewing on the other side. The patch of blue was a mirage to sucker you in. Then it was too late. There was no going back.

An errant ray of sunshine came out of nowhere and glistened off my little plane's port bow. A pure white light that grew in intensity engulfed the plane's fuselage and me until everything glowed as one. Where the hell had that come from? I looked down at the controls but couldn't make them out. I had to fly on instinct. The same instinct that back on the ship had told me to turn around and kiss Garbo. The very same instinct that had told me it wouldn't be our last kiss.

I was floating midair in a pool of light when I realized I wasn't worried about death anymore. Aware for the first time that I had been fearful of the end my whole life but was now free of fear. I lifted my hands off the controls and raised them into the air. The plane responded, the nose slowly dipping into a descent. In another minute I'd be in a tailspin, but I didn't care. I wanted to be on the other side, where there was no fear, no more misunderstanding.

Then, as quick as it came, the sunray was gone. The sky returned to a cloudy gray. I lowered my hands back to the controls, unsure of what had come over me. I pulled the little plane's nose up and approached the Sucker Hole. My gateway out of the storm clouds. Then the thought of turning around struck me. Hard.

If I turned around now, I'd be swearing out my own death warrant. Be blown from the sky as sure as that First Officer from the *Athenia* had been picked off her port side by a Nazi sniper for even thinking of coming to Garbo's aid. Become one in a faceless sea of honored dead.

Garbo. She was under Nick's spell as well. He was using her as bounty, booty, or whatever the hell the pirate lingo was? He was the *Athenia's* dark passenger whose intention all along had been for Garbo to be his meal ticket. She thought she was destined to save the world. I feared how she'd react to the news that instead, she was to be sold on the world's biggest auction block? Made a mockery of in front of the entire planet.

Hold on a minute.

Maybe I'd been thinking about all this ass-backwards. Nick had acted like he was the one who had sent for me. Knew my history and had planned everything down to the very last detail. But what if he hadn't? What if the opportunist had merely capitalized on my being aboard? Had improvised yet again and enlisted me into service? After all, hadn't Garbo been the one hiding in the men's room? The one who had sucker-punched me over the head?

She had played a velvet-gloved hand in my destiny, not him. What if?

Nick had appealed to the old Seth, the gambler. The one that got the story and got away clean. He hadn't known about this new Seth. The committed, love-struck schmuck who stayed and stood his ground. I couldn't blame him for not knowing of New Seth's existence. New Seth had only been born just recently. Just now. In flight. Brought into being the same moment that stray beam of light appeared and, like a fulcrum, switched up the controls. Now New Seth spread his wings and turned on a dime. Pulled back on the throttle and took on torque. Steered the airship around and back. The little plane yawed.

"Fuck it," I said as I turned her into the wind and gunned the engine. "No Sucker Hole for me."

Nick thought he'd figured all the angles. But he hadn't seen anything yet. I was headed back to Garbo without a chance in hell of surviving. But that wasn't the point anymore. Now-or-never had become now-and-forever. A solemn vow to see things through to the bitter end. To get my hands dirty for the first and last time. To take a stand and fall with Garbo, Keeper of the Light.

The cloud cover was thick. A storm system was moving in and had lowered the ceiling of visibility over the *Athenia* since I'd left. But even before I dropped altitude and burst through the clouds, I knew I was on the right track. A beacon of light on the water's surface was guiding me in. I believed Garbo herself was bringing me home.

I knew the second they saw me. Order gave way to mayhem aboard Garbo's tiny transport boat. A mad scurry of Nazis blurred around her, while Garbo remained perfectly still. Garbo and Nick beside her, who wasn't a Nazi after all but a con man extraordinaire. Both turned in unison and watched me, each one's facial expression in perfect contrast to the other. Garbo smiled while the last rays of sunlight played in her hair. Meanwhile, Nick darkened and, I imagined, bit his lower lip.

I came in hot. Brought the little mail plane around and down toward Garbo's transport boat. My plan was to buzz them. Close enough to let them know I meant business, without colliding and killing myself along with the most beautiful woman who ever lived. I knew the Nazi battleship wouldn't dare fire on me for fear of killing Der Führer's would-be prize possession and meal ticket to immortality. Or so I hoped.

As I passed overhead, I saw Nick beside Garbo. He'd gotten over his shock at my untimely return, taken out his gun and trained it on me. He fired off a couple shots as I returned fire with my camera. Meanwhile, several of Nick's Nazi play pals turned tail and jumped ship. They weren't into taking any chances on a crazy American with an apparent death wish.

I pulled back up into the heavens and banked right, intent on circling and doing another run. That's when I first saw the small bullet holes in my right wing. Nick had good aim, and he wasn't shooting blanks. The canvas wing flapped in the G-force of my ascent. I prayed she didn't rip any farther. Small holes I could live with. Big ones became big problems.

This time, I lowered my altitude quickly, purposefully. I'm sure everyone onboard Garbo's ship thought I was making a suicide run, because even more of them bailed over the side. The ship's pilot began evasive maneuvers and was no longer headed for the Nazi pocket battleship. I knew so long as he held a bearing for the battleship, her powerful deck guns would remain silent for fear of hitting Garbo in the cross fire. Now he forced me to open my flank to the battleship in order to follow him. In a few short moments I'd be a goner. I had to act.

I brought the plane down and began my final descent to the ocean's surface. I felt my stomach rise up in my throat. My gut wanted to jump out of my mouth in order to save itself. Even my internal organs were turning against me. Who could blame them?

I touched down on the ocean's surface, not three hundred yards from Garbo's transport boat. I pulled back on the seaplane's stick and brought her little nose up while sailing ever closer toward Garbo's boat. That's when I saw the Goddess stand up, when everyone else onboard crouched down around her, even Nick. They raised up their hands to her, imploring her to take cover. But she paid them no heed. Remained righteously defiant.

Then calmly and slowly Garbo began to disrobe. First, she removed her overcoat. Then her silk blouse. Then her skirt. Momentarily distracted from my own imminent death, I snapped several shots of her intoxicating striptease.

Everyone stopped. Even the ship's captain turned to watch Garbo step out of her clothes. Truly a sight to behold if ever there was one. Garbo's naked body shone and shimmered bright white against the darkening atmosphere, like starlight in the shape of the most beautiful female form God had ever created. I slowed the engine to coast in closer.

Nick stood back, his gun at his side. He was slack-jawed, his mouth hanging open at the hinges. I wondered what he was thinking. Fancied he was forced to reconsider his position. Even the devil himself, when faced with something as stunning, pure, and elemental as Garbo in the raw, must give pause. Surely such reverence for absolute beauty was an unwritten, supernatural law?

I taxied in toward the Nazi vessel and used Garbo's nakedness as my cover for sneaking up close. She remained nonplussed, uninhibited, strong, standing in her birthday suit. Then, with those beautiful blue eyes of hers cast down, she turned and in one fluid motion swan-dived off the side of the ship into the ocean.

All eyes followed Garbo overboard. Her body glowed white within the blackness of the Atlantic while she made long, confident strokes toward me. I willed her to swim faster. I wanted her to make up the distance before anyone got any smart ideas. Any ideas at all.

Then someone started taking potshots at my Garbo. I looked up and saw Nick. He had somehow recovered from his shock and was aiming his pistol at Garbo's submerged heavenly body. Thank God bullets hit the water harmlessly around her. But I feared his aim would soon be true and find her. That's when I was the most scared, truly frightened for the Divine One's safety.

Then inexplicably, masses of white bubbles rose up from the depths all around Garbo's body. Nick stopped shooting. But Garbo continued to swim, surrounded by froth and fury. Was it a torrent unleashed by the elemental Goddess herself? I snapped away several more photographs as I slowed the seaplane down to an idle. Garbo was now equidistant between the plane and the transport boat. No more than one hundred fifty yards from me. But I was no longer able to distinguish Garbo's body from the sea. The disturbance in the water escalated ever more. I was horrified.

Water swirled and shot out of the ocean in funnels. Sea foam formed everywhere and shined bright in the last vestiges of sunlight. Garbo was gone. Oh my God, she was gone. Had Titan himself claimed her for his queen? I raised my camera's viewfinder to my face, unable to imagine what was to happen next and wanting to capture the unimaginable.

Then Garbo came, rose up out of the sea between Nick and me, arms held out plaintively before her. She literally stood on the water parting at her feet. Her beautiful, perfectly proportioned feet stood as if they were on *terra firma*. I shot off exposure after exposure of film. Clicked away as I watched thick strands of Garbo's shoulder-length tresses flow in the wind. Her body centered in my viewfinder, Garbo glowed brighter than the planet Venus rising behind her. Yeah, I clicked away, all right. Long after I had run out of film.

Beneath Garbo, the Nazi U-Boat emerged. The one I'd seen off the *Athenia's* port bow the first night I was aboard ship. The conning tower was marked "U-30." Garbo stood on the foredeck, her expression never wavering. Her eyes fixed on the horizon, her body caught in the last of the sun's burning amber reflection. Garbo turned to me and silently commanded me to her.

I put my camera down and worked the seaplane's controls. I brought the seaplane right up beside the surfaced U-boat. Came so close that my right pontoon scraped loudly against its dark metal hull. I bet it made a hell of a sound to the Krauts inside that can. A soundtrack to go along with the improbable image in their periscope of a naked sea goddess, climbing aboard a seaplane and into the seat in front of me. No, I wouldn't have believed it either, if I hadn't been there myself.

Garbo put her bare-naked bum on her seat as I pulled back on the throttle and headed our little plane for open water. The engine roared as we gained speed, experienced some chop. We cut long white lines in the sea before gaining altitude and lifted off the ocean's surface completely to ascend into the heavens. I looked right and caught a glimpse of our shadow on the clouds. Saw it surrounded by a circle made up of brilliant red, green and blue bands. A glory Lucky Lindy had called it. Then the sun vanished a moment later, making it impossible to tell water from sky.

That's when I looked down and saw the carnage begin. The *Athenia* under siege, first by the U-30 and then The Vaterland. The first explosion blew a large volume of water into the air and destroyed the *Athenia*'s bulkhead. It also shattered an oil tank and destroyed the access stairs to the upper decks from the third-class and tourist dining saloons. The lower-class passengers were trapped below.

The oil slick caught fire immediately and covered the water surrounding the ship with a thick blanket of flame. I found out later that it was impossible for passengers trapped in the dining-room to escape, so given a choice between drowning or burning to death—they descended into the frigid darkness below decks and snuffed out their own lives in oil.

Shortly afterwards the *Athenia* was struck again by a missile projected through the air that was not from the U-30, which had already submerged, but The *Vaterland*. The second explosion hit portside with terrific force, destroyed the ship's radio shack and created a column of black smoke that quickly billowed to a thousand feet in the cool, night air. A funeral spire for the *Athenia* and her spiraling death count.

The swarm of Nazis ravaged the civilian ship while Garbo and I watched from above, helpless. And in my mind's eye, I imagined Lars standing between the two smokestacks waving us on. Waving goodbye from the ship he had called home.

Neither Garbo nor I said a word as we lifted above the cloud cover, emerged into the night sky. I listened for the report of rifle fire, but none came. I didn't need to look back. I knew Garbo's little showstopper had left everyone in shock and awe. I knew because I felt exactly the same way.

I was lucky I could function at all. But function I did. Under a canopy of stars, I managed to wriggle free and give my naked companion Nick's jacket. Garbo put it on, buttoned up the front, then sank low in her seat and remained there, silent with her thoughts. A falling star streaked across the night sky above us. The largest one I had ever seen, before or since.

I flew our plane through the rare thin air, navigated between heaven and hell with only my wits and the instrument panel to guide me. But with Garbo in front of me, I felt like the luckiest man alive. I was on the greatest high of my life. No one and nothing would ever take that feeling away from me. I was in my glory, all right. Even all the suffering and pain below us could not bring me down. I was in nirvana with Garbo.

I had saved the woman of my dreams, drawn down the Goddess of Eternity from a fate worse than death. I felt like a god. Felt like Bacchus wanting to throw a party and introduce Ariadne, his blushing bride-to-be, to all his immortal friends. I belonged with Garbo now, beside her celestial body as we flew through the heavens together.

I didn't worry about sticking the landing anymore. Why worry about landing when the knockout of the ages sat in front of me, the sweet smell of her body wafting back to keep me awake? Alive. Why think about anything but how much I loved and worshipped her? How much I wished this moment never to end. I had risked everything to witness Garbo's last gleaming. And in doing so I awakened a love inside myself that has never faded. I never wanted to come down.

25. DOWN TO EARTH

JAMES

Seth, his eyes now glazed over and fixed firmly on the video camera lens, lay sunken into the pillows of his hospital bed. We had recorded him for the last hour and a half with only a few short breaks. He'd described how he'd seen the light, turned his plane around, and faced certain death. Instead of dying seventy years ago, he had lived to see Garbo, the love of his life, survive. And he had survived as well to now tell the tale.

"Seth," Sarah said. Her arms cradled herself, rocking herself lightly from side to side as she cried. "You were willing to sacrifice yourself to save Garbo. So beautiful."

Beautiful, yes. Ballsy, definitely. Seth was the poster child for jumping-head-first, diving-into-the-deep-end and fuck-the-consequences involvement. But I was scared. I chalked up the more fantastical elements of Seth's story to the fact his brain was dying. A product of lack of oxygen mixed with an awareness of one's own imminent demise. But then what was my excuse? Was actually believing in what Seth said a sign I was losing my own mind?

I didn't know what Sarah and Video Guy were thinking, but I wasn't letting Seth go without finishing the not-so-happy ending. I'd follow him into heaven—even hell, for that matter—with a video camera if I had to, to get the rest of the story. I needed to know where this ultimately led.

Seth finally blinked, turned and looked in Sarah's direction. His face lit up, and he smiled at her.

"You remind me," he said, the words forced out with labored breath, "of her."

Sarah brought her hands up to her face and covered her mouth. She blinked several times over moistened eyes and leaned forward. I started for her, thinking she was about to be sick. Then I realized she was reacting to what Seth said.

"Garbo?" she said and blushed bright red.

Sarah's smile trembled, then her lips separated into a bright, gleaming-white-teeth smile. Video Guy and I shared a glance. Seth still had it, for sure. Dying, he was still better at charming the pants off a woman than I expected I would ever be in my life. But I'd still try and learn.

The new woman in my life, my Garbo, was standing next to me. And I wasn't about to let her get away. That was why I needed to know the end of Seth's story so badly. Know what happened to Seth and Garbo. She was long gone, but she had never left his thoughts since. Garbo had been Seth's co-pilot these last seventy years, only for him to finally crash and die in a hospital bed having never told the story to anyone before. Never told a living soul before me.

"What happened after that, Seth?" I whispered.

Seth kept his gaze on Sarah's glowing face, savoring her. I knew I was pushing his limits. Maybe the others were happy to let him go in peace. Not me. The kid gloves were off, and I was grabbing for the fucking story while it was still within reach. Still on earth. Once he passed over, we could all relax. I knew it sounded cold. But it was my reality. My life.

"Seth." I avoided the eyes of the others.

"We landed," Seth said, his steady gaze still fixed on Sarah. "Hard."

"Yeah," I said. "Where? Come on, Seth, make it that extra mile for me."

"Jones Beach," he said.

Jones Beach? Off Long Island, New York? Could a seaplane the size and configuration Seth described have gone the distance? Again, I wanted to believe, but it was too late for details like that now. Say they had made it, what then?

"Seth," I said, "why not tell your story before now? You beat the Nazis and Nick. You and Garbo."

Seth turned from Sarah and looked at me with a vacant stare. The glimmer in his eyes was fading.

"The plane was on fumes," he slurred and leaned his head back on his pillows. "We crashed in the surf. Garbo dragged me ashore."

Fuck. Garbo saved him. They had come so far together in such a short time. Why hadn't they ended up together? Seth took a shallow breath. Then with great effort, he leaned his head up to look me straight in the eye.

"We could never be together. I knew—" he said. "After what happened."

"What, Seth?" I was about ready to jump out of my skin with anticipation. Rip my hospital gown off and run around naked and screaming in frustration. "What happened?"

I could feel Video Guy and Sarah staring straight at me now. Maybe even a little scared. I knew they wanted me to stop badgering Seth. Have some respect. But I wasn't ready to let him go yet. No, the old man and I had unfinished business.

"Seth, tell me," I said, stronger. "Tell me why you couldn't tell the story."

Then Young Seth came alive and joined the conversation. I saw him in Old Seth's eyes. Conjured for what I had to believe would be the last time. He stared at me through the portal of time. Pain in his eyes. Pain and sadness.

"The Nazi bastards sank the *Athenia* that night," he said. "Didn't want any witnesses."

A shiver ran through me. Of course, the Nazis had sunk the ocean liner. They were Nazis. Looking through Young Seth's eyes, I felt the impact of the loss for the first time. People's lives had been cut short for something they had taken no part in. Punished for simply being in the wrong place at the wrong time. Civilians.

"The *Vaterland*, the Nazi battleship, was sunk three days later," Seth added, "by an English destroyer."

I came around Seth's bed. Video Guy made way for me to kneel down beside Seth. I was in front of the camera with Seth now. The blinking red light above the lens reminded me that everything was still being recorded. Recorded for the first and last time.

I looked over at Sarah, off camera. She looked sad with her watery eyes and runny nose. I'd met her not even seventy-two hours ago but couldn't imagine ever being without her again. I still had a lot to learn about women, and I hoped she would be the one to teach me. Teach me for the rest of my life. Sarah gave me a slight smile of encouragement. *Thank you, God.*

"Garbo," I whispered in Seth's ear. His eyes had not followed me when I drew closer but had stayed on Sarah. "What happened to her?"

I already knew what had happened to her. Garbo came back a changed woman. Ever guarded about her privacy, she was only recorded on film by the paparazzi after her last screen appearance in 1941. An insipid comedy Garbo would call "her grave."

Garbo would become a shadow of her former luminous self. No longer bold and brazen, her image became fuzzy and undefined, in long-lens paparazzi shots taken around her adopted New York home. She was virtually unrecognizable as Garbo, except to people like my mom.

"All those people," Seth whispered as tears formed in his eyes. "Dead and gone because of what we had done. Garbo was guilt-ridden. She said it was because of her plan to save the world, that all those people on the *Athenia* perished. I promised her I would never tell."

I leaned in closer to Seth to listen, shocked to feel him rest his head on my shoulder. My own vision blurred as I turned and fixated on Sarah. I fought to retain my composure while he told me of his own survivor's guilt.

"It was war and the Nazis were playing for keeps. And if what you say is true," I whispered, "Garbo didn't fail. It wasn't her fault."

In the nick of time, Seth had foiled Nick's plan and saved Garbo. But she'd been free to make a choice. She could have stayed in the boat with Nick and gone on to Germany to be sold to Hitler where he'd keep her as his pet goddess. But she knew the Nazis would have blown Seth and his seaplane to smithereens if she stayed with

Nick and boarded the Vaterland. So, she'd stripped naked and swan-dived into the frigid ocean and climbed into the plane with him. She chose to save Seth because he'd chosen to save her. Wasn't that the bond that connected Seth and Garbo forever? A connection that was still alive in this very moment? For me, there was only one question left.

"Why me, Seth?" I choked back a sob. "Why keep your pledge all these years and then decide to tell your story to me?"

Seth grabbed the collar of my gown with his hand. His chest rose with another breath.

"Because," he said, "you're my kin."

"What?" I said. "What are you saying?"

"Your good-for-nothing father," he said, "was my son."

I pulled away. I broke our connection and stood straight up. Looked at Sarah for help. She stared back at me through her veil of tears with a look of innocent resolve.

"It's true, James." she said. "You're Seth's grandson."

I didn't answer right away. Just stood motionless above Seth, trying to process too much information too quickly, experience too many conflicting emotions at once. I tried to swallow, but my saliva had turned to cotton. I had to fight to form words, force them out into the world with all the breath I could muster.

"My biological father. A Moseley? How is that possible?"

While Seth worked up the energy to speak, my mom materialized in front of me. Young and vibrant, she stood next to Sarah and gazed into my eyes. I was about to call out to her. Wanted her to speak. Confirm that I hadn't gone stark raving mad. But all our attention was drawn back down to Seth.

"Theo died six months ago," Seth said in a whisper. "We hadn't talked in decades." Seth was fighting to get every word out now. Words I needed to hear. "In his things, I found a letter your mom sent. Telling him about you."

All my mom had told me about my father was that he was older. Older and a bum. I asked her once why she had been with him. She said it was to have me. That was all she'd ever said about him. Then she'd died.

I looked down at Seth. The light in his eyes all but faded. I reached a hand down and touched his shoulder. He looked up at me, smiled impishly. The paparazzo who'd fallen in love with a movie star, was now all but gone. Then he looked back at Sarah.

"I never got over Garbo," he said. "Never gave my family the love they deserved." Seth's eyes widened as he stared off into space. The space beside Sarah.

"Seth?" I leaned down and looked at his vacant eyes, Sarah reflected in them. I looked over with my own eyes and saw Sarah standing there, crying. Next to my mom. Mom turned to the young woman, then back to me. Then smiled.

Sarah came around the other side of the bed. Stepped into the light. Joined Seth and me. Grabbed me and hugged us both.

I looked back at Mom. She lingered a moment longer then disappeared in the blink of an eye. Meanwhile Garbo, the star, the icon, the woman responsible for my very existence by saving Seth, took Mom's place. Young and glowing in all her ferocious beauty, she stared into my eyes for one incredible moment, then turned and silently walked out of the room. I looked back down and saw that Seth was gone now, too. Had gone with Garbo. Finally, together again.

Then I remembered Video Guy was still in the room. The poor guy had hung back a respectful distance, his camera still recording. I couldn't imagine what he must have thought. What he and his camera had or hadn't seen. Didn't yet know what I thought of what had just happened. All I knew was he was waiting patiently for my command. Waiting to be told we were done.

"Cut," I heard myself say and held onto Seth and Sarah even tighter.

The death certificate read 8:18 p.m., but Seth had actually died ten minutes before, at 8:08. That's the time it took to get Video Guy and his equipment packed up and back out through the window into the dark snow. Sarah had given me a running start. Still off duty, she had to find the attending nurse to officially call the time. I didn't think Seth would mind. I now knew how he felt about the history books, how they were mostly wrong anyway.

In those precious few minutes after Video Guy had gone and before Sarah and the attending nurse came, I stayed with the body of the man I'd come to admire. Love, even. I sat in silence and felt the urge to feel nothing, instead of experiencing the grief of losing the best friend I ever had. A friend I'd talked to a maybe four or five times on the phone and then met in person just three days before, a friend who happened to have been my paternal grandfather.

Why hadn't he told me before, when he'd first called in about the ad I'd placed for previously untold stories on Garbo? Told me that "oh, by the way, I'm also your long-lost grandfather." Why wait until the very last moment of his life, to tell me the incredible truth? That I was a Moseley, too.

I wasn't thinking straight. I was fatigued beyond belief. But even more tired of my life amounting to a constant lament at what I'd lost. The loss of friendship, of family I didn't even know I had, of not knowing what I'd lost until it was already gone. Then there was my own survivor's guilt to deal with.

I got up off my own bed and stood over Seth's body. Looked down at it. Before she left the room, Sarah had laid Seth to rest. Crossed his hands one over the other on his still chest and pulled the covers over his face. I should have guessed the old man and I were related. So similar in so many different ways that it couldn't have been coincidence. I studied the shape of his body shrouded in that white sheet from head to toe. The image sent me spiraling back. Back to a moment I'd never forget.

I was a boy again. Sitting in a hospital hallway not unlike the one in Norfolk, Connecticut. I was alone, outside my mother's hospital room. Doctors had gone in and out throughout the night and morning. I stared at the closed door.

No one really looked at me. A few nurses cast furtive glances laden with something as yet undefined, but what I would come to recognize as pity. I would grow to hate pity. Find it as vulgar and offensive a human emotion as envy or jealousy. But at that moment, I obediently concentrated on my mom's hospital room door.

Then the door opened, and several doctors streamed out in a wave of white coats. Some were somber, yet others smiled as if they hadn't a care in the world. Dropping any pretense of caring as soon as they turned away from the patient. To them, Mom was just another Stage 4, terminally ill young woman. To them, she was already history.

A pretty, young nurse also emerged. She came to me, leaned down in front of me and looked me straight in my young blue eyes.

"You must be Jimbo," she said.

I nodded in agreement.

"My name's Rebecca," she said and smiled. "Your mom says you're a very special little boy. Said I should remember your name, so when you're rich and famous I can say I knew you back when."

Rebecca gave me a wink. I just blinked, unsure how to respond. Mom was always telling people how special I was. How when I grew up I'd rule the world. Rebecca looked at me for another moment. She had beautiful, violet-colored eyes. Like Elizabeth Taylor. I'd never seen that shade occur in nature, before or since.

Then Rebecca took my hand, brought me to my feet and led me into my mother's room. Her hand was warm and reassuring as it held mine. I liked Rebecca. There was none of that ugly pity discernable on her kind face.

"Jimbo," Mom said. Not "Hey, Jimbo," her usual catchphrase.

Mom was short of breath, her mouth hidden behind an oxygen mask fogged with condensation. The mask cut into her face, and I could tell it was hurting her. Rebecca lifted me onto a chair, so I could stand next to my mother's bed and look down on her.

"I'll be right outside," Rebecca said and departed behind the door. The door I had spent two eternal days of my young life on the other side of.

Now I was inside with Mom. All was well again. She opened her hand, the one nearest mine. I minded the tubes coming out of it and grasped onto her. Her skin was cold and clammy.

"I'm worried, Jimbo," she said.

Her brow furrowed above the mask. Then huge orbs of clear liquid formed in the corner of her eyes as she looked up to me. I braced myself, determined not to cry. Mom needed me to be strong. I'd sooner pee myself than cry.

"Come to me," she said.

I gingerly crawled into bed and lay down beside her. Put my head on her chest. There was barely anything to her, but I embraced what was left and cried in spite of myself. She brought both arms down around me and held me with her remaining strength.

"You're different," she explained amid gasps for breath. "In a wonderful, curious way." She clasped me tighter. "That makes you so vulnerable."

I sensed her pain and hugged back. She rested her chin on my head, and our tears ran together.

"I'd take you with me," she said, and I felt her chest compress with the effort of speech. "If I could ... you won't survive without me."

Mom's chest never rose again. I listened with my left ear pressed up against her chest. Listened to her heart beat slow, then stop. Rebecca, the nice nurse, found us however many minutes later lying in our embrace. A dead woman protecting her only living kin. A burned-out chrysalis surrounding the unformed creature inside.

Mom was twenty-six when she died. For years after, I worried the weight of my head against her heart had been what killed her. Mom had wanted to die like Garbo did in *Camille*, beautifully and in the arms of her young lover, Robert Taylor. Instead, she died weak and wasted away holding her ten-year-old son, tormented by the thought of leaving him behind. Died with the weight of worry over how I would survive without her. Of leaving me alone.

"Get to the heart of things," my mom used to say to me. "If you love someone, get to the heart of things and stay put. Don't ever stray."

Mom had lived by her own words her entire, short life. I had the same X-Ray vision she had had into people's hearts. Right up until the day I listened to hers stop. Ever since then I'd been turning my head. Turning away and refusing to listen to any heart that came in my direction. That was the only way I knew how to survive. To avoid people. Not love or be loved. Ever again.

Between my skill for invisibility and sixth sense to distance myself right before people tried to get close, I'd grown up in the shadows. I'd been able to protect my own broken heart and it only cost me everything. The last fifteen years or so had been abrupt stops and starts as I navigated between my desire to be in the glamorous movie industry my mother had idolized and avoiding meaningful interactions with people. It's definitely the reason I found Martin, or he found me. He was as incapable of making human connections as I was intent on avoiding them. We were perfect for each other. Two dysfunctional peas in a rotting pod.

Seth had known I was closed off. That I wasn't looking to make friends. Maybe that was why he waited to fill me in. To fill in the blanks of our familial bond. Maybe Seth figured his Garbo story was our true bond. The only way to get me to stop avoiding my own life and start listening to love.

Mom's heart began to beat in my ears while I gazed down at Seth's body. And I finally realized what the old man had been saying all along. How I needed to spread my wings and learn to fly on my own. Become someone my mom could stop worrying about and be proud of. Finally become my own man.

I turned from Seth's body to watch snow falling silently out the window. I knew I'd been brought here for a reason. Believed that the story I'd been told held a greater truth. I'd come to Seth a cynic about life and been transformed into a true believer. A Keeper of the Light.

The cynics of this world would demand proof before they'd let themselves believe in such a fantastical story. They'd cry out for substantiation. A body of evidence to dissect. I'd been that way once, a long thirty minutes ago.

I turned from the snow back to Seth's corpse. Went to the foot of his bed and quickly undid the covers. I took a deep breath then exposed the dead man's feet. Sure enough, Seth was missing both his pinky toes. The digits, now stumps covered in age-old scar tissue, had been severed at the base.

Seth had been good to his word. He had never sold his Garbo story. Not even when it came down to losing his precious piggies to Bernie and Toes back in New York City. Probably walked right into their hangout upon returning stateside and offered them up to the thugs. Seth was a new man after Garbo. She had changed him forever. And, good to his word, his love for her never faded. Losing a few toes could never change that.

Now I had to be just as strong in my convictions. From now on, no more bargaining with scumbags for crumbs to subsist on. I knew I had to take a stand in my own life before I could convince anyone of Garbo's last stand. And in the process, I'd bring Garbo back down to earth like Seth had. Make the connection live once more.

Bring her back for one more encore.

26. HOME, JAMES

JAMES

I had to believe Seth had waited to tell me he was my grandfather on film, not so much for the shock value but more for the record. If the story held true and I was indeed his kin, Martin couldn't touch me. I would have won our little pissing match and been officially done with him in a way neither of us could have predicted. The way Seth had always intended.

The next morning, I was officially discharged from Mercy Hospital in Norfolk, Connecticut. It felt strange to sit on my hospital bed dressed in my street clothes. Maybe the fact that my ass was covered up again gave me a false sense of security. Or maybe it was the hot nurse assigned to escort me out.

Sarah came into view in the open door frame, pushing an empty wheelchair in front of her. She looked at me, gestured her head down to the chair.

"Need a ride, mister?" she said acting every bit the sexy chauffer. I smiled at her tongue-in-cheek, come-hither routine. I could get used to being pushed around.

I looked at Seth's empty bed. Images of the previous night sprang forth like flashcards, one after another.

Learning that Seth was family still stunned the morning after. And knowing he and I had shared more in common than a bloodline changed the way I looked at my world. Seth had taught me more about life in three days than I had learned in the last two decades. My eyes were opened wide and still adjusting to a new light.

But the image that stuck with me the most, the one that kept repeating over and over inside my mind, was one I hadn't seen with my own eyes at all. I was in the back of that seaplane watching Young Seth from behind while he turned that plane around and headed back to certain death. He would confront Nazis in a kamikaze run that ended up saving Garbo, screwing Nick, and giving himself a second chance at life. Is that what it took? Seth had turned and faced the darkness, certain he would fail, only to succeed beyond his wildest dreams. Is that what I needed to do?

"Time to go," Sarah called from the open doorway.

Every time I looked at her now, I knew she was the one person I could trust. When Seth had confessed, then met his maker before Tom's video camera, I had looked in Sarah's eyes and realized she believed in me. Believed in the two of us. I wouldn't let her down now. Not ever.

I looked up at Sarah as she opened the footrests of the old-school wheelchair, then tapped the cracking leather back beckoning me to get in. She saw me hesitate. She saw everything now that I'd stepped into the light.

"Everything alright, Tiger?" she said.

"Yeah. I just realized I'm not really sure where I'm going."

Sarah came around the side of the wheelchair and sat down with me on the bed. She lifted her arm and put it over my shoulder, while we both stared at the door entrance to the room.

"Well, where do you want to go?"

I turned toward her. Her profile was strong and white like alabaster with a sprinkling of freckles. I was hesitating again. I felt the old, familiar sensation of fear crawling up my spine. Fear of rejection. Fear of wanting something that I didn't deserve. Fear of her finding out that I might be related to old Seth Moseley but that's where the similarities ended.

Sarah turned to me, like a statue of a Greek goddess come alive before my eyes. I blinked, waiting for the inevitable fatal blow.

"I think you should stay with me." She said.

"You do?"

"Why not? Do you have someplace better to go?"

"No."

"Okay then," she said. "Then get your cute tukkis in this wheelchair. I don't get paid by the hour, ya know."

We got up off my bed and I grabbed the handle of the plastic bag marked "Personal Effects." There wasn't much of anything in it, except for a change of clothes that I'd brought with me from LA. I'd traveled light on my trip back East with Martin. Always afraid of losing what few possessions I had. Always ending up carrying Martin's crap for him instead.

Dear Martin. When Sarah and I wheeled by his doorway, he was in his hospital bed on his cell phone, leaving his agent yet another message. I raised my hand up to halt my driver.

"I need to make a pit stop," I said.

"You don't need to do this." Sarah put a warm hand on my shoulder to keep me in my seat. "Not now."

Ah, I loved this woman. Sarah was giving me the easy out. And only a couple days before, I would have taken her up on it. Turned tail and run, in fact. Anything to avoid a confrontation. Then I saw again in my mind the vision of Seth turning the plane. But now I was in front of those controls. I was steering straight for what I wanted. And what I wanted was to be free of Martin, once and for all.

"Only be a moment." I got up out of the wheelchair under my own power. Now on my own two feet, I leaned in and kissed Sarah on the cheek. "Keep the engine running."

By the looks of him, Martin was pre-pissed when I stepped into his room. Come to think of it, Martin always looked pissed. He was the only human I knew who left a debris trail behind him. A swath of destruction through every person's life he touched. Including his own.

"Motherfucker," he said into his cell phone, then slammed the flip-phone shut with a metallic snap. He threw it on the night table, next to a bouquet of big-cup, hothouse yellow tulips arranged with baby's breath and fern. "Fucking cell reception is for shit in this God-forsaken place."

Martin turned and looked up at me with a dull, slightly ponderous expression. Slow-witted that he was, he could tell something was different with the picture his brain was receiving. Whether it was me back in my street clothes, or the new air of confidence I exuded that tipped him off, I just couldn't say. "What the fuck is your problem?" he asked.

I smiled. No, he didn't disappoint.

"Nice flowers," I said, calm and diplomatic. "From your wife?"

"Are you kidding?" he said and looked at them as if seeing them for the first time. "She's never spent a nickel of her own money on me. They're from my agent. A reminder that it's my own funeral if I don't get back to L.A. and get this fucking show done."

Los Angeles. Martin couldn't stop thinking about LA. Like he would suffocate away from the smog for too long. No doubt the abundance of fresh oxygen here was messing with his mind. Meanwhile, I hadn't thought of L.A. for an entire forty-eight hours and felt fine.

"I'm leaving, Martin," I said. "For good."

Martin's face registered shock. Then just as quick, he became stone-faced. But try as he might, he couldn't iron out his crinkled brow. His tell that he was in serious panic mode.

"Going back to L.A. without me, huh?" he said. "Well, think again."

I took one more step into the room and reminded myself that this wasn't a sophisticated individual. Martin was the guy who had once eaten half a dozen stuffed tamales before I could inform him that he should unwrap them from their corn husks first. He had ended up in the bathroom for two days straight.

"I'm not going back to Los Angeles." I raised my chin a little higher. "At least, not right away."

"Fine," he said, his forehead crinkled into a capital-M. "I've got enough footage of the old fuck anyway. Who needs you?"

Martin couldn't see Sarah waiting for me in the hallway. I turned and beckoned for her to join us. Wanted her to bear witness to what I had to say next. I watched the beauty enter Martin's room, come and stand next to me. Then I turned my attention back to Martin in his bed.

"I wouldn't try and make anything up," I warned.

Martin looked at me. Then Sarah. Then back at me. He wasn't having too much luck piecing the puzzle together.

"Why?" Martin said. "The old guy's dead, isn't he?"

"Yes," I said. "Seth has passed. But there is his heir to consider."

"His heir?" Martin chuckled, put both hands up and behind his head. He thought he'd caught me bluffing. "Don't fuck with me, James. You told me he didn't have anyone. You said."

I smiled. I couldn't help it. Martin had always relied on me to tell him the truth. And I had, even when it had been to my own detriment.

"That was before," I said. "Things are different now. His life rights revert to his surviving family member."

Martin looked at me then to Sarah, standing beside me. I'd added a layer of complexity to our little pissing match he hadn't anticipated. Martin lowered his arms and defaulted to his fall-back position: When in doubt, lash out.

"Who? Rhonda Rottencrotch here?"

"No, Martin." I said. "Me."

Martin looked back at me. Scanned my facial features, grew even more confused. Then confusion quickly gave way to anger.

"Bullshit," he said, spittle flying from his lips.

Then Sarah took my hand in her own. She made a commanding presence. Her height, beautiful face and the way she filled out her scrubs conveyed to Martin everything he needed to know. What he didn't know and what I'd learned and now loved most about her was that she was the smartest person in the room.

"He's telling the truth," she said. "And you'll be remembered as the schmuck who missed out on the story of the century."

Martin didn't need brains to tell Sarah wasn't bluffing. She had that way about her. That no-nonsense way that cut through the bullshit like a warm blade through butter. God, what a turn-on.

"Now, wait a second," Martin stuttered. "Wait, wait, wait just a second here. Let's not punch a gifted horse in the mouth. We had a deal, James and me."

Before I could respond, Sarah turned, grabbed me by the collar and brought my lips to hers. Kissed me like I'd never been kissed before. A deep passionate kiss that tickled my toes and made me weak in the knees. Literally. She drew back and turned to look into Martin's eyes.

"James has a new deal now," she said. Sarah licked her thumb and gently wiped red lipstick residue from my upper lip. "Come on, partner."

Sarah and I turned, joined hands and headed for the door. Meanwhile, Martin ranted on about being stuck in the middle of fucking nowhere because of me. How the doctors said he'd probably lose both his piggy toes to frostbite. I smiled at the thought.

Sarah and I walked straight out of the room without a backward glance. Then Sarah turned and closed the door on Martin. Shut out the sound of his voice. I had emerged a free man. Free and full of confidence for the first time.

Sarah, back behind the wheelchair, winked then slapped the bottom of the wheelchair seat.

"Get in, Jimbo."

I got in and we started down the hallway toward the bright light of the lobby. And I closed my eyes and imagined I was in the seaplane Seth Moseley, my grandfather, flew through the heavens with a naked Garbo asleep in the front seat. The one he may have landed but had never come down from.

★　★　★

Sarah pushed my wheelchair to the lobby of the hospital, where Tom, the Video Guy was waiting. I could see his van parked out front. He had been gracious enough to offer me a ride the night before, but my discharge was delayed until this morning. I got up and received an unexpected bear hug from the mountain man. Sarah looked on and laughed.

"What now?" he said.

I turned to Sarah. She was calling the shots, and I was only too happy to follow her lead.

"Now," she said, "we go to the bank."

Sarah produced a safe-deposit box key from the pocket of her uniform. She held the key up high, between her index and forefinger. The metal jigsaw-puzzle piece with "Diebold" stamped into it glistened in the morning light.

"Is that what I think it is?" Video Guy said.

"Yep," she said. "Seth's safe deposit box key. He gave it to me yesterday, and I'm guessing there's something in it we all need to see."

"Not me," Video Guy said. "I've got another gig across town. I just came by to say goodbye."

Then Video Guy, the loveable bear of a guy, fell silent.

Sarah was first. Stepped up and gave him a great big hug and a kiss. His cheeks blushed the color of his beard. I was no good with goodbyes. So I shook his hand and handed him a personal check I knew was no good.

"If you could wait a week to cash that," I said. "Maybe two."

"Don't worry," Video Guy said and smiled. Stole a glance at Sarah. "I know where to find you. But hey, don't forget this."

He reached in his jacket pocket and produced a plain manila envelope, handed it to me. I grabbed the envelope and looked inside. A mini-digital-video cassette marked "Seth Moseley Interview" the date scribbled in thick, black Sharpie on the bottom.

"You know," he said and pulled on his beard with his right hand, "I never expected to see you again, after that day at the old man's apartment. Funny how things work out."

"Funny," I said and reached for Sarah's hand.

The paperwork I had to fill out at New Haven First Security Bank was amazingly simple. When Sarah and I came through the front door, they acted like they had been waiting for us. Everyone working there had known Seth Moseley for decades. And apparently, he'd recently told them he'd found me.

"Sorry to hear about Mr. Moseley," the bank manager said as she led us to the vault where rows and rows of deposit boxes lined the walls. Sarah and I held hands to steady one another. We were both shaking with anticipation. This was it.

I watched while the bank manager inserted her key into the tiny door of deposit box number 313, situated almost in the exact center of the wall of tiny metal doors. Then I inserted mine, the one Sarah had given me. The manager turned both keys and the little door opened. She removed a long, rectangular metal box.

"Follow me," she said, box in hand.

She led us to a little room off the vault. Placed the box on a table with two metal chairs beside it.

"Let me know if you two need anything else."

Then she turned and drew the curtain that enclosed us in the little room. Sarah and I stood and stared at one another. I looked down at the box on the table. We both eased into the chairs in front of us.

"Well," Sarah said and pushed the box in front of me. "Aren't you going to open it?"

"Yeah," I said, "sure I am."

But I hesitated. The little room was too quiet. I half-expected Seth to pop out from behind the curtain and say something sarcastic. Or give me instructions. Sarah looked at me, read my nervous face, and smiled.

"Let's open it together," she said.

Inside the box, a folder contained a series of photographs and their negatives the likes of which this world had never seen. Their stunning black & white images clearly conveyed the same amazing story Seth had told. Fat Harriet Brown caught naked in her tub. Nick and Captain Cook on the Lido Deck of the *Athenia* with their men. But most of all—Garbo.

Garbo looked every inch the goddess Seth had described. The one Mom and I had worshipped together.

The images captured an elemental goddess, before and after her rebirth in the pitch-black waters of the North Atlantic during that fateful sunset of September 3rd, 1939.

Garbo's body shimmered, bound within the frame of Seth's lens, captivating but not captive. Seemingly ready to take flight at any moment when the wind was right, like so much glamorous gossamer. Garbo glimmered supernaturally. A ghost caught on film between two worlds.

Along with the photos came the fan letter from Hitler, written on Nazi letterhead. The one where he invited the Great Garbo to be his Aryan Goddess. The letter stained with Ingrid's blood.

Next was a yellowed clipping from a Long Island local newspaper:

Seaplane wreckage washes up at Jones Beach
By *Newsday* staff, Thursday, September 7, 1939

A piece of wreckage, which local aviation officials confirmed is a portion of an aircraft, washed up on Jones Beach, Long Island, yesterday. The immediate vicinity was littered with what officials characterized as 'burnt envelopes'.

Surfcasting fisherman Dennis Bottomly said that he first observed the twisted metal pieces moving back and forth in the surf in the early morning hours of Tuesday, September 5th. "When I find it I say it got to be a part of a plane," he told this newspaper. He said that he brought what appeared to be a part of a pontoon further onshore and returned on Wednesday morning to bring it further in. Later on Wednesday, he transported it in his 1936 Dodge Fore-Point pickup truck to his home in Massapequa. The piece of material is white on the outside with a little dark portion.

Officials from the Nassau Civil Aviation Authority took custody of the piece yesterday. It was confirmed that it was a portion of an as yet unidentified seaplane. Bottomly gave a statement to police.

"What does it mean?"

I looked up at Sarah's profile. Her hazel eyes shimmered in the fluorescent light like mica.

"It means," I said, "Seth was telling the truth the whole time."

Sarah looked through the remaining photos and letters. She handed me Seth's graduate degree in rhetoric from Amherst. Then several pictures of his wife Helen holding their son, Theo Moseley, my father. I stared at the solemn young man in the photos, looked for any resemblance to Seth. Looked for any resemblance to me.

Then Sarah stopped, stared at one particular document. Her jaw slackened and her face paled. She seemed like she was about to faint. I brought my chair right up beside hers and took her in my arms. She turned and rested her head on my shoulder.

"Your mom," she said.

"What?"

I looked down and saw a black and white photograph of my mother, young and in her glory, holding me as an infant. Attached to the photograph was a short letter, written in my mother's hand and addressed to Theo.

I read the letter over several times to myself. My mother informing my biological father that I had come into the world, my name was James and that he need not concern himself. Ever. Their one night together was to remain just that. She was strong and unequivocal on this point. My mother would take care of everything. And that was that.

My father, Theo Moseley, remained an enigma. I would never know whether he knew of my mom's passing. Never know if he ever thought of her, of me, of anything. All I knew for sure was that he must have had Old Seth's talent for flirting with much younger women. That and he had never made an attempt to connect with me.

I held Theo's photograph. Finally put a face with the anger I'd felt toward my father, a ghost, for so long. I had blamed him, sight unseen, for everything that happened to me after Mom died. Now I felt I could put all that to rest. All because of Seth.

"Seth told me." Sarah whispered. "When you left to go get Tom in the lobby." She leaned back up to put her arms around me now, drew me to her in a close embrace. "He told me how he tracked you down after reading your mom's letter. Found out from an ad you'd placed how you were looking for Greta Garbo and what an incredible coincidence it was. Or, then again maybe not. But then he was scared. Scared to tell you who he really was and how he loved you at first sight. Afraid you wouldn't believe him."

I put Theo's photo down and concentrated on holding Sarah. I couldn't find my voice. I could only hold onto her and feel my heart beating rapidly against hers. Breathe in her lavender scent.

Then I looked over Sarah's shoulder and caught a glimpse of Garbo, rising naked from the ocean. The most startling image Seth had ever taken. The one he thought he'd missed, run out of film before capturing. Before the light of day had failed completely and he'd kept her image hidden from sight ever since.

I believed everything Seth had said, everything that had taken place those three days in early September 1939. Not because of the photographs, but because the old man had shown me how to put my anger aside and trust again. How to listen for love again. In less than three, short days.

I put everything back in the box and closed the lid. The photos would keep. Then I turned to Sarah. Life finally felt right. That's the only way I could explain it. I hoped it was love. The kind of love that Seth had for Garbo.

My Goddess turned toward me, and we fell into a long, passionate, take-no-prisoners kiss. Sarah pulled away, surprised. Surprised and then delighted. She reached up a thumb and forefinger and tugged on my chin, like she had the very first time I laid eyes on her.

"Let's go home, James."

Not to "your" place, or "my" place. Home. Was I reading too much into it? Definitely, and having a helluva time doing it. I turned toward the door and slipped my arm around her waist.

"Yeah, home."

★

ACKNOWLEDGMENTS

This work would never have been possible if not for the help and support of a dedicated group of friends, family and fellow scribes who never pulled their punches, even when I wanted them to. Thanks to Wendy Aten, Andrea Cavallaro, Jim Chegia, Sydney Chute, Kevin Cleary, Mary Coleman, Charlotte Robin Cook, Francesca Dinglasan, Lauren Hill, Jon de la Luz, Anne Fox, Margaret Gutowski, Mariah Klein, Ea Ksander, Mary Ann Koory, R. Lee Paulson, Marc Manzo, Chris Matz, Chris Miller, Thomas Charles Miller, April Rouveyrol, Jefferson Randolf, Geraldine Solon, Ruth Schecter, Jacqueline Stagg; Tom, Betzi & Harry Sylvan, Rollo Tomasi, Tom Ward, and especially my agent, Jill Marr at Sandra Dijkstra Literary; and Kristy Makansi, my editor extraordinaire, at Blank Slate Press, and Lisa Miller and Laura Robinson at Amphorae Publishing. Finally, I have to thank Mia Sampaga for her patience and loving support, and legendary Associated Press Reporter and my good friend, Seth H. Moseley, who inspired me to never give up on this story of Greta Garbo, the movie goddess and the black and white cinematic world she rules over to this day.

ABOUT THE AUTHOR

Jon James Miller has always been passionate about literature and film and pursued a career in the latter at Ithaca College in upstate New York, earning a degree in cinematography. He moved to Los Angeles and worked as a researcher and segment producer on cable documentaries for A&E, Lifetime Intimate Portraits, and The History Channel.

In 2008, Jon won Grand Prize of the AAA Screenplay Contest sponsored by *Creative Screenwriting Magazine* for *Garbo's Last Stand*. The World War 2 mystery inspired by true events won the 2009 Golden Brad for Drama. But advice Jon received from legendary screenwriter and novelist William Goldman proved most valuable. After reading Jon's screenplay, Mr. Goldman said, "This is a great story, now go write the novel." *Looking for Garbo* is that novel.

In addition to writing novels, non-fiction and screenplays, Jon is a frequent presenter of live webinars on the craft of writing. His presentations can be found at *SCRIPT* Magazine, The Writers Store, and Writers Digest University online. When he's not writing or presenting, Jon loves to hike, play tennis and go to movies. He lives, works and plays in Northern California.